WOLF ICE

Additional novels by Melissa Yi

Code Blues
Notorious D.O.C.
Terminally Ill
Stockholm Syndrome
Human Remains

The Italian School for Assassins
The Goa Yoga School of Slayers

High School Hit List
Dancing Through the Chaos
Mr. Chef & Ms. Librarian
The List

Short stories and novellas

No Air: a Hope Sze radio drama
Blood Diamonds
Student Body
Reckless Homicide
The Sin Eaters

WOLF ICE

MELISSA YI

Windtree
Press

For the wolves:
the four-legged kind,
and wolves at heart.

Cover design by Yocla Designs Copyright © 2017

Published by Olo Books
http://olobooks.com/
In association with Windtree Press
http://windtreepress.com/

Join Melissa's mailing list at www.melissayuaninnes.com

Yi, Melissa, author
Wolf Ice / Melissa Yi.
Issued in print and electronic formats.
ISBN 978-978-1-927341-52-0 (softcover).
--978-1-927341-01-8 (PDF)

For typographical errors, please contact olobooks@gmail.com

CHAPTER 1

I hopped into Elena's red Honda Odyssey, which vibrated so hard from the White Stripes' bass line that I felt, more than heard, my door thump shut. Elena tossed her blond hair and bared her teeth. "Ready to rumble?"

I threw back my head and howled my answer. It kicked ass to desert Montreal once a month and go wild. If my biological clock didn't demand it, I'd have to do it anyway.

Elena threw the van into reverse. "Good. You're gonna need it, Leila."

At first I thought she meant she was going to spar with me when we got to the campground I'm negotiating to buy, but her glance flicked to the rear view mirror. She grinned.

I checked out our compatriots in the van's rearmost seat. We always carpool. It's more environmentally sound, plus, worst case scenario, if one of us 'shifts too much on the way, someone else can drive. Usually Elena drives, and I ride shotgun. Mac and Laurent fill the back seats, plus one to three other pack members join us.

I said hi to Mac, our resident redhead. "Big Mac" is a few years older than us, which means he broke through the big 3-0, but he still looked like a taller, broader Richie Cunningham. Like me and Elena, he doesn't 'shift until almost the last second the sun disappears and the full moon rises, so he drives occasionally.

Laurent's the opposite: small and lean, bad five o'clock shadow two days before the full moon. We practically have to smuggle him out as our wolf dog if we leave too close to evening. Today he hung out by himself in the van's rearmost seat, like a French Canadian version of Slash. What makes it more hilarious is that in the Real World, Laurent is a clean-shaven lawyer.

I twisted to look directly behind me and hissed involuntarily, baring my teeth.

"Nice to see you, too," said Jack. Also known as Jack Meng, paramedic, or as I prefer to call him, scum-sucking motherfucker.

I turned back to Elena. "His lips are moving, but all I hear is, 'Hey! I'm an asshole!'"

"Yeah, I'll bet that's what you're hearing." She merged on to the Décarie Expressway, gunning ahead of a police cruiser.

Was I that transparent? I sure hoped not. Of course, I also hoped I was impervious to Jack's Chinese-Canadian werewolf charms, but my triple-digit heart rate testified otherwise. My parents had always hoped I'd marry a guy who a) was Chinese like me, b) scored a good job, c) had sprung from a decent family, so we could d) make nice yellow babies. Until Jack, I'd never met an Asian guy who rang my bell. Before I could bring him home, though, Jack showed off his true player colours. Finito. RIP, Jack and Leila, forever and ever, amen.

I changed the radio station, and the first, familiar chords of "Werewolves of London" came on. I stiffened.

"Aroo," said Elena.

"I'll change it." I reached for the button. The song was pure cheese. The only one that bugged me more was "Layla," by Eric Clapton, because kids used to tease me that the song was about me.

"*Laisse-le,*" growled Laurent. Leave it.

"Yeah, don't you have any team spirit?" said Mac.

Elena laughed. I snorted.

Only Jack didn't say anything. Maybe he remembered how we used to laugh and kiss and do the wild thing to this song.

The chorus kicked in, and we all howled along with it. Jack's tenor rose in the air. The hair on my neck prickled, and my nipples stood at attention. I crossed my arms, but there was no way to get around it. Scummy motherfucker still sounded—and smelled—like heaven.

Eventually, I relaxed to Sheryl Crow while Elena munched beef jerky and gunned it along Highway 20, weaving through April's early tourists and bad-tempered commuters. An hour later, we crossed the provincial border into Ontario. First exit, Curry Hill, toward the fifty acres of land our pack's going to buy.

I love nature. I love mosquitoes, sweat, and mud that sucks off your sneakers. I love to run and scream out of pure joy, and it doesn't matter because no one can hear you, or if they can, they're running and screaming too.

In four short weeks, this would be our new stomping ground.

Elena still drove like she was in Montreal, passing a tractor even though a black GMC truck was already pulled over on the shoulder. She took a left at the faded sign for A PLUS CAMPGROUNDS. Maples, ash, and pine trees unfurled their new leaves and needles in welcome. We bumped over the frost heave potholes in the dirt road.

"We'll have to fix the road," grumbled Laurent.

"The water and sewage hookups still work," I countered. "And wait 'til you see the river."

"The mighty Beaudette River," Laurent said.

"You can fish in it," I said. "Maybe not now, but next month."

"Awesome," said Elena. I grinned at her until she rolled down her window to toss a beef jerky wrapper on to our new homeland.

At my look, she stuffed the wrapper back in the cup holder.

"Thanks," I said. I sniffed the fresh air. I loved the smell of damp earth, that gentle hint of warmth and spring. I inhaled deeply, closing my eyes, and smelled Jack. Even for a werewolf, I've got quite the nose.

I blushed, which made me mad. I tried to concentrate on Elena instead. She smelled like herself, calendula, and beef jerky. She gets hungry before she 'shifts. Like PMS times a thousand.

"Great place," said Jack. "What's the closest city?"

I laughed. "Two towns, about 20 minutes north and west. This land'll be all ours. The Ottawa wers have been calling me, though. They want in on it, too."

Elena couldn't pull right up on the campground because the ground was too boggy. We carried our tents about 20 feet from the dirt road.

I set up my tent, trying to ignore Jack working on his to my right. My tent is a two-person job from Mountain Equipment Co-op, kind of like a little white nylon igloo held up by retractable metal poles. A tall five-year-old could set it up.

So I had plenty of time to watch Jack's forearm muscles and biceps as he set up his blue four-man wonder, the kind with an awning that's practically a porch. He probably held orgies in there. Somehow, this did not detract from his arm muscles. I love well-used muscles in a guy. Not steroid-induced, tanning bed, poser muscles, but the kind you get from hauling wood, running, and generally being a man.

Or a wolf.

"You have good taste," he said.

"What?" My eyes snapped back up to his face. Conceited bastard, saying I have good taste for gawking—

"This land. I like it."

Oh. Right. Only the entire focus of my work life. "Yeah, thanks. I wanted a green space not too far from Montreal."

When I tore my eyes away from Jack's intense brown irises, Elena's little red tent caught my eye. It was still sitting in the open trunk of her van.

I started toward it, still feeling Jack watching me.

"Leila!" Mac flagged me to the south side of the campground.

I glanced at Elena's tent again before I jogged toward Mac. Jack matched me stride for stride.

"What's up?" I asked Mac.

His face looked paler than usual under his growing ginger beard. "Elena's missing."

CHAPTER 2

Elena. Missing.

"No," I said. Laurent sometimes took off right away, stretching his legs, sucking in the air, to get the edge off before he 'shifted. But not Elena.

Laurent galloped toward us, his face contorted behind his ever-thickening beard. "I could smell her up to the river."

The river! It made no sense that she'd walked away from her van, her tent, and her pack to dip her toes in the river 200 feet south of our campsite. And then I remembered something else. "She can't swim."

"Let's move," said Jack.

We raced toward the river, still on two legs, yet swifter than most humans. Laurent scouted along the bank, pointing out where he'd smelled her on the bush along the riverbank.

The river was swollen with spring run-off—not fast-moving, but high. Elena could have lost her footing on the muddy bank. But what was she doing out here in the first place?

We split off, instinctively fanning out. Jack dashed downriver, Mac shot east, and Laurent waded into the river while I took the riverbank, hunting for another clue.

Down in the dirt, I caught a tang of the stupid calendula deodorant Elena insisted on wearing. I refused to get choked up. Find her first. *Find* her.

I clambered down into the river after Laurent, slipping despite my boots. Elena had driven up in ballerina flats. Had she slipped into the river?

And then I spotted her size eight footprint in the mud. And another, heading west. "Hey!" I said.

Jack's howl split the air.

He was dragging something heavy on to the riverbank.

I lost sight of Jack for a minute when he dropped to his knees in the dusky brush, but when I raced to his side, he'd braced his arms to pump up and down on Elena's chest.

I screamed.

He hadn't found something. It was some*one*. Elena.

I scrambled to feel for a pulse in her cold, slippery neck. Her chest bounced every time he released a compression. But I couldn't feel any pulse.

Her lips looked purplish blue.

"Do you know how to do mouth-to-mouth?" yelled Jack.

I started to tilt her forehead before I noticed the bloody knot on top of her head.

Jack yelled, "No, do the jaw thrust! Or take over the compressions!"

Mac knocked me aside. While I sprawled into the burrs, he started pumping his hands up and down on Elena's chest.

Jack swiveled his body around to Elena's head. His thumbs opened her mouth while the rest of his fingers hooked around the angles of her jaw and forced it forward. He exhaled into her mouth.

"No chest rise. It's blocked. Leila, get in there!" Jack shouted. "Scoop out her mouth!"

While he held her mouth open, I stuck two fingers between my friend's rows of even white teeth. I felt her tongue, and then something else. A piece of bone.

I yanked it out, scraping the backs of my fingers on her teeth, and flung it on the ground.

Jack immediately gave her two breaths before he yelled, "Good work!" To Mac, he yelled, "Keep up the compressions!"

I whipped my cell phone out of my jeans pocket and started to press 9-1—

Laurent gripped my arm so hard, I nearly dropped the phone. "No doctors," he growled.

That was the code. No outsiders. But this was Elena's life. I ripped my arm out of his grip.

Or started to. His hand tightened until my hand bulged with engorged blood.

I snatched the phone with my other hand.

Laurent cursed and grabbed my left arm, too.

Jack stabilized Elena's head. "Call 911. She could make it."

Laurent pointed at the indigo sky and stark black tree silhouettes. When the sun's last rays faded below the horizon, we would all 'shift into wolves. Including Elena.

CHAPTER 3

Laurent growled, "We've got to do this on our own."

"I want an ambulance," I said, but softer now. The pack came first. 'Shifting into wolves in the middle of the ER would not help the pack. We all knew this.

But I didn't want Elena to die.

Tears pricked my eyes. Laurent released my arms. The blood rushed back into them, but I dropped my phone and had to kneel to scoop it back into my pocket.

Mac kept pumping on Elena's chest so hard, he pushed the breath out of her body. I could almost hear her chest indent with every blow.

Jack bent over her face and gave two more breaths. Her waxy skin contrasted with his healthy tan, even in the dusky light.

Jack's head jerked up, and dark brown eyes fixed on me so intently, I squirmed. I flashed back to a morning when he rode me in bed with the sun shining behind him, haloing him like the caramel-skinned god he was.

My heart throbbed in my throat, and every hair in my body felt electrified.

Then Jack shook his head, snapping me back to the present. He said, "I need to secure her neck. And we've got to warm her up. I've got a bedroll and tape in the van."

"I'll get the van," I said.

Jack's teeth glinted at me, a sudden smile in the growing darkness.

"I'll come with you," said Laurent.

He didn't trust me not to call 911. I didn't waste time arguing with him, just started running back toward the camp. The trees cast shadows against the darkening sky. Every second counted.

I heard Laurent's heavy footsteps pounding behind me. Minutes later, he caught up and passed me.

I gritted my teeth and sprinted full-out toward the Honda Odyssey. I hit the driver's side door first and threw it open. The keys hung from the ignition, right where Elena had left them. I glanced in the back and spotted Jack's fluorescent orange backpack. I buckled my seat belt and gunned the engine while Laurent slammed his door.

I flicked on the headlights, threw the van in reverse, and squealed out of there.

I knew there was a circuitous dirt road to the river. I just had to find it. For a werewolf, my built-in GPS was weak. "The road," I said.

Laurent pointed left at the fork.

I had to trust him, but I didn't particularly like him right now. "She needs a hospital," I said.

Laurent looked at me. His brown irises seemed to fill his eyes more than usual, and I knew what he was thinking. The pack. Almost everything we do is for the good of the pack, not ourselves. It's instinct. Kinda like Japanese vs. American culture, only more so. If we took Elena to the hospital and she 'shifted—if we all 'shifted—we'd be carted off to a lab and doomed. Our whole species would go down, hunted as a scientific oddity.

"Jack has connections," I said. He was a paramedic. But I had no idea how far those connections stretched.

Laurent didn't bother to answer. He pointed me right, and soon we were bumping alongside the river. I hit the gas as hard as I dared without tipping us over the riverbank. The road hadn't been maintained and wasn't designed for passenger vans in the first place.

Laurent had rolled down the window and was sniffing the air. I did the same, but I figured out from his dilated nostrils that Elena was nearly in heat, and it was easier for him to track her, even if she was almost—

Our headlights picked up Jack and Mac over Elena's body.

Laurent grabbed the door latch, ready to leap out of the still-moving van.

I slammed on the brakes. He dashed down the riverbank. I bumped along the road a few metres closer, then snatched Jack's backpack and followed him, leaving the engine running and headlines on to help us see.

I could hear Jack yelling over the motor. "No. I need you to hold her neck. Don't move. Laurent, take over compressions!...What'd'ya mean, you don't know first aid? What good are lawyers, anyway?"

I darted to their side, holding Jack's bag up like an Olympic gold medal.

Jack's eyes lit up. "I've got a face mask in there. In the right side pocket. Black case."

I unzipped it and handed him a triangular plastic mask with what looked like a crooked chimney coming out of it.

He said, "Great. Now you take over compressions, Leila, while Mac gets her neck again. Careful, Mac. Hold on to her shoulders. Use your forearms to brace her. That's it. Good. Leila, tell me when you get to thirty compressions."

I hadn't done first aid since I practiced on a dummy three years ago. But I got on my knees, locked my arms, laced my fingers together, and started pumping up and down on Elena's breastbone.

I tried not to think that this was my friend. That I'd never gotten this close to her C-cups before.

That I didn't know what I was doing.

That she still wasn't breathing.

Jack slipped the top point of the triangle over her nose and the bottom over her mouth. His long fingers expertly opened her jaw, and he bent over the mask to ventilate her.

My arms were shaking already.

"Use your body weight to do the compressions," said Jack. "Lift up. Yeah, that's it."

Fine, except now my knees gouged the cold mud. My teeth started to clatter. To distract myself, I said, "How's she doing?"

"She's been down twelve minutes since I found her. But she's cold, so she's not dead until she's warm and dead. Speaking of which, we've got to cut her clothes off. Laurent, I've got a pair of trauma scissors. Left side pocket, Laurent. Sorry, my left."

"Thirty," I gasped.

Jack gave two more breaths while Laurent started snipping the clothes. Then Jack helped tug her wet clothes off and unrolled his sleeping bag over her.

I said, between compressions, "Do. You. Have. Con. Nec. Tions. At. A. Hos. Pi. Tal?"

"Not good enough. She needs resus and then ICU. I can't see any way to bring her in without her 'shifting and throwing the whole hospital into pandemonium. Is that thirty?"

I nodded. He gave another two breaths.

"What about a vet?" said Mac.

"Yes!" I ground out.

Jack said, "I don't know anyone who's got that kind of set-up. I brought a kid in once who survived cold immersion, but they put him on a heart-lung bypass machine. It would have to be the most advanced vet hospital in the world. We're in the middle of nowhere." He glanced at the van. "And once we 'shift, we can't drive. We can't do CPR. And we can't stabilize her neck."

Tears swam into my eyes. I blinked them away and pounded harder on Elena's chest. Sweat trickled down my back. He was right. By the time we drove the hour plus back into the city, we'd all have 'shifted.

Elena would die.

Jack cut through my tears. "Let's get her in the van and warm her up as best we can. Is there something we can transport her on? A board? I don't want to carry her if I don't have to. Laurent, check the van."

While Laurent loped back to the van, Jack reached into his magic bag and grabbed three white plastic packages. "Warming packs," he explained while he squeezed the packs and shook them. Then he tucked one under each armpit and one on her inner thigh.

He touched my arm. "Stop compressions."

I blinked back more tears.

"Leila, stop compressions."

I did. I shook out my arms. I worked out every day, but my biceps and triceps felt like they'd been steamed.

Jack pushed two fingers on the side of her neck. He frowned and pushed harder. His shoulders tensed.

He met my eyes. "She has a pulse."

CHAPTER 4

Jack's teeth gleamed, but all he said was, "Mac. Keep holding on to her neck. Leila, grab my stethoscope out of the front pocket." He felt her pulse, and then I tossed it to him. He pressed the stethoscope against her chest and shook his head, but he was grinning. "We're not out of the woods yet. Still, that's amazing."

Laurent hustled out of the van, hauling something rectangular. "She had a carpet remnant on the floor."

Right. Elena kept an extra carpet in her van because of "dog hair." For a wolf, Elena sure was—is—picky about that kind of thing. I wanted to laugh and cry at the same time.

"Best I could do," said Laurent, rolling it out. He folded it in half to stiffen it up, and it was still big enough to carry Elena.

"Good enough," said Jack. He exhaled into the face mask he held over Elena's face. He lifted his head and explained, "She's breathing now, once in a while. I'm helping her."

I nodded. When I got home, I'd brush up on my first aid. I'd still never know as much as Jack. He wanted to be a doctor, but there was no way he could excuse himself from call every full moon, so he became a paramedic.

Jack felt her pulse again. "It's there. Slow but steady."

Under Jack's direction, we rolled two shirts into cloth logs and taped them on either side of her head to help stabilize her neck on the carpet.

"Keep the carpet as straight as possible," said Jack. "I wish we'd taken my truck. I've got a real board. One, two, three."

We heaved her into the van. Luckily, Elena was tall but thin, and we had lots of muscle power between Jack, Mac, and me. Laurent took the foot end because I didn't trust him so close to 'shifting. At any second, his hands could warp into paws.

I glanced at Jack, trying to convey my worry with my eyes. He directed Laurent to fold down the rear bench so we'd have room to lay Elena down, even with the guys crouched around her. Then he said, "Leila, drive. Crank up the heat. Laurent, unroll the other bedroll over her. Mac, are you all right with the head? Good. I want her back at the camp before the moon rises."

I floored it. Laurent grunted to point me the way, but even I could follow the river road back now.

Over the engine's roar, I heard Jack say, "I'm losing her pulse."

CHAPTER 5

I tensed, waiting for his verdict. I could hear him shuffling in the back, but I couldn't make out much in the rearview mirror at nightfall. As it got closer to 'shift time, my peripheral and motion vision sharpened, but central details and colours faded.

After a pause, Jack said, "Restart the chest compressions."

I swore under my breath and kept driving. I could hear Mac and Laurent's breathing, almost panting, in the enclosed space of the van.

Just before I screeched into camp, Jack said, "Let me check again."

I eased off on the brakes, as if that would help him feel or hear better, but Jack's grim voice floated into my ears. "More compressions."

I killed the ignition and glanced at the sky. I could feel the moon's incipient rise like a discomfort, like a calling. It was as if someone were staring at me. Even if I ignored it, I felt an increased awareness, almost unease, along my spine.

Moonrise was less than ten minutes away. More like five.

I hit the automatic "door open" buttons and bounded around to the back to lift open the trunk hatch. "What can I do?"

Jack shook his head.

Even in the grey light, I could see the stillness in Elena's face and the passive way her body rebounded with each of Mac's compressions. As if she were a life-sized doll.

Or a corpse.

I suppressed a howl.

Laurent leapt out of the back hatch, a blur of black. He howled for me, his wolf voice rising into the night sky.

Mac tried to speak, but it turned into a moan. His forearms were marked by thicker fur.

He was 'shifting. I jumped into the van and thrust him aside. As I started up CPR, giving it everything I got, I barely noticed Mac hit the ground on four legs instead of two.

"OoooooooOOOOOOOoooooo…"

Laurent. Mac. Howling together, already a chorus of mourning.

My heart cried along with them, but I kept my arms locked and pumped with the entire strength of my body.

Jack's hands trembled on the face mask.

Oh, no. I spared a glance at his face.

His agonized brown eyes.

His growing muzzle.

The face mask dropped from his paws. He scrambled to pick it up before he whined and nudged the mask with his muzzle.

I scooped up the mask and tried to arrange it on her face the way I'd seen him do it. Triangle shape. Pointed top over her nose. Right?

Jack nudged my hands with his muzzle. Yes, that was right.

My hands shook, but I pressed it on to her face. I bent over it and exhaled two breaths into her chest. Did I need to coordinate with CPR?

No one was doing CPR.

My fingers sprouted fur and claws.

I could no longer support all my weight on my hind legs.

The mask tumbled out of my paws.

I howled.

CHAPTER 6

I dropped on to all fours, dancing to avoid Elena's still face and Jack's furry body.

I leaped out of the van, still howling.

Jack burst out after me, his call even more desperate than mine.

I raised my head to the full, serene face of the moon. She who commands us. She had risen, as she always did.

Elena lay swathed in the bedroll, her face and central chest exposed.

The moon had risen.

Elena had not 'shifted.

She was dead.

I had tended to elders who died, but this was the first time I had lost a friend.

My agony was sharpened by guilt. If, instead of fussing with Jack, I'd insisted that Elena help me unload the van, she wouldn't have run off.

If we'd left Montreal an hour earlier, we might've gotten her to a hospital in time.

If I hadn't picked a piece of land so far away.

If. If. If.

I howled.

Jack pushed his shoulder against mine, trying to comfort me.

I shoulder-checked him. I was hurting.

He barely swayed with my shove. Then he pushed his shoulder against me, harder this time. He wasn't going to leave me.

My howl turned high-pitched. Why did this happen? Why couldn't we save her?

Jack's long tongue swiped over my face, his lupine version of a kiss.

Comforted despite myself, I let him.

Mac yapped at me.

The pack was moving.

I trotted back to Elena and nosed her foot, the one still trapped in her ridiculous shocking pink ballerina shoe.

The foot shifted with my muzzle, but when I let go, it immediately flopped outward again. Almost like she was doing final relaxation pose in yoga.

Corpse pose.

I could smell the difference in her body. Not decay, exactly, but a flattening of her usual scent into something heavier.

Jack nudged my shoulder with his muzzle.

After a moment's hesitation, I followed the pack into the forest next to the campsite.

Mud squished under my paws. The smell of pine and loamy earth surged up my nose. Yet I kept glancing back toward the van. We couldn't abandon her.

Jack nudged me again.

What if a human came and found her? I whined deep in my throat.

Jack trotted ahead, leading the pack deeper into the forest, leaping through bush, and skirting trees.

He obviously didn't care, the scum-sucking mofo, no matter what guise he took. No wonder we'd broken up two years ago. I trailed behind Laurent and Mac, brooding.

Jack capered around a maple tree and reached a small clearing. He sniffed, stopped abruptly, and began to dig with his front paws. Mac joined him, followed by Laurent.

Out of curiosity, I sniffed around the site. I smelled pine needles, squirrels, old urine, and Jack. Did he find a clue? What was going on?

Still, I joined in with my front paws, digging more and more ferociously, as if I could tear away the memory of Elena's death.

We managed to dig a large, deep hole. Deep enough that, when I bounded into it, the dirt loomed taller than my head.

Long enough to fit almost two of us in wolf shape, end to end, not including our tails. Maybe seven feet long.

And finally, I understood what Jack had initiated. We were digging Elena's grave.

I reared back on my hind legs and dug all the harder with my front paws, although I had no idea how long we'd be able to maintain the discipline. The desire to hunt grew stronger with each passing moment.

Laurent's hackles raised. He growled softly.

Our instincts were more powerful in this form. We couldn't hold back much longer.

A squirrel raced across our vision. Mac bounded after it.

I soared out of the grave after him.

We were off, running as one. Dashing through the night, free and alive, remembering Elena, but also feeling the wind ruffle our fur and the humid spring air against our bared teeth.

Jack streaked ahead of me. I put on the juice, but he powered past me, even glancing back with a lupine grin. Bastard. But a smart one, the one who would have saved Elena if it had been at all possible.

I sped after him, mock-snapping at his tail. Jack was very vain about his tail and its fine plumage. For whatever reason, werewolves tend to grow more meager tails than wolves. Jack's was quite long and well-furred. He liked to groom it.

About fifteen feet from the riverbank, Jack stopped so abruptly that I almost ran into his hind end. I rolled head over heels through the mud, yelping.

Jack panted out his laughter: ha, ha, ha.

I would have laughed too, except I looked like such a doofus. I jumped at him and managed to yank a tiny tuft out of his tail.

His turn to yelp. He turned glittering yellow-brown eyes on me, and my heart accelerated. Now I was in for it.

I spat out the hairs and dashed behind a cluster of rocks and a dead stump.

Jack sailed over the stump and landed lightly beside me.

Show-off.

A show-off who'd trapped me next to his long, furry body. The heat radiated from his frame so strongly that it felt like he was stroking me.

My nose twitched, relishing the dark scent of his arousal.

He growled deep in his throat.

I arched my neck. I ached to rub my side against his and nip the skin of his neck, inviting him to mount me.

Instead, I eased my body between him and the stump and tore west along the riverbank.

This close to the river, my paws squelched in the mud, slowing me down. Jack ripped after me. His long strides ate up the ground, and soon I could hear him panting almost directly behind me.

I twitched my tail off to the left a half-second before Jack dove for it. I heard the click of his jaws snapping closed on empty air.

My turn to ha-ha-ha. Only for a second, though, before Jack shoulder-checked me.

Not hard, but his greater bulk pushed me toward the river.

River. Elena.

We were only about ten feet from the spot where we'd found Elena.

I stumbled on the root of an oak tree. I rolled on the side of my front left paw. I yelped and slowed to a stop.

Jack immediately backed off, whining in apology.

I ignored him and tested my paw. I could still walk, or at least limp on it, so it wasn't broken, just strained. I snapped at him in mock anger.

Jack nosed my paw and licked the fur. His tongue felt warm and wet. His touch loosened something deep inside me.

Scum-sucking motherfucker, I reminded myself, but that didn't break the spell. I stood still, waiting for more.

Jack licked upward, exploring the rest of my foreleg. I trembled. My muscles felt rigid now with the effort of holding myself in place.

I waited for him to lick my nipples. That was the usual sequence of events for human guys: kiss on the mouth, finger the breasts, fuck. And Jack was in wolf mode, something we'd never explored during our brief fling two years ago, but which I knew from personal experience made you even more likely to spring for the main event.

But Jack, the delicious, daring Jack Meng, licked back down toward my hurt paw.

He paused and sniffed the ground near my paw.

Sniffed it again.

His muscles seized with tension.

He growled softly.

Growling at dirt? What on earth?

I would have laughed in human form. Even as a wolf, I grinned. My long, pink tongue hung out of my mouth.

Jack growled again, raising his nearly black eyes to compel my own.

We stood almost muzzle to muzzle. I smelled something on his nose, a faint, musky odor that made blood shoot directly into my groin.

Desire electrified me.

I moaned deep in my throat and crouched closer to the ground, throbbing with want.

Before I had time to take my next breath, Jack leapt behind me and slammed his cock into my wet and ready opening.

I ululated with pleasure. Jack panted against my neck. The moon beamed down on us and the river rushed by while we rocked and howled, howled, howled into the night.

CHAPTER 7

When I woke up in the morning on the nylon floor of my tent, I was stiff and sore and aching in all the right places. I stretched my arms and legs luxuriously and sniffed the air. I smelled good, clean earth, a delicious male in his prime—

Oh, Christ.

I seized the soft burgundy sleeping bag lying on top of me. I was pretty sure I hadn't placed it there myself.

I squinched my eyes shut against the sunlight—and the dread rising over me—but I could still hear someone breathing hard. Someone trying not to laugh, in fact. And I'd already caught a glimpse of spacious blue nylon walls. Jack's tent. Not my own little white igloo tent.

I don't always remember exactly what happened in wolf form. But slowly, the memories percolated back, kind of like after a night of drinking. The scent of his arousal. His fur against mine. His breath against my neck. Him riding me until I nearly fainted with pleasure.

I said, "Scum. Sucking. Mother. Fucker."

"You called?"

He sounded amused, which annoyed me even more. I eased all of my bits under the sleeping bag so only my head stuck out. The cold, uneven earth underneath my body had woken me up early, but I'd be damned if I exposed my body to crawl inside the bedroll in front of Jack.

I cracked open my eyes to peer at SSMF, my ex-boyfriend and recent wolf lover.

Who was also naked.

No hiding under a sleeping bag for him. I belatedly remembered that he was a furnace, naturally warm-blooded. Some guys stick their feet out of the covers; Jack liked to sleep buck-naked and with everything sticking out.

And I mean everything.

My eyes trailed down in order to check out the everything before I yanked them back up to his face.

Jack's grin was one of the most wolfish things about him in human form and therefore one of his most seductive. He could wear the same grin in bed or while gamboling in the forest.

I realized I was grinning back at him.

Then I remembered. Forest.

River.

Elena.

Dead.

My face must have crumpled, because Jack placed his hand on my naked shoulder. His warm, callused fingers awoke nerve endings I hadn't remembered I possessed until last night.

I forced my thoughts back to Elena. I twitched my shoulder away from Jack, although I smiled to make it seem more natural. Well, I bared my teeth at him, anyway. "Thank you for the sleeping bag."

"You're welcome."

I blushed. My complexion is darker than Jack's, so I thought maybe he couldn't tell, until his smile spread across his face, and I had to glance away. I hadn't thanked him for the sex. That was a one-time thing, a wolf thing, a my-friend-is-dead-and-I'm-so-fucked-up-I'm-fucking-you thing. Not to be repeated. Not even to be acknowledged. As soon as he left, I'd wrap the sleeping bag around myself, hold my head high, and walk back to my tent to get dressed.

I said, "We have to take care of Elena." I couldn't quite bring myself to say, "Elena's body." But we'd dug her grave last night, and we certainly couldn't leave her remains in the van.

Jack nodded. "I know. I was talking to the guys—"

"Mac? And Laurent?"

Jack nodded. For some reason, it surprised me that the trio had made plans without me. This was my pack, not his. They didn't even know each other before this trip, and now Jack was schtupping me and high-fiving the guys. "Go on," I said ungraciously.

"We have to report this to the district leaders."

The earth felt even colder under my back. Elena's death was starting to feel all too real. I could smell her body even from inside the tent.

I tried to concentrate on our conversation. I had nothing against Bernard and Sylvie St-Hubert, the Glengarry district heads. I'd met the alphas briefly before making the offer on the land. I'd also invited them on our inaugural run last night, but they'd declined because of a prior engagement. If they'd come, could they have helped save Elena's life?

If, if, if. I said aloud, "I don't know what Elena was doing by the river."

Jack's brow pleated. "I was going to ask you about that. I don't know—didn't know her, but it was kind of strange for her to run right over."

"She couldn't swim," I said. "She didn't even like the water. I remember her saying she didn't mind sitting on the beach with a martini or taking a quick drink as a wolf, but she never wanted to play in it, even as a kid."

The unspoken "So why…?" now hung in the air between us, instead of sexual tension.

Jack rummaged in his backpack and tossed me a white T-shirt. He even turned his back as I slipped the T-shirt over my head. It hung well past my hips.

My heart sank further. Even though my friend was dead, a selfish sliver of me wished Jack would pay me the courtesy of ogling my body. Still, I felt a little better now that I was dressed, like I was in more control.

Meanwhile, Jack grabbed a pair of boxers and jeans. I womanfully averted my eyes, but I was conscious of the lean muscles of his ass and his long legs sliding into the jeans.

Okay, maybe the sexual tension hadn't completely dissipated.

The sound of the zipper pierced the tent. I shivered.

"It's strange that she went to the river, but we don't have any evidence of foul play," he said, snapping his jeans.

"True." Now I could meet his eyes again, even though his well-defined pectoral muscles looked good enough to lick. I seemed to remember me nuzzling his furry chest last night, but my hands wanted to play with that smooth brown skin today.

Focus, Leila! I swallowed hard and said, "There's no evidence. I just have this feeling."

He glanced sidelong at me. I don't get feelings often, but I knew he remembered the time I called him and told him to check his apartment.

Someone had broken in and stolen his laptop. His home insurance covered it, but neither of us discounted my feelings after that.

"We have to bury her today," he said finally.

I averted my head. I did not want to think about this, but I had to. "I know we couldn't bring her to a hospital last night in case we all 'shifted. But we're human now. Do you think someone could do an autopsy?"

"I know the coroner for my district," said Jack. "He's not one of us. We could never explain why we did CPR but didn't call 911."

"Aren't there any wer doctors around?" We're a shrinking breed, but not that shrinking.

Jack slowly shook his head.

"It's still impossible to work around the call schedule." He wouldn't meet my eye. It obviously bothered him that he hadn't made M.D., even though he'd almost saved Elena's life last night. "There's one guy I met from Romania. He's a foreign doctor trying to get his license in Canada. I'm pretty sure he's wer. But he's not legal yet."

The key word was "yet." Like Mark Twain said, one word made the difference, like lightning versus a lightning bug. "We don't need anyone legal. We need some answers."

"We'd need a pathologist, not any doctor. And I don't remember the guy's name."

I drew up my legs, still cocooned in the sleeping bag. Jack's eyes flickered toward my chest, but he kept listening while I brainstormed aloud. "How 'bout a wer vet? Or a taxidermist?" Both of us grimaced. I hate people who kill animals and stuff them, but they'd know anatomy, at least. I said, "Just, something. I'll have a look through my phone book and maybe everyone else can, too."

"Good idea." He smiled. I loved when he loved me for my mind and not only my body. "I know a wer vet. I'll give her a call. I'll take a look at Elena, too. See if there's anything major. I didn't last night, but—"

"It would have been a miracle if you had," I said. He'd pulled Elena out of the river, started CPR, and coordinated her rescue from the bush, which was crazy enough for a human, let alone for a werewolf at moonrise. "I'm going to make some calls. Do you, ah, have some extra pants?"

"Aww," said Jack, but he tossed me some plaid shorts and left the tent.

CHAPTER 8

Clad in my own clothes, I joined the guys clustered around the back hatch of the Honda Odyssey. I didn't want to look at Elena, but I did.

Her face was terribly still and grey. Her dirty blond hair was tangled and knotted and clotted with blood. From under her nearly closed eyelids, her now-dry, filmy blue eyes peeked out between the lids. I was grateful that someone had unrolled her own shocking pink sleeping bag over her, since she was still naked.

I tried to hold my breath. I did not want to smell her, but I couldn't help it. Her flesh had started to decompose.

Jack pointed at the bloody lump at the top of her forehead, bordering her hairline. It looked as wide as my pinky was long, but maybe that was partly the matted, bloody hair. I winced.

"She must have hit her head," said Mac.

I nodded. I still couldn't speak.

"I didn't see any blood," said Laurent.

"We didn't look in the river, though," said Jack.

I closed my eyes. I tried to imagine Elena alive and chomping on beef jerky. That felt better than standing before her corpse. Next, I remembered her modeling her "jeggings," or jeans/leggings, and telling me they were the greatest invention since the curling iron. I started smiling a little, imagining her in heaven, dancing with a random hot guy—or two—in those jeggings while they fed her some beef jerky. The G-rated kind.

My fists started to uncurl. I could breathe again.

"Sorry," said Laurent. "You were the closest to her."

Mac nodded. "You were Elena's best friend, weren't you?"

I hesitated. Best friend was a little strong. "We hung out a lot," I said.

Mac glanced quickly at me and away. I remembered that he and Elena had dated a few years ago. It never took off, but Elena hadn't offered details and I hadn't asked. Should I have?

Jack sighed. "Sorry, Leila. I wanted to check on Elena before Kelly—my vet friend—gets here. But I completely understand if it's too disturbing for you."

I swallowed hard and shook my head. "The more people who get in on this, the better. Like I said, I have no idea why Elena would run off, especially down to the river."

He watched me for a long moment. "If you're sure."

"I'm sure." I didn't realize I was tugging at the sleeve of my windbreaker until his gaze flicked down toward it. I stopped fidgeting. "You're practically a doctor. Go for it."

He winced. "Listen. I could drive her away, closer to the entrance, if you want to have some breakfast."

I licked my dry lips. "No way. I'm in."

"You want to watch him examine her?" asked Laurent.

"Uh huh." I crossed my arms in front of me and wished I'd thrown on a warmer jacket.

Jack nodded slowly. "Okay. But if you think you're going to faint, let us know. Or at least lie down or sit with your head between your legs."

I snorted. I've never fainted in my life.

Of course, I've never had a friend die on me, either. And I've certainly never seen an autopsy except on TV. But I waved Jack on. "Forget about me."

"Okay." Jack turned back to Elena. "Like I was saying, I'm not a doctor. I don't even play one on TV. So I want to take a quick look and get an idea what might've happened."

Laurent pointed at the bump on her head. "We know what happened." He glanced at me and muttered, "Sorry."

I ignored it and waited for Jack to answer.

"But what caused that head injury? Are there any other clues?" Jack said.

Mac nodded. "I thought she drowned."

"Could've been both," said Jack. "Let's keep looking." He pulled out a small cobalt camera. "If you don't mind…"

I shook my head. It'd be better if they forgot I was here, so I'd decided to shut up until they forgot I was Elena's friend, and that they'd voted me Most Likely to Have a Breakdown.

Jack shot some pictures of the lump on Elena's head. He said, "I don't want to move her if I don't have to, so I'm going to move down her body." He pulled the sleeping bag down to show her neck and shoulders. "We protected her C-spine because of her head injury—"

I flinched, remembering how I tried to do a head-tilt chin lift on her.

"—but I don't see any obvious neck fractures."

Phew.

He quickly uncovered her breasts. Elena always posed proudly with the girls in the locker room, and I have to say, she still had quite a rack, even after death. Laurent and Mac goggled for a second before Jack moved the pink bedroll south and kept talking.

"She's got a few bruises and scratches, especially on her right side." He pointed at her right hand, cheek, and a few dull bruises on her right ribs. "I think she was trying to break her fall."

"Do you think she slipped on the riverbank?" asked Mac.

Jack made a face. "I'd have to ask a pathologist, but I'd be surprised if a young, healthy wer got hurt this bad slipping on a riverbank."

Not to mention why she'd gone on a river run in the first place. I mulled over that while Jack took a few more pictures, including some close-ups of her bruises and scratches. Her right eye had started to swell, too, now that he'd mentioned it.

When Jack checked under Elena's acrylic nails, Mac said, "What are you doing?"

Jack flushed slightly. "I remembered hearing about this. If she was being attacked and she fought back, you can find stuff under the fingernails."

We all fell silent, but we each took a quick peek under the red and white polka-dotted nails. She'd broken the right index nail, and I saw a bit of dirt under the rest, but no blood or flesh or whatever it was supposed to be. I felt better.

And then I caught a whiff of musk. My legs wobbled. My mouth dried up and my eyes shot straight to Jack, telegraphing two words: *do me.*

Jack's eyes widened. Message received and noted.

Mac stirred, glancing at us. His back straightened, but I was staring too hard at Jack to care.

Laurent's harsh voice cut the tension. "Hey, what's going on between you two? Didn't you get enough last night?"

Jack ripped his eyes away from mine.

I stalked away from the guys, breathing hard. What had gotten into me? Yes, I wanted Jack. Yes, he attracted me more than any other guy, human or wer, I'd ever met. But when we first hooked up two years ago, it hadn't been this intense. Or inappropriate.

After my head cleared, I walked back in time to see Jack quickly separate Elena's legs and glance at her most vulnerable area. I'd shoved a hot pack above this region before, but somehow it felt even more wrong to see the lightning bolt shaved into her "landing strip" of pubic hair in broad daylight.

Jack shot a quick photo of her entire body before he covered her back up, and we all started breathing again.

"Do you think someone raped her?" Mac said.

Jack said, "No. We haven't detected anyone else around here and I don't think she had time to be raped. We got here after five. It would have taken her at least 20 minutes to walk down to the river."

"Less to run," muttered Laurent.

"Even so. I found her at 5:38. I can't rule out sexual assault, but it seems unlikely." Jack shook his head. "I don't carry around a rape kit."

Of course not. I felt ill at the thought.

"I don't think a vet would have one, either," said Jack.

We laughed uneasily.

It was bad enough that my friend was dead. What if it hadn't been an accident? My gut clenched. Even though that's what had been gnawing at the back of my mind, I hadn't let myself contemplate it.

"You think she might have been murdered?" asked Laurent. His tone was belligerent, like a student who asked the teacher a question but already knew the answer.

Jack delivered a flat brown stare to him. "I'll leave that to the experts."

"Whoever they are," said Mac.

I wiped my hand across my forehead. Jack was doing his best, and so would his vet friend. But would it be enough?

Mac checked his watch. "I've got to make a call."

His human girlfriend kept him on a short leash. Laurent snorted. Mac gave him the finger. We all laughed a little.

I retreated near my tent to grab a granola bar out of my backpack and curse myself for not preventing Elena's death.

Jack sat beside me on a rock. He watched me tear open the package and chomp on the oatmeal apple bar. I could feel the humidity in the air and smell the rain building in the low-slung clouds, but in the meantime, my granola bar was dry as toast.

Jack said, "It's not your fault."

"I wasn't paying attention to her. I was—" I bit back the words "distracted by you." No need to add humiliation to guilt. "—setting up my tent. I didn't even notice she was gone. Someone else had to tell me. And then I flipped out. I couldn't even do the jaw thrust right. You had to do it, on top of everything else—"

"Leila." He stood and folded me in his arms.

For a second, he felt so right, I let myself lean against him and bury my nose between his shoulder and his neck. He smelled like wood smoke and coffee and wolf and man.

Tears pricked my eyes. Elena was dead, and even in the middle of mourning her, I wanted Jack so badly. I let myself hug him back. I ran my hand up the back of his leather jacket, feeling the muscle and bone and sheer strength beneath.

He made a noise in his throat. I knew he was feeling it too. "Leila," he almost growled. And then he kissed me.

His lips were firm. I hesitated a second before I tilted my head back and returned the pressure. His lips softened and he ran his hands up my back. I could almost *feel* him saying, *I missed you.*

I closed my eyes. I'd missed him too. His smell. His taste. His tongue. The way he could raise goose bumps on my arms with a single look.

He placed his hands on either side of my face and inhaled deeply. I knew he was smelling me, and I was glad. I wanted him to want me in the same deep and primal way I wanted him.

He kissed me until I was breathless with want. Then he dotted one last kiss on my lips and said, "Leila." That was all. But the word felt like another caress and also, faintly, a warning.

I kissed him again. It was like I'd been starving for him for the past two years. I'd been doing okay, ignoring my hunger, concentrating on my work and saving the world as best I could. But one car ride with Jack Meng and I was ready to press my naked body against his and run with him under the moonlight.

For a second, his lips responded. He inhaled deeply and wrapped me in his embrace, and I felt like I could live there forever. Then he pulled back, more firmly this time.

My heart thudded. I do not take rejection well. I yanked my arms away from him and glared up at him. "What is it?"

"First of all, I'm about one second away from throwing you back in the tent and having my way with you."

My heart started beating again. "You just try it."

"I might. But first, we should talk about what happened before."

My chin snapped up. "You mean how you were a scum-sucking motherfucker two years ago?"

He sighed. "If you want to call it that. I want to talk about that, too. But I meant what happened to Elena. I want to go down to the river before everyone wanders over and destroys the trail."

Guilt ripped through my stomach. Once again, I'd started lusting after Jack—and even bringing up ancient history—instead of focusing on my friend. What was wrong with me?

I rubbed my palm against my forehead. I felt grit rub against my skin, and dust made my eyes tear, but I didn't care. I'd rather cry over dirt than over Jack. He was so intelligent and so practical, but now I remembered how that sometimes left me cold.

He was the smart one, which made me the dumb one. He thought with his head and I led with my heart. Theoretically, we were equal, but it didn't always feel that way.

Out of the corner of my eye, I felt Laurent and Mac's eyes on us, adding to my humiliation. I turned away.

Jack said, "I'd rather kiss you. But I want to find out why she died."

My head jerked up at the pain in his voice. Our eyes met and I noticed dark shadows under his eyes. I hadn't remembered him looking this beat up two years ago, even following a bunch of night shifts. After a minute, I realized it was the sorrow buried in his deep brown eyes. And I realized that although I felt guilty about Elena dying, because I hadn't noticed her running off, Jack truly blamed himself for not saving her. Detective work was the only way he could atone.

I wanted to find out how she died, too. I knew we shouldn't mess up the crime scene for the experts, but it couldn't hurt to take a look. "Do you know how to track?" I asked Jack.

"No. But you do," he said.

Finally, I smiled. "Follow me, city boy."

CHAPTER 9

Mac ambled in front of us and blocked our way. "When's your vet getting here?"

Jack paused. "About lunch time. She's coming from Montreal. The district heads might make it here first, but I'm not sure. I left messages on their voice mail."

"I think the St-Huberts live pretty close to here," I said. "That's what they told me before, anyway."

Mac nodded. "I've gone snowmobiling with them on the trails. They're only about half an hour's drive away from here. I'd expect them anytime. I should text them."

"Cool." I jerked my head toward the river. "Jack and I are going to check the trail."

Laurent snorted. My cheeks flamed. I felt like yelling, "That was not a euphemism!"

Jack ignored it. "We want to take a quick look through the woods before the whole gang arrives."

"I'll come with you," said Mac.

The last thing we needed was a mass exodus to Elena's drowning point. The trail would probably be messed up enough by the resus and the truck. We'd never find anything. I opened my mouth, but Jack spoke first.

"No. Call Bernard and Sylvie. The fewer people on this, the better. Leila knows how to track, and I've got a good camera. We'll report back to the group in a few minutes, before it starts to rain."

Mac made a face and eyed Jack up and down. I calculated that "Big Mac" had to be over six feet, so at least three inches taller and twenty pounds heavier than Jack.

Jack stood with his feet braced on the soil. The wind stirred his hair while he stared back at Mac without blinking.

After a long moment, Mac grunted and looked down. No words were exchanged, but I figured that Jack nearly saving Elena's life had made him the temporary alpha.

Mac looked at me and said, "Be careful. I'll expect you back within the hour."

Be careful? With Jack? I hid a laugh and shrugged. "That'll give us time for a preliminary scout."

"Don't touch anything," said Laurent.

I waved him off. Even I knew that from *Dexter* and the rest of the crime shows.

Anyway, my first destination was a lot closer: the minivan. It was surrounded by footprints, but I was looking for a woman's prints. Only Elena and I qualified.

I explained to Jack, "I don't know where she went after we pulled up. I went to set up my tent. See, this is me." I pointed to some boot prints in the mud, already drying out, on the passenger side of the van. "Women's prints tend to be smaller than men's, with a shorter stride, and we walk more pigeon-toed, which means the toes are pointed in. So even though I'm wearing boots like the rest of you, you can see the difference between you—" I pointed to Jack's prints, bigger and pointing straight ahead. "—and Mac. He's the biggest. See how the prints dig into the mud more?"

Jack nodded, drawing his brows together in concentration. I felt good about being the one teaching him.

I walked more slowly over to what had been the driver's side. "Elena's not hard to spot. She was the only one wearing flats instead of boots."

Jack pointed at the footprints. Elena had walked more on her toes than I did, probably because of her shoes.

"She usually changed into her boots first thing at the camp site, but I don't see that. I see her walking to the back of the van, but before she got to the back hatch, she spun to her right and started walking toward the river."

We followed the trail. At first, Elena had followed the path, but then she veered west, into the trees. The spaces between her prints widened, and the toe prints became deeper than the heel.

"She's running now," I said. Fear rose in my chest. I stamped it down with anger. What was Elena running from, or to? What made her take off from the safety of the pack? How and why did she die?

Her prints were less obvious off the trail, but still clear in the mud and trampled grass. I pointed silently at twigs and even a few rocks that had been kicked out of the way. Elena hadn't been watching the ground. She'd been intent on her goal. What goal?

Jack said, "We're getting closer to the river."

I nodded. The muddy water neared the lip of the riverbed during spring run off, so we could see it from a good fifty feet away. Although the current didn't look strong, it had been enough to kill Elena.

I was breathing faster now. Exertion, tamped-down panic, and—I glanced at Jack out of the corner of my eye—ever-present lust.

He did it for me. He always had. His black hair stuck straight up, spiky. He was starting to sweat, too. I had the sudden, crazy urge to start rolling with him in the grass and make some tracks of our own.

He caught me looking at him and frowned. His frown deepened as he spotted the look in my eye. "Leila—"

The breeze batted the collar of his windbreaker. I smoothed it with my hand without taking my eyes off his.

I reached forward and traced the side of his neck and then his face, echoing the way he'd held my head as we kissed.

His lips pressed together. He looked angry, but his Adam's apple bobbed up and down, and I knew desire outweighed his sense of duty.

I fit my body against his. He felt so warm. When other guys wore down coats, Jack could get away with a lined leather jacket. He radiated heat. I inhaled his scent. Now that I'd found him again, I didn't know how I'd be able to let him go.

I rubbed my hips against his and felt how much he wanted me.

"Leila," he said, sterner this time. Jack's pupils were dilated and his nostrils flared, but he wove his fingers in my hair in order to lift my head away from his neck.

Great. I couldn't keep my hands off him, and he played little Mr. Prude. I jerked my entire body away from him and stood two feet away.

The wind had changed, now blowing from the east. His collar lay flat. No further excuse to touch him. Not that I cared.

I shook my head and bit the inside of my cheek. *Ouch.*

There. Now I didn't need to touch him anymore.

Right.

To distract myself, I turned back to Elena's trail. It stopped at an ash tree overhanging the river. I paused. "This is bizarre."

"What?" Jack said from five feet behind me. He was trying to keep his distance now.

I could act professional, too. "It's not unusual for people to try to throw off a tracker around a tree. They'll keep up on the trail for another 5 to 10 paces, then walk backwards in their prints to take a 90-degree turn at a big tree. The tracker's supposed to think he lost the prints on the trail, but the tree helps to hid the real trail."

Jack stared at the mess of prints at the base of the tree. "You think that's what Elena was doing? You said you thought she wasn't paying attention to where she was going."

"I still don't. She did something even weirder. She was pacing all around this tree, especially here." I pointed at the tree side facing the river. "I think she was jumping up and down. Normally, if you're walking without thinking, the print is deeper at the heel, and the soil gets scuffed in the direction of movement. But here, I see a lot of prints where both her feet are facing forward and the prints are deeper at the toe. Plus there's bits of bark on the ground."

Jack pointed to the trunk, which looked a bit scuffed. I raised my eyes to the lowest tree branch. Most of it was covered in green lichen, but some areas were definitely worn off. Some of the higher, thinner tree branches were broken. I glanced around, but none of the other trees had sustained such obvious damage.

"You think she climbed up the tree?" I asked. "But you found her in the river."

Before he could answer, I smelled blood.

CHAPTER 10

If the wind hadn't started blowing from the east, I would have smelled blood sooner. I picked my way through the rocks and mud, conscious of our many footprints. I didn't want to mess it up too much for other investigators, but it was probably too late for that, and now curiosity had gotten the best of me.

I found it. A heavy smear of blood on a rock. I bent over it. This had to be Elena's blood.

I felt light-headed. I would not faint. Would not. I gritted my teeth and tried to summon up a memory that would keep me grounded.

The sniper can determine a wound's location from the quality of blood. I almost laughed when I recognized the source of that memory. An old army guy had taught me how to track a few years ago. I wanted to get back to the land, but since I'd been raised as a Chinese princess and not a wilderness survivor, I didn't know how. I hired the old guy to take me out on "wilderness training." I thought he'd teach me about making a fire and how to find north. He did, but he really loved the blood and guts. He'd say stuff like, "A lung wound is pink and frothy. A head wound is wet and slimy. Guts leak bile, so the blood is lighter and it smells like acid."

At the time, I rolled my eyes and said, "Sounds real useful." But now I clung to that memory to try and figure out what happened to Elena.

I crouched to stare at that rock jutting out of the riverbank. The part that showed was the size of my two fists put together, although of course, like an iceberg, most of the rock would be submerged, and the jagged point at the end was the important part.

That was the part with the two-inch smear of my friend's blood. On closer inspection, I spotted a single blond hair.

My throat closed up.

"Stay with me," said Jack.

I took a deep breath. I could do this. I didn't even feel nauseous anymore.

"Good work," he said. "Do you mind if I talk?"

I shook my head. I just didn't want to talk myself.

"I found her downstream from here," he said, watching me to make sure I could handle it.

I nodded. My hands clenched into fists.

"I marked the spot with my bandana in case I had trouble carrying her back."

I spotted a worm of red and black fabric material two feet from the rock. I focused on that instead of the bloody rock.

"How did you find her, anyway?" I asked.

He turned his head west. A muscle flexed in his cheek. He said, without meeting my eye, "I could smell her."

I stared at him. I was a top smeller in my pack, second only to Elena. Women traditionally have a better sense of smell. Why hadn't I picked her up first?

Then I remembered that Elena had been nearing heat.

Here I'd been thrusting myself at Jack all morning, and he hadn't wanted to anything about it beyond the usual male reaction, which was probably as personal as a pogo stick.

Meanwhile last night, he could track Elena down to the river. Water cuts the scent, so he must've really been gunning for her.

I closed my eyes. Did he have sex with me last night because he'd smelled *Elena*?

"Don't go there," I muttered to myself.

Eventually, I tuned into Jack's voice. "And I could hear her. Or at least, I thought I heard something. Like a tree branch break." He frowned and glanced at the ash tree again.

I shivered. Was it possible Jack had heard Elena fall out of the tree? If so, she must have barely tumbled into the water before he found her. Why didn't she make it?

"I was going to the river anyway," he said, almost to himself. "I figured that was the most dangerous place she could be, and we could work our way back from there."

Great. Very logical. I could try to forget about him and the other guys sniffing after Elena.

I unclenched my jaw. *Don't take it personally. Don't take it personally,* I chanted to myself. Elena used to coach me on that, actually. She said it was from "Toltec Wisdom," whatever that means. I think she got it off Oprah.

But she had a point. As wolves, we were ruled by biology. In human form, most of us are fertile every month and we get periods like everyone else, except we're more prone to irregular cycles and other problems. That would be me.

We're supposed to be most fertile in wolf form, but that only happens once a year. For me, it was back in February. And when that happens, the male wolves—all of them—think you are the hottest thing on four legs. It doesn't matter if you're fat or thin or bandy-legged or cross-eyed. To every male, you are desire incarnate.

I don't think Elena was in full-blown heat, or the guys would have gone collectively nuts. She was probably a month away, but still shooting up on the lust scale.

I pinched the bridge of my nose and pretended to study tracks so I didn't have to look at Jack. You'd think I'd be immune to him after two years of radio silence. Particularly when I already knew he sucked scum.

"You okay?" he said.

I nodded without looking at him. Even his voice did it for me, a mellow tenor that used to make me curl up in bed with the phone pressed against my ear. Back in the day, I once teased him that he could be a phone sex operator. He said, "I'm not a girl." I told him I was sure a gay sex line would hire him, especially since he was bilingual—actually, trilingual, with English, French, and Cantonese. He tackled me and showed me how he could operate my sex anytime.

Why was I thinking about the nasty again? Not like me. At all.

I cleared my throat and pointed at the river. "I don't want to go too close in case we mess up your tracks. I can see where you went down." And, although I didn't mention it, we both eyed the obvious impression where Elena's body had lain, surrounded by numerous footprints.

Next, we walked to the van's tire tracks, where I'd pulled up and we'd loaded Elena in the back, but we already knew that part of the story.

"That didn't help that much, did it," I said, mostly about the tracking. I started walking back to the camp, crossing away from the previous prints so we wouldn't mess up the track more than we already had.

Jack didn't speak for a moment. I noticed that his pace matched mine. It was something we'd always done effortlessly in synch.

Then Jack said, "I found it helpful. She left the camp on her own. No one kidnapped her. She was running, so it seemed like something urgent."

"But the whole tree thing was so bizarre. Why would she climb up a tree? And remember the bone I pulled out of her mouth? How'd that get in there? She liked beef jerky, especially before she 'shifted, but it'd have to be a really bad batch to have a bone stuck in it." Anyway, I couldn't imagine Elena sprinting toward the river, still noshing on beef jerky. "She didn't get it out of the cooler in the back because she never got to the back hatch. So she found chicken somewhere around here."

"Good point." But I could tell Jack was distracted. He glanced over his shoulder and headed back toward the ash tree. "When we get the all-clear, I'd like to check this out more."

"You mean like fingerprint it?" I was curious, too, so I matched his pace back to the tree.

"I'm not sure. I'm no police expert, but I know a few guys in the force. I could ask them." He paused. "If the St-Huberts don't mind."

Once the district heads got here, they'd run the show. I glanced toward the entrance, but I hadn't heard or spotted them yet.

Jack stopped a few feet from the tree, frowning at the bark.

I took a deep breath of fresh air. I couldn't get enough of this after the exhaust fumes of Montreal.

Wait a minute.

I sniffed again, more attentively. Even in human form, after a full moon, when my nose was less acute, I could detect mud and pine trees and—what was that?

I smelled *meat*.

I sniffed once more, but the fickle breeze had shifted again. Still, I knew I hadn't been hallucinating.

I began circling the trunk of the tree.

I felt Jack's eyes on me, but he didn't demand what I was doing. That was one thing I always liked about him. Instead of asking questions to hear the sound of his own voice, he watched. He listened.

I sniffed once more and caught a good whiff.

Chicken.

Chicken tinged with something else. Maybe a seasoning.

I'd heard of wild turkeys breeding in the area, but not wild chickens.

And definitely not seasoned chicken.

It meant a human had been around this tree.

The obvious candidate was the man selling the land to us, Mr. Tabassian. He could've checked out the grounds before signing the last of the paperwork. But I doubted he was the one strolling by the ash tree. He had the kind of gut he had to adjust when he sat down. I knew he hired a guy to take care of the mowing and snow removal instead of doing it himself. A real hands-off kind of man.

"Do you smell that? It's chicken," I said to Jack.

He burst out laughing, but stopped at the look on my face. He frowned and smelled the air. His brow pleated even more.

He bent to sniff the tree base and worked his way up the branches. "It's strongest here." He pointed to a branch that dangled about a foot out of his reach.

I wanted to climb up the branch and get a good whiff, but I knew I shouldn't. I closed my eyes and inhaled. "You're right." I'd call that point maximal. I noticed the end of the branch had broken off, exposing fresh, pale wood.

"Why would someone hang a chicken from a tree?" Jack squinted into the sun as if he was trying to visualize it.

"Well, that's what you're supposed to do in bear country. But I doubt there are any bears here. It's mostly farms and a few houses. Not bear habitat."

"So one of the campers might have left it," said Jack.

"Mr. Tabassian hasn't rented out to campers in the past 18 months. He let his insurance lapse because he wasn't making enough money on it. That's when he put it up for sale."

Jack closed his eyes and smelled as hard as he could. He was concentrating, but it reminded me of a sommelier smelling a fine vintage. Or a man in the throes of a different kind of ecstasy.

When he opened his eyes, the irises had darkened slightly, the way they did in bed.

I swallowed. All morning, we'd done the push-pull sex tease thing, but I felt like I'd been the instigator.

This time, though, Jack walked up to me and kissed me with such thorough hunger, my knees buckled.

In answer, he kissed me harder. He tasted my mouth, exploring my tongue and teeth.

My heart pounded in my chest. I kissed him back. I wasn't capable of hiding my emotions. I still wanted him, even though I'd forced myself to forget about him. In fact, my desire was even more acute after two years of deprivation. I moaned deep in my throat.

He muttered what sounded almost like a curse before he tangled his hands in my hair and sank his fingers into the curves of my ass.

I jumped. This was very aggressive for the buttoned-up Jack I used to know.

As if reading my mind, he thrust his hips against mine, rubbing against me, making me dizzy even before he shoved his fingers under my bra and pinched my nipple.

I cried out. Usually, I liked tenderness, but I felt so crazy, I wanted it like this.

He ripped open my bra. I hardly knew what he was doing except within seconds, I felt a cool breeze on my skin, closely followed by his hot, smooth mouth and tongue, with just a nip of teeth.

I shoved my hand down his pants and grabbed him, long and hard and already slick with anticipation. I squeezed him.

He swore. We both tore open his pants so I could tease him with my mouth, too. He was so urgent, I had barely tasted the salt on the head of his cock before he shoved it as deep as it could go.

I didn't choke, but only because I automatically pulled back. That brought me to myself for a second. This was madness. We were investigating the spot where Elena had died. With the tiny remaining part of my brain, I gasped, "No," pulled myself off of him, and started to run back to the camp.

I hadn't gotten ten feet before he tackled me from behind. I'd been half-expecting that. I tumbled to the ground, cushioned by Jack's arms and muscular body, but still getting well-rolled in the mud and dead leaves and the barest shoots of green grass. We rolled around, laughing, before he kissed me and unbuckled my jeans. Then he looked into my eyes and paused. For the first time, a hint of uncertainty crossed his oak-colored irises. "Leila—"

Oh, no, you're not. No more games . I rolled over so I was on top. I yanked his own jeans—no boxers—down to his knees and straddled his hips, bare flesh against bare flesh.

He grimaced, almost a silent scream, before he flipped me over and entered me slowly, so slowly, making sure I was ready.

He felt so right. God damn it, I was ready. I wrapped my legs behind his hips, urging him onward. I urged so hard, my hips lifted off the ground. Sweat gleamed on his face, his nostrils flared, he smelled like all man, and the tendons stood out in his neck and arms, but he still wanted to go slow.

"Leila," he breathed. "This isn't—"

"You're fucking right this isn't! Fuck me, you fuck fuck fucker!" I tried to slide down on him.

Instead, his eyes narrowed. He looked almost like he loathed me, but instead he shoved his cock into me so hard I screamed. "Like that?"

"Yes, like—" I arched to put more pressure on my clit. And then I couldn't speak any more, it was so fantastic, my vision blurred. I saw red and blue and green and yellow and he smelled like heaven and he rode me like an animal while he played me like an orchestra. He teased my breasts with his mouth. He kissed my stomach, my armpits, my neck, my mouth, my hair. He hit my pleasure points with his cock, over and over, and augmented them with his thumb.

I exploded. I shuddered. I screamed.

I think he was having a good time, too, but I was having too much of an out-of-body experience to care. By the time he collapsed on top of me, my throat was raw from screaming, and the rest of me was pretty tender, too. I became aware of twigs trying to pierce my skin and the wet earth chilling me.

We were both still breathing fast. In fact, our breath was coordinated. I smiled at that. We still matched.

"Leila," he said.

I tensed. Here came the recriminations. I didn't want him to admonish me, or to point out we were mindless boobs who had probably destroyed key evidence, not to mention done it without a condom. I wanted to bask for one more second. "Jack—"

"That was phenomenal."

My mouth stretched into a smile. I relaxed into the cold ground for another few minutes. At least Jack's body was still heating me up on top. "The best I've ever had," I agreed.

"Hey, what about me two years ago?" He narrowed his eyes in mock anger.

"You've gotten better." I refused to think who he must've practiced on. Now was not the time to dwell.

"I think it's you," he said. I snorted, but he kissed me until my cynicism melted. He said, "No, seriously."

"Let's say we're both sex bombs and leave it at that." He was so beautiful. I loved the tenderness in his eyes and the way he threw back his head and laughed at my joke.

"Sex bombs?" he repeated, still laughing.

"Right. You know. Like the Tom Jones song." I smoothed out his hair. It stuck up in the back. My fingers found a twig, which I removed. I did not want to stop touching him. He must have felt the same way, because he was still inside me.

"Am I too heavy?" he asked.

"Never." I heard the fervency in my own voice and flinched. "Well, not unless you gain another 30 pounds."

He snorted, but I did have to shift my legs, and he ran his hand down my arm. "You have goose bumps."

I shrugged, but he rolled so I was on top and he took the ground. He managed to stay inside me. "Damn, this is cold," he said.

"Yes," I agreed. I was starting to shiver from the cool air. Jack was a furnace on my front side, but I was always kind of thin-blooded for a wer. The fact that we were about ten minutes away from a spring shower didn't help. The humid air carried a chill, almost an angry pinch.

"We have to get back." He paused.

"I know," I said.

Neither of us stirred.

"I didn't mean to…take advantage of you. I mean, I wanted to, but this was…" He paused again. The corners of his mouth jerked up in the smile I loved. Used to love. Loved again. Whatever.

"Phenomenal?" I said innocently.

"Precisely. You have a way with words."

"I remember them well. Especially when they're complimentary."

Jack kissed my cheek. "I never said one bad word about you."

I couldn't muster the energy to dredge up bygones. Not after the best sex of my life. "Keep it that way."

"You're smart. You're obviously"—his breath changed—"so sexy, you should be illegal." He ran his hand over my backside and my breathing altered too. He said, "You keep your head in a crisis. I admire that."

Crisis. Elena. Dead. The afterglow drained away, and we stared into each other's eyes. What had we done?

Jack cocked his ear. He had the best hearing of any wer I knew. He said, "Someone's coming."

CHAPTER 11

Jack and I barely made it back to the campground, clothes on and hair smoothed-down, in time to see a black Honda CRV pull into the lot.

I relaxed minutely. "It's Bernard and Sylvie," I whispered to Jack. The district heads had beaten the veterinarian.

Bernard held the door open for Sylvie. Even from a distance, I detected his nostrils flaring. He could smell all the new wers in his territory. He nodded at me, but his lips stayed parted in a half-smile/snarl. He didn't trust anyone. Maybe that was a good thing in a leader.

Bernard was wiry, about 50 years old, with salt and pepper hair, but obviously still sharp and strong enough to lead the district. Sylvie, the female district head and also his common-law wife, held on to his arm as they walked toward us. Even though we'd called them before 7 a.m., she was beautifully turned out, from her cap of chestnut hair to her black low-heeled boots. I imagined that as a wolf, she'd be the first to rip the burrs out of her tail and lick the hairs back into place. Elena and I liked to dress up or down for fun, but Sylvie was a woman for whom appearance was a serious consideration.

Laurent, Mac, Jack, and I stood in a line beside the main building while we waited for them to approach. When they neared striking distance, we lifted our chins, exposing our necks.

They surveyed us for a long, silent moment. I could feel my blood throbbing in my throat.

Bernard spoke first. His voice rang into the trees. "Why did you call us?"

For obvious reasons, we hadn't revealed much over the phone except that it was urgent. Since I headed the campaign to buy this campground, I stepped forward, but I kept both my voice and my face lowered as I spoke. "One of our members died last night."

"I see," said Bernard, while I studied his shoes. Good quality brown leather hiking boots, broken in, well-polished. He and his wife both cared about appearances. Bernard said, "Explain what happened."

First, I introduced Jack, Mac, and Laurent. They continued to expose their necks until Bernard gave them a curt nod to relax.

Although Jack kept perfect form in following the ritual, his dark eyes didn't blink. He had not fully accepted Bernard as his leader.

Bernard waited for me to continue. I said, "Elena drove us here. That's her van." I pointed at the Honda Odyssey. "As far as we can tell, she ran off the campground almost immediately and headed toward the river." I paused, unsure if I should add the chicken smell and the broken tree branches. No, better leave that until later. "Mac and Laurent noticed she was missing and told me and Jack about it. We searched for her. Jack found her in the river. He's a paramedic, so he started CPR. Laurent and I got the van to bring him more equipment. We almost saved her. I mean, her pulse came back, but the moon—" My voice broke. My hands flexed into fists. I forced them to relax and took a deep breath so I could continue. "The moon rose. We all 'shifted. She died."

Bernard nodded, averting his eyes from my emotion. Sylvie stepped forward to pat my hand. Her skin was cool. "What are you not telling us?"

I glanced at Jack. He said, "This morning, Leila and I searched the area where we'd found Elena. I wanted to know if there were any clues."

Bernard exhaled, but I heard the growl underneath. The hair rose on my arms and neck. He said, "Why didn't you wait for us? We arrived within 90 minutes."

Beside me, Jack's stance remained fixed with his legs apart and planted on the ground. He said, "Leila's a good tracker. I thought it might rain and wash away the evidence. We tried to call, but we couldn't reach you."

Bernard stepped close enough to smell Jack. Bernard's snarl-to-smile ratio now reached 70/30. He was also taller than Jack and accustomed to being obeyed.

"We apologize," I said.

Jack's lips tightened. I held my breath, but Jack retained enough sense-to-testosterone ratio not to object.

Bernard snorted. "I'd rather hear it from this one." It was a mild form of disrespect not to name Jack.

I eyed my lover again. He locked eyes with Bernard.

If they were going to fight, it would be now. With their bare hands.

After a long moment, Jack's shoulders relaxed even as his quadriceps muscles tensed. "We apologize for searching the area before you came."

It was a specific apology, less submissive than my own. Bernard knew it. His brows drew together, but his tone was mild. "I accept your lack of judgment. You were probably concerned about your friend. However, you must know how seriously we take a death. We do our own investigations, and we can't afford to compromise any evidence."

Jack and I nodded. I fought the urge to chew the inside of my cheek. Wers are very attuned to body language, and I was probably already telegraphing too much with my face and hands. If the rest of them figured out we'd had sex at the scene, we were toast. Burnt toast.

Sylvie watched me with a particularly haughty expression. She raised her nose and sniffed the air once. Twice.

Oh, no. She could smell the fluids on us. Women tend to have a better sense of smell than men, both in human and wolf form.

I turned scarlet. My lungs squeezed into apple-sized chunks of flesh. My heart paused.

"I believe the scene has already been compromised," said Sylvie.

Bernard waited for her to explain, but she shook her head, still watching me. I didn't dare look at Jack, but his stance didn't alter. Either he didn't catch this new threat, or he didn't feel threatened. Sweat broke out on my forehead and prickled my armpits. My heart started up again, but faster than a jackrabbit's. I'd been so proud of myself, negotiating a piece of land for my pack. Now Elena was dead, and Jack and I were whores who'd ruined the investigation before it even began.

Thunder rumbled in the distance, low and threatening.

A drop of rain hit my cheek. Then my hair.

Rain.

Washing away the evidence. Evidence of what happened to Elena, but also of Jack and my foolishness.

I wanted to cry and laugh at the same time.

Bernard said, "I must make some phone calls." He squinted at the sky, assessing the upcoming downpour, before he marched toward the main building with his cell phone in his hand.

Sylvie stayed by my side. "May I see you for a moment?"

"Of course," I murmured. She was the district head. Old term: alpha female. Either way, she outranked me, and it was my duty to obey.

CHAPTER 12

Sylvie pitched her voice low, almost seductive, in the close confines of the CRV. "Tell me everything that happened. Don't leave out a single detail unless I stop you."

I glanced out the passenger window of their vehicle. My breath was already fogging up the window. My legs sank into the black leather car cushions. I could smell the new car scent overlaid with Sylvie's floral perfume and natural musk. I felt trapped. And, although I wouldn't admit it aloud, I wished Jack could stay by my side.

Sylvie's classic red nails tapped on the driving wheel. "Let me make it easier for you. This is why I ask. Bernard is very good at evidence. He pieces together information. He is logical. He uses reason."

I breathed a little more normally. Jack was like that. I found it either comforting or aggravating, depending on the circumstances.

"I use more intuition, Gestalt, and a certain amount of human psychology to put the picture together. That is why Bernard and I are such a good team. Now. He is calling his policemen friends and getting advice. And I am putting the story together. For that, I need you. I know you are hiding something, whether it's consciously or subconsciously. That is not helping your friend. So tell me everything." She straightened her already-impeccable posture and reached for the door handle. "We will start from the beginning, when you drove here from Montreal. You can show me where everything happened. Where did Elena pull up the van?"

I licked my lips. "I know Bernard was worried about too many people on the trail, especially—"

She waved her hand. "I insist."

I opened my car door, leaving smudges on the polished metal handle. I had to obey her. My only move was to delay her. "Well, okay. From the beginning. We pulled up next to the old camp building, where they used to sign in the guests."

"Show me."

There was only one road into the campground, but it fit into my plan. I pointed at the road and the camp building. I could still see our van's tracks in the mud, so I pointed them out. She looked at the tire tracks and flattened grass, where Elena hadn't quite managed to stay on the gravel road, and said, "Hmm."

"We got here not long before moonrise. About 5 p.m. We were setting up our tents when Mac and Laurent noticed that Elena had... disappeared."

"They saw her go?"

"No. But she wasn't setting up her tent with the rest of us, and Laurent smelled her heading away from the camp. He was worried because she was moving toward the river, and she couldn't swim."

Sylvie's gaze shifted to her husband, who was still talking on his cell phone. He'd moved closer to the camp building, presumably looking for better reception. "Laurent knew her well?"

I was surprised. I thought she'd go right for the money, how we'd found Elena, but she meant it when she said she wanted all the details. "No. Or, I don't know what you mean by 'well.' We were all friends because we were part of the Côte-des-Neiges pack, and we hung out once a month. But Laurent didn't socialize much. He's a lawyer. He's always working. In fact, he's helping me close this land deal. Elena was a businesswoman and she—" I paused to try and phrase this. "She liked to have fun. She wouldn't hang out in Laurent's office or anything."

"What about Mac?"

"She and Mac went out for a while, but that was over a year ago. He's a good guy, and she was trying to date werewolves, but it didn't work out."

"He's her ex?" Sylvie swung to check out Bernard again as she spoke. Her husband had closed his cell and was walking toward us.

"Yes, but no hard feelings. They're friends now." Mac was one of the good guys.

Sylvie gave me a cool look. "We're not finished. I will talk to you again later."

"I'm sure." I lowered my head to hide my relief. Saved by the rain and by Bernard. Now I could concentrate on trying to figure out what happened to Elena. Well, once Sylvie and Bernard were finished with us.

CHAPTER 13

Bernard eyed each of us in turn. We stood in a loose semi-circle while the rain dripped off our windbreakers. We could've all squeezed into Jack's tent, but I got the feeling Bernard wanted us to stay off-kilter.

Bernard stared a little longer at Jack, who stood on my right. "Sylvie and I have made a plan."

"Please sit down," Sylvie added. "This is a difficult time for you."

That made me even more wary. It must be bad news. Still, we slid onto a picnic table that was so old, its grey wood bench sagged under our weight. The four of us chose to sit together, across from the district heads. Jack stayed on my right. Although we weren't touching, I could feel the warmth radiating from his body. I felt more confident with him at my side.

Bernard cleared his throat. "I have spoken with my connections. They will investigate the area today. No one is to go there in the meantime. It is common sense. Let the professionals do their job." I didn't realize I had gulped until his eyes darted to my throat. He was very perceptive. "Now for the more difficult part. When humans die under strange circumstances, their pathologists can do an autopsy to try and determine the cause of death. We do know of a pathologist who is sympathetic, but he is now in Calgary. In any case, many of our members are wary of allowing any tissue samples in case they are sent for DNA testing."

I resisted the urge to crack my knuckles. It was hard for me to sit still when I was pretty sure I didn't like where he was going.

"For that reason, we have asked a...colleague to take a look at Elena. She is not a pathologist. She is a veterinarian. She will not do a formal autopsy. However, she can learn what she can and then she will report back to us."

As a wer, I'm used to strange stuff. I wasn't surprised about the no-tissue-samples thing. It's a huge debate in our community. Some people

52

want to try and figure out what makes us what we are, biologically, and the rest of us are terrified government wackos will hunt us down and put us in concentration camps if they get the slightest genomic hint of our existence. In case you're wondering, I'm in the second camp. Keep your hands off my body. I'll raise money to fund a private wer lab with heavily guarded information, but I wouldn't trust it to any regular human pathologist.

Still, I needed more details. "Who's the vet?"

"Dr. Valentina Flores."

I'd never heard of her. Not too surprising, since we were out of my regular territory. But I kept talking, ignoring the rain dribbling into my eyes. "Jack called a vet—"

Sylvie answered. "No. We are keeping this within the district. Dr. Flores is our vet. She lives about 15 minutes away."

"Is she one of us?" asked Laurent.

Bernard nodded once.

I relaxed.

Jack didn't. "Is she trustworthy?"

Bernard snorted. "We wouldn't have called her if she wasn't."

Jack shook his head. "Where will she perform the P.M.? Here or in her clinic?"

Bernard and Sylvie exchanged a look. "We haven't arranged all the details."

"I'm sure she'd want all her equipment, but I think it's dangerous to transport Elena's body to her clinic. What if Dr. Flores were stopped on the way? The police certainly wouldn't understand what she was doing."

A muscle clenched in Bernard's jaw. "Point taken."

"So she'd have to bring whatever equipment she could. She might want to take photos. And what about lab tests? We might want to do a toxicology screen to make sure Elena hadn't ingested something. Would you feel safe if she took blood or urine samples, as long as she cleaned the equipment afterward? It would probably be safe to transport the samples, if not the body. Dr. Flores might need ice—"

Bernard began to look pained. "Perhaps you would like to speak with her."

"I'd love to."

Mac gave me a look. I shrugged. That was my man. Always thinking, right down to the details.

And then I caught myself. Jack wasn't my man, my wolf, or my anything. It was too easy to get caught in that loverboy trap. We were exes. We'd gotten stupid on the trail, maybe thrown by Elena's death. But we weren't going to take it any further.

Still, I found myself watching Jack walk away. I adored the proud way he held his head and straightened his shoulders against the raindrops. I admired his trim waist, recalling the satiny skin over his taut abs. Not to mention his godlike ass.

Oops. If he wasn't my anything, I really shouldn't drool over his ass.

When Jack glanced my way, I found myself blushing so hard, I turned into the wind to cool myself down.

Mac shook his head. Laurent snorted. And worst of all, Sylvie's cool eyes rested on me.

CHAPTER 14

Dr. Flores showed up within half an hour, during a brief lull in the rain.

I liked her immediately. First of all, she wasn't much taller than me, which is pretty rare when you only stand five foot two. Secondly, her tanned face showed more laugh lines than frown lines. Thirdly, I liked her accent, the streaks of white in her long, wavy black hair, and even the fact that she wore pearls with her jeans. Not the most practical mode of dress today, but cool. She'd make a distinguished wolf.

Right after we introduced ourselves, Jack said, "I'd like to help. I'm a paramedic, and I did two and a half years of medical school."

I filed that away for future reference. He never talked about med school.

Dr. Flores surveyed him from behind her wire glasses. "Fair enough. I'll need a private area to work."

"I was thinking about that. We don't have a key to the main building yet."

Dr. Flores said, "Yes. We have to consider the need for privacy, if a stranger comes to investigate, versus the very real possibility that someone might investigate a building later and find evidence of our work."

My knees wobbled. Evidence. She meant Elena's blood and other body parts.

Dr. Flores's sharp brown eyes turned to me. "You. Leila Fan. You were friends with this girl?"

I nodded.

"You had better stay far away. Stand guard at the main road, perhaps. We don't want anybody fainting on us. Do you understand?"

I nodded. She certainly wasn't touchy-feely, but I understood.

So I didn't hang around for the grisly autopsy stuff. I patrolled near the road, along with Laurent and Mac. When I heard a saw buzzing, I hummed K'naan's "Wavin' Flag" and tried to think about soccer instead of saws. Then I gave up and said a quick, wordless prayer that if there was an afterlife, Elena might get to see her parents, who'd both died years earlier. Even though she'd joked about being little orphan Elena, I knew she'd valued friends even more because she had very little family left.

When the saw finally paused, a few birds chirped. I walked back toward the main dirt road and ran into Mac leaning against a tree. When he spotted me, he yanked himself upright and shoved his hands into his pockets.

"Are you all right?" I asked.

He shrugged. He looked pale. Redheads often do, but I thought he'd reached one shade away from puking.

I realized I'd asked a stupid question. None of us were all right. Our friend had died.

Mac said, "I'll manage. But you watch out, Leila."

I frowned at him. It was the second time he'd warned me about Jack, but I had no idea why.

"It's obvious that you and that guy have it going on. But you don't know him. He's a stranger."

"I know him from two years ago."

"Yeah. Elena told me."

I did a double take.

He smiled slightly. "Yesterday, before we picked you guys up on the ride over. She told me and Laurent that you and Jack had a history, but not to worry about it."

"There. You see?" It ticked me off that Elena had warned Mac and Laurent but not me. No, I had to find Jack lurking behind me and leading me into temptation on the ride over.

Then I smiled and shook my head. The girl liked to tease. I'd miss her.

Mac said, "All I see is you losing control. I can't stop you, but I'm pointing it out. As a friend." He nodded at me and walked back out on the trail, toward the main road, still patrolling.

Leaving me with my thoughts. Okay, everyone here knew I craved Jack. And they'd figured out that he'd burned me two years ago. Which made me a chump a million times over, both as a wolf and as a human.

I couldn't keep playing the "my friend died and I lost my head" card. I had to develop self-control around the guy.

56

Had to.

Uneasiness rippled along my spine. I trusted Jack instinctively. He'd been right beside me, setting up his tent when Elena took off. The only time he'd been out of my sight was when he pulled Elena out of the river.

He'd almost saved her life.

Hadn't he?

Mac was paranoid. I couldn't let him affect me. But I found myself patrolling deeper in the forest, crunching through the brush, trying to ignore my spiraling doubts.

I spotted a shadowy figure creeping toward the river. Skinny, dressed in a black windbreaker, still heavily bearded. Laurent.

I didn't feel like talking to anyone after Mac, so I retreated back toward the main road. I couldn't help wondering what Laurent was doing, though. The district heads had expressly forbidden us to go back to the site.

CHAPTER 15

Dr. Flores surveyed us around the campfire, where we'd all congregated under the leaders' instructions. Even in the flickering light, I could see the whites surrounding her nearly black irises, which usually made people look startled, but somehow made her more intimidating. She held my gaze for a long, unblinking moment before she moved on to Laurent. The faint but detectable odor of blood hovered around her.

The St-Huberts flanked her left. Jack stood on her right. The fire cast light and shadow over his face, masking his expression. He stood with his arms behind his back and his feet separated, reminding me of a soldier at ease. He smelled a little like blood, too, but also like himself and soap and deodorant, and his hair was wet-combed, so he'd tried to clean himself up.

With a sponge bath?

I imagined Jack stripped to the waist, running a wet cloth over his smooth pecs. A drop of water fell on his jeans, so he unbuttoned them...

No, no, no, no, no. No more Jack. I'd declared myself a Jack-free zone. Zero tolerance for Jack.

Fortunately, Dr. Flores began to speak. "I will issue a formal report on Monday, after further tests in my laboratory, but Bernard and Sylvie suggested I share my preliminary results with you today."

I licked my lips and tasted my fake cola lip gloss. I could also smell Laurent's nervous sweat.

Dr. Flores frowned. "Again, I must stress that I am not a forensic pathologist or even formally trained in human anatomy. However, as you all know, Elena suffered a head wound." She pointed to the top of her right forehead, at the hairline. "It bled considerably, as scalp wounds do, but I didn't locate any extra bleeding under her skull." She paused. I tried not to imagine how she must have checked for the bleeding under the skull.

"The biggest question is if Elena died from this head wound or from drowning. The short answer is that I can't tell you at this point."

I exhaled and Jack looked at me. I raised an eyebrow at him to ask: bullshit or truth?

Jack's mouth quirked, and he nodded almost imperceptibly. It was true. She wasn't holding out on us peons.

"But isn't there some way you can tell something? You spent hours on her," said Mac.

Dr. Flores sighed. "Are you asking me for my opinion, or for fact?"

"Both," said Mac. I nodded. *You go, boy.* Until now, he'd always struck me as the strong, silent type. He said, "I did a quick search on Wikipedia. I didn't understand all the stuff about wet drowning and dry drowning, but they basically said you can tell if the person drowned."

Dr. Flores said, "Yes. Naturally, if we had unlimited resources— multidetector computerized technology, for example—I could scan her body and tell you if the fluid in her airways, sinuses, lungs, and stomach looked like she had drowned. I wouldn't have to make a single incision."

"And in the real world?" asked Laurent, with a hint of sarcasm. Both he and Mac were testing the limits of politeness with her.

Dr. Flores managed to stare him down, even though she was more than half a foot shorter than him. "I took photos and samples of everything. We will run the tests we can and destroy the samples afterward. I will do my best."

"Dr. Flores. If I may," said Jack.

She nodded stiffly.

He looked at Mac. "I know this is hard. You knew Elena a lot better than I did. And believe me, I don't understand all the science even though we did some searching ourselves this afternoon." He turned to Laurent. "But this is what we know. Most people panic when they hit the water. They hold their breath, which makes them flail around and use up their oxygen reserves. Then they panic more. After a while, your body won't let you hold your breath anymore, and you *must* breathe. Then you suck in water, and your throat closes, and you choke. That's how you drown. So if Dr. Flores finds water in her lung tissue, Elena was conscious when she drowned."

I twitched involuntarily.

Jack nodded in sympathy at me. "The problem is, some people close up their throats so well when they drown that their lungs are dry anyway. It's called 'dry drowning.'"

Laurent said, "If I understand you correctly, you are saying that if her lungs are wet, we will know that she drowned. But if her lungs are dry, we are still at an impasse."

"That is a close enough approximation," allowed Dr. Flores.

Mac asked, "So how accurate is your testing? How can you tell if her lungs are wet?"

"I could weigh them. But since we haven't decided what I'll be able to transport, I might have to take samples to examine under the microscope instead."

Bernard interjected, "Sylvie and I think it's too dangerous for you to transport anything intact. We would not be able to explain human body parts to the police. Although we have some sympathizers, our network does not extend that far."

Dr. Flores inclined her head in acknowledgement.

I dropped my eyes to the fire. It popped on some wet wood, and I tried to sort out my feelings. This sure wasn't as satisfying as watching CSI, because we were guessing. And my real, flesh-and-blood friend was still dead.

I tasted blood. I had bitten through the inside on my cheek.

Dr. Flores took over again. "The most likely scenario is that she hit her head and drowned. I can't speculate how or why she hit her head. Drugs or alcohol could have played a role."

I cleared my throat. I wanted to say, "No fucking way," but I tried to match their more formal tone. "That seems doubtful."

Dr. Flores's eyeballs pierced me. "Have you done a toxicology screen on her already?"

"No. But she wouldn't drive impaired. And I can tell you she almost never took anything—"

"Almost?" Dr. Flores's mouth hooked upward.

I decided to be honest. "Well, a few drinks if we were going out on the weekend. And ecstasy once in a while. Like, maybe three times a *year*. But otherwise, she was totally clean." I didn't mention that Elena avoided pot because she was afraid the munchies made her fat. Let her have some dignity.

Dr. Flores shook her head. "I will go to my clinic and begin running tests. Mr. Meng, would you care to join me?"

She wanted Jack to join her. The blood seemed to freeze in my veins. My upper lip lifted in a snarl.

Jack said, "Thank you for the offer, Dr. Flores. I've learned a lot from you today. However, I'll stay here, if that's all right."

"Certainly," said Bernard. "We've hired a private investigator who'll want to speak to all of you tomorrow morning."

An investigator tomorrow morning.

Even so, the tension eased out of my body. Jack was staying. For now.

Chapter 16

Wers aren't squeamish, and most of us aren't too religious, but we have our rituals. One of them is that we bury our dead as soon as possible. Maybe that's common sense from when our ancestors lived in the forest, but it felt right.

Soon we could lay Elena to rest. As soon as the investigator arrived and gave us the green light.

We took turns working on the hole we'd started as wolves. Bernard and Sylvie had fetched some shovels and flashlights. The nearly full moon lit our way as well. Bernard apologized for not bringing his tractor, but said we needed to be as quiet as possible.

My shovel bit the dirt hard enough to jar my shoulders. I heaved the dirt out of the grave, thinking about Elena.

We'd dropped into an easy friendship almost from the first day we met at McGill University. If there was a movie I wanted to see, or I felt like going for a run, I might call Elena. But it wasn't deep. We probably wouldn't have kept in touch if we weren't both wer girls in the same neighborhood.

You know how with some friends, you can talk about whatever's on your mind and not censor yourself? If I brought up the war in Iraq or greenhouse gas emissions with Elena, you know, as fun party talk, she'd let me run on and then she'd change the subject. Same thing if I complained about my family or current boyfriend. So I never went deeper with her. She didn't offer confidences or seem particularly interested in mine, and she obviously didn't get fired up about injustice the way I did, so we didn't connect. We did okay in a group or over another activity, but I didn't *know* her know her, even after—holy smack, could it really be?—ten years.

I had a Cree friend who told me that the Cree are not too friendly when they meet you. In fact, people might think they're cold. But if they take you in, you're like a brother to them. The Inuit are much more friendly, all smiles right from the start, but you never get past that veneer.

Elena was definitely the Inuit kind. Fine on the surface, but we'd never taken it to another level.

Still, she was my friend. My crazy friend. The one who went skydiving regularly. The one who breezed through boyfriends and toasted them with tequila before moving on. The one who introduced me to Bal en Blanc, kind of the world's last rave, where 15,000 people wearing white dance to house music all night. Elena donned a white ball gown and held out for the full fifteen hours last year.

She was fun. She was life. She was Elena.

When I finished digging, I wiped the tears away, rubbing grime across my face. My shoulders ached. I placed the shovel carefully against the tree.

Bernard ran his construction flashlight over the grave and nodded his satisfaction. It was done.

I looked up into Jack's shadowed eyes.

There were so many things I could have said. How bone-weary I felt. Or how conspicuous this crater of freshly dug dirt looked in the middle of a clearing. We'd have to buy this piece of land now, no question.

Jack walked around the grave to my side. He placed his hand on my lower back as lightly as a friend might have done, but my skin tingled underneath my clothes.

I bit my lip. I'd sworn off Jack, but surely a small touch couldn't hurt.

"We will all mourn Elena Shapko, a bright spirit who died too soon." said Bernard. "May her soul rest in peace."

Did werewolves have souls? Did anyone? I liked to think of Elena roaming the happy hunting grounds, chasing rabbits or hunting men, depending what form she'd take. Would we 'shift in the afterlife, or stay locked in a single form?

Sylvie said, "We've prepared a bonfire tonight."

I made a noise low in my throat. No. When Elena and I had talked about a bonfire this weekend, I'd said we should blast Nickelback's "Rock Star." She'd said, "Only if we dance naked."

Sylvie said, "It will be her wake. She would want us to celebrate her life."

I turned away. I hefted the shovel over my right shoulder, the side Jack wasn't on. We walked back toward the fire pit, Jack's hand still lightly resting on my back. He said, "We could eat beef jerky."

I felt comforted that he'd noticed that about Elena. I added, "And drink Corona."

"That's what she liked to drink? I thought she might like frilly girl drinks."

"Sometimes. She liked wine, too. But if we went camping, she broke out the beer. She said beer went better with three things: barbecue, Indian food, and camping."

Jack laughed.

"She liked those putrid coolers, too," Mac said from behind us. "She tried to make me drink a Caramilk one."

"And did you?" Laurent's voice swooped out of the darkness, also behind me, but off to the left.

Mac said, "We played a poker hand over it."

"Who won?" I tossed over my shoulder.

"She did," he said. "I chugged that frigging thing."

Our laughter rang through the woods. Even Sylvie murmured in pleasure.

"But I won the next few games. Strip poker," said Mac.

I heard a slap while Laurent high-fived him. The guys laughed, but I sobered a little, remembering my last sight of Elena's cold, naked body.

Still, when Bernard lit the fire and Sylvie invited us to roast some deer sausage, the mood felt lighter. I impaled my sausage on a real stick.

"I brought skewers," said Sylvie, hoisting up a picnic basket.

I shrugged. Everyone else grabbed a skewer, including Jack, but I held on to my stick.

"You're the rebel," said Jack.

"I just think she would've done it like this," I said, pointing to my long, slightly crooked, mildly dirty stick.

"You mean she'd let her stick burn off and waste good meat in the fire?"

I laughed. "You're supposed to hold the meat *above* the fire. Got it?"

Jack made a face. "What's the fun in that?"

But while the fire crackled, we held our sausages above the flames, smelling smoke and barbecued deer. Our shoulders bumped every so often. My eyes filled with tears. Elena would have loved this so much.

64

Jack slung his arm around me. He used his other arm to keep roasting his sausage, turning it lightly above the flames.

I punched him lightly in the stomach. "The meat's more important, huh?"

"Baby, the meat is always more important." But he kissed the top of my head, surprising me, before he handed me the sausage. "Ladies first."

I pulled my stick out of the fire. "I think mine's ready, too. Oops. A little toasty." One side was blackened.

He sighed and removed the stick from my hand. "I'll take the hit. C'mon."

I accepted his deer sausage in exchange. It tasted a little dry compared to the usual beef or pork, but it was cool that Bernard had hunted the deer himself. Mac passed me a beer. His eyes flicked from me to Jack.

I shrugged a little. As far as I was concerned, we were pretty G-rated. At least, we'd managed not to hit it again, which practically deserved a medal.

I felt Jack's body stiffen against my side and, seconds later, I figured out why.

A car purred up the driveway toward our parking lot.

Bernard held out a hand, silently telling us to stop moving. But we already stood on alert, sausages forgotten.

The car's engine cut. A door opened and slammed. Soon a man's figure weaved its way through the trees toward us. I could see him, but I could hardly hear his light footsteps, despite my sensitive wer hearing.

He moved like a wolf even in human form: light, long-limbed, and sure-footed in the darkness.

When he stepped closer to the bonfire, I saw that his skin was darker than mine, more the colour of chicory. I could hardly make out his deep-set eyes, but I admired his smooth-shaven head and his large, capable hands.

He smelled *right*. Powerfully male, almost dizzying.

Was he one of us?

He smelled delectable, he moved like one of us, but my wer-dar stayed stubbornly silent.

Who was this dark-skinned stranger?

Bernard said, "Ladies and gentlemen, may I present Mr. Jefferson Hollingsworth, my friend and a private detective."

The private detective.

Oh. My.

I straightened, subconsciously drawing away from Jack. I held out my free hand and said, "Pleased to meet you."

CHAPTER 17

His skin felt warm and dry. He shook my hand firmly enough to feel it, but not hard enough to crush bone. Just right.

"Call me Jeff," he said.

Secretly, I preferred Jefferson. I'd probably met a dozen Jeffs over my lifetime, but none of them contained a tenth of the magnetism of this man. I dropped my eyes to his legs, well-outlined in dark wash jeans, but partially hidden under a black trench coat.

Trench coat. I'd never really noticed that item of clothing before, but suddenly, it seemed sophisticated and mysterious and eminently desirable.

Jack didn't make a sound, but I became aware of the tension vibrating in his body, still only inches away from mine. He shook Jefferson's hand, a quick, bone-crushing jerk, and said, "Jack Meng."

Jefferson nodded. He looked from me to Jack and back to me, standing very still.

I licked my lips. I usually stick to one guy, and Jack was very stick-able. On the other hand, I'd sworn off Jack the scum-sucker, and here was a toothsome alternative.

Jack growled once.

Jefferson's nostrils flared. He didn't back away. He simply watched us, which made Jack growl again, louder.

Bernard stepped forward. "That's enough."

Jack silenced himself, but I could imagine his wolf hackles raised and his teeth bared.

Bernard went on, "I told you to cooperate fully with the investigation. Professionally speaking," he added.

Mac cleared his throat. After a beat, I realized Bernard was waiting for my response, so I nodded and kept my head lowered while Laurent and Mac shook hands with Jefferson. This allowed me to study Jefferson's black leather boots. Smooth, polished, but not flashy. Kind of like the man himself.

"Thanks for inviting me, Bernard," said Jefferson, turning toward the rest of us. "I know you've lost a friend, and I want to find some answers for you. That means I'm going to have to ask all of you some questions."

"We started searching for her right away," said Mac.

Jefferson turned to him. Now the half of his body facing me pivoted away from the fire and became shrouded in darkness. I found myself studying the contours of his shaved skull and wondering how his skin would feel under my fingers. Smooth, I bet.

Jefferson said, "Let's start at the beginning. What time did you arrive at the campsite?"

Mac said, "We got here at 5:07." He glanced at Bernard and added, "I noticed because the radio blew the five o'clock whistle and played their end-of-work-day song."

Now I remembered. They'd played Todd Runion's "Bang on the Drum All Day." Elena had sung off-key and banged on the steering wheel. I said, "Yes. That sounds right."

"And then what happened?"

"Leila and I set up our tents," said Jack.

"Right away?" asked Jefferson.

"Pretty much," I said.

"So you didn't notice Elena missing?"

I shook my head. "I wish. But Mac and Laurent did."

"Both of you, at the same time?" Jefferson asked.

I watched Mac's Adam's apple bob in his throat before he answered. "I noticed first. I grabbed a drink from the van. Then I was going to set my tent up. Sometimes I set hers up, too."

I smiled a little. Elena never did anything if a guy was ready and willing to do it for her.

"I went to ask her where she wanted it, but I couldn't find her. I asked Laurent if he'd seen her."

Jefferson quirked his eyebrow at Laurent.

"I went for a run," said Laurent. "I was rounding the camp when Mac flagged me down and asked if I'd seen her. I hadn't noticed, but I'd done a few laps around the main building. I returned to the campsite and picked up her scent heading for the river. I circled a few times, but she was definitely going for the river, so Mac alerted Jack and Leila."

"We all went looking for her," said Jack. "I found her in the river. I tried to hold her head steady and get her out of there. She wasn't breathing. She didn't have a pulse. I'm a paramedic, so I called for backup and started resuscitation. Leila and Mac know first aid."

"So do I," said Laurent.

I'd forgotten that, but he'd been too close to 'shifting to do much good. I left that part out as I picked up the story. "Jack needed some supplies from the van, so Laurent and I drove it down to the river's edge. We ended up loading her in the back of it. Her pulse came back—"

"Return of spontaneous circulation," said Jack. "But we lost it, and then we ended up 'shifting, so we lost her completely."

"You didn't think of calling an ambulance."

"Sure we did," said Jack. "But if we'd 'shifted in front of them, we'd all be as good as dead now."

I closed my eyes. Maybe that could be my next mission: a werewolf medic team. I'd have to talk to Jack about it afterward. I had the ace resuscitator on my team this time, and it hadn't saved Elena, but maybe with some more equipment…

Jefferson nodded. "I'm going to talk to all of you individually, but that can wait until the morning. I'd like to explore the campground in the meantime."

Any human man would want to explore in the daytime, when he could see. Hell, any human man would stay away from a pack of grieving werewolves, period. Who was Jefferson Hollingsworth? Not a typical man, but not clearly a werewolf, either.

"I printed out a map of the campground from a cached website. Is this accurate?" He held it up to Bernard, but I took a step closer, inhaling Jefferson's potent male scent while studying the map.

"That looks about right," I said. "You come in through the main road, by the main building and office." And the overhang where Dr. Flores and Jack had performed the autopsy, but I didn't bring that up. "Mr. Tabassian had some RV hookups on the front sites, but mostly it was tent camping. That little building closer to the river is marked as laundry and restrooms, but he told me the washing machine broke and he never fixed it. He went out of business 18 months ago. The water and sewage has been disconnected, and he's selling it as is."

Jefferson frowned. "Most of the camping sites are quite far from the river. Do you have any idea why Elena would have gone down there?"

"No. She liked to look at water, but not go in it, either as a human or a wolf."

Jefferson tucked the map under his arm. "This should be interesting, Bernard. Thanks, everyone. I'll ask each of you more questions in the morning." He waved and switched on his flashlight.

I took one last, discreet sniff before he disappeared toward the overhang. Or at least, I thought I was discreet. Sylvie raised her eyebrow at me. And Jack's dark eyes blazed at me in betrayal.

CHAPTER 18

The rest of the bonfire passed in a blur.

Jack paced around the fire, toward the forest, and back to the fire. Never next to me, and never staying still, but I was perpetually conscious of him, and not only because he broke more branches than usual and swore under his breath.

Sylvie smiled and sipped from her wineglass like we were her own personal reality TV show. She murmured to Bernard, who surveyed us all with half-narrowed eyes.

Laurent and Mac ignored us, for the most part, but after midnight, Laurent waved good night.

At almost 2 a.m., Mac signaled to me. "You want to sleep in my tent tonight?"

I glanced at him sidelong. He used to be Elena's. She and I never touched each other's men, past or present.

"Not like that. Just so you're not…alone." He didn't look at Jack, but we both knew that was what he meant.

"I'm okay," I said, even though I shivered a little. April is not warm in Canada, and my fleece gloves let the wind in. The bonfire had died down, too, which meant more embers and fewer leaping flames.

Mac said, "I know you. I know you're usually careful. But this is different. You're grieving and vulnerable."

I didn't usually think of myself as vulnerable. Tough. Ardent. But not weak in any way.

"You're probably not in your right state of mind."

I backed away from him. "Mac, I know you're trying to help, but I'm not stupid, okay?"

"I never said you were."

I pushed my fingers through my hair and tried to calm down. "I know I look out of control to you. Maybe I am a little nuts. But I still know what I'm doing. I took your point about staying away from Jack—"

Mac glanced at Jack, who was stomping back from the van with a beer bottle in his hand. Then Mac looked toward the river, where Jefferson had disappeared.

I felt like thumping Mac on the head. "Do you see me with either of them right now?"

He shook his head.

"So trust me on this one, Mac. If your big brotherly instincts kick into high gear, you have my permission to knock on my tent door and ask if I'm all right. But no more hovering. I'm a big girl. I can handle this."

Mac sighed. "So be it." He walked away from me, but he tossed over his shoulder, "Elena was a big girl, too."

So then I felt like a social quad. Mac had also lost Elena. True, they weren't going out anymore, but he still cared about her. Hell, he was going to set up her tent.

I jogged after him. "I'm sorry."

He smiled a little. "It's all right."

"Not really. I guess I got really…wrapped up in myself." I winced. I'd always accused Elena of being self-centered, and now I was doing the same g-d thing.

In fairness, I wasn't used to guys dropping out of the sky for me. A lot of human guys smelled wrong or hated dogs or any other deal-breaker. To tell you the truth, Jack was my biggest hope two years ago, which seems about six kinds of pathetic. And right now, when I should be paying attention to Elena's death, I fixated on not one, but two guys who hit it for me.

And they say guys think with their groins.

I held out my hand. "Are we good?"

Mac shook it. I could feel the rough skin of his calluses from playing guitar. "We're always good, Leila. Don't sweat it. But my offer still stands."

"That's cool," I said. "I appreciate it."

I walked to the van. We'd brought our own water in a tank, so I filled up a cup and grabbed my toiletry kit from my tent. I walked to the edge of the forest to perform my nightly ablutions, only to hear swift footsteps behind me.

I wasn't really scared. I even thought I knew who owned those boots crunching through the brush and the last bit of snow at the edge of the forest.

I swiveled around to face Jack advancing on me.

CHAPTER 19

"Having fun?" he asked, in a controlled way. If I hadn't noticed his rigid shoulders and his hands flexing, I might have been fooled.

As it was, I shrugged. I dug through my bag for my toothbrush and popped off the travel cap. I wanted to pretend everything was as normal as possible. Also, worse come to worst, I could jab the toothbrush into Jack's stomach and call for help. Hey, it would work in the movies.

"What are you playing at?" he asked.

"I'm not sure what you mean."

"Don't pretend with me, Leila. We know each other too well for that. You're mine."

It sucked my breath away, him saying it like that. I snapped the case back over my toothbrush and placed it back in the bag. I wouldn't be performing any dental hygiene during this conversation. I said, "That's funny. I thought I belonged to myself. The religious people would say we belong to God."

"Very funny. Look. You belong to me."

"That's the second time you've said it, but that doesn't make it true."

"Leila!" He didn't touch me, but his voice was like a whip.

I stood still. Inside, I was quaking. Part of me, the deep, dark, un-politically correct part of me, maybe the wolf part of me, wanted to roll over and let him dominate the hell out of me. The other part of me, the feminist twenty-first century ass-kicking Buffy the vampire slayer part of me, said, "That's funny. That's not what you would have said two years ago."

He closed his eyes. "I wanted to talk to you about that."

"Great. You're only a quarter of a lifetime too late."

"Hey. You cut me off. You shut the door in my face, you didn't answer my calls, you deleted my messages, you sent me a virus that almost killed my computer—"

"You fucked another woman!"

"No, I didn't." And before I could object, he grabbed my head, yanked my face next to his, and kissed me so thoroughly, my lips ached and my head swam. He made a muffled noise, and after a minute, I realized I'd spilled my cup of water all over his boots and the cuff of his jeans.

"Good," I said, even though my lips still burned from his imprint and my hands trembled. "I ought to drop an elephant on your foot for cheating on me."

"How many times do I have to say I didn't do it?"

"I guess you can say it as many times as you want in the Never-Never Land where you think we belong to each other." My hands had stopped shaking. Good. I raised my chin and eyeballed Jack. "Look. You can't have it both ways. Either it's all a game and we do whatever we want with whomever we want, or we play boyfriend-girlfriend. I didn't know the rules had changed—"

"They never did. Wolves mate for life."

I hesitated for a second before the biologist in me corrected, "Actually, that's not true. If they lose their mate, they'll mourn, but usually they'll find another one."

"Fine." He took a step closer to me so his face surrounded my vision and the heat from his body seared into mine. "I mate for life. And you do, too."

I wanted to spit on him and his words. Humans lie. So do werewolves in human form. But I stayed in place, so close I could feel his breath on my face. I said, "You certainly mate as much as you can, so maybe it seems like your life. But that's not what I'm looking for."

"Are you talking about Fabienne? Because I can explain."

I crossed my arms, even though he was so close to me that it meant my forearms pressed against his chest. "This ought to be good."

"Here's the short version. I lost it after I dropped out of medical school. Fabienne was like crack for me—a way of killing myself without actually pulling the trigger." He took a deep breath.

I stood still. I tried to imagine the hurt in Jack, losing his dream of medicine. Would he really have killed himself? Could that woman have been his weapon of choice?

He rubbed his forehead and lowered his voice. "I was clean by the time I found you in that McGill running group, but Fabienne started stalking me. I didn't think much of it. Actually, I was kind of flattered."

I tensed, but I could understand that.

"That day you found us—"

His birthday. I wanted to surprise him at the end of his shift. Even though it was 2 a.m., I brought balloons.

"—she broke into the paramedic change room."

"Naked," I said.

"She wasn't naked when she got a guy to let her in. She could sweet-talk her way around anyone. She stripped down in the change room and waited for me. I think she'd hacked my messages and knew you were coming."

I closed my eyes. Even after two years, it still hurt to remember me opening the door, beaming, wearing a ridiculous white ballroom gown trimmed in feathers, with a matching scarf. Jack bought it for me and declared it fantastic. And like I said, I was carrying balloons. Five red balloons, one for each week we'd been together.

I thought it was weird that the lights were off when I came in, so I said, "Jack?" and flicked them on.

Only to see him with a naked woman's hands down his pants.

I fled the scene. I never spoke to him again. Stupid, stupid, stupid Leila for thinking I found The One at age 25.

But a few things didn't add up. I said, "If she broke into your workplace, you should've called the police, not let her fondle you."

"First I thought she was you, but she smelled wrong. So I figured it out and asked her to leave. She said she'd lost her clothes."

I rolled my eyes.

"Yeah. I guess I was a chump. I told her I'd help find them—anything to get out of there. Finally, I found them on the windowsill. But the lights went out and—well, you know the rest."

I shook my head. Sure, I saw her groping him, but there was more. "I saw you guys together."

"When?"

76

"Two weeks later." When I was wondering if I should forgive him. When a few of his buddies pleaded his case and told me Fabienne was an unofficial psycho. When I was running away my pain. "On top of the mountain." That's what everyone called Montreal's Mount Royal, our city's biggest peak, and it was one of my favourite places to run, especially in good weather. "You were playing *Frisbee* with her." I know it doesn't sound like much, but him laughing and launching the yellow disc in the air toward her twisted the knife in my gut even now. "That's not how you act with a psycho."

He swore. "I don't even—oh, okay, I think I know what you're talking about. She promised to bring me a box of my stuff if I met her at the mountain. She kept me waiting around, as usual. I started playing Frisbee with a bunch of guys. Eventually, she came joined in for, like, a minute before she left." He shook his head. "I can't believe that you saw us."

I almost believed him. But what were the chances I'd glimpse him and his ex having a good time for the few seconds they'd met up? Much more likely they'd been hitting it and I'd caught them.

"She didn't even bring back my Live CD, and that was the one thing I kept asking her for. I ended up downloading it so I didn't have to talk to her anymore."

I said, "Whatever. It doesn't matter now if you were a lying, cheating bastard."

"I thought I was a scum-sucking motherfucker."

"Yeah. You're right. Enjoy." I took a step back from Jack.

He followed me. "Wait a minute. Did you usually run at the same time every day?"

"I guess." On weekdays, I run on my lunch hour or, if I miss it, after work. On weekends, I run before a late breakfast.

He frowned. "I wonder if Fabienne could have figured out your schedule."

"C'mon. That's a little too paranoid."

"The woman was a genius at wreaking havoc. I'm telling you."

"It doesn't matter now."

"Sure it does. I don't want to let you go."

"That's a real shame. Watch me go." I spun around, still clutching my toiletry kit and my empty cup. I didn't know what to believe. But I knew I didn't want to get hurt anymore.

CHAPTER 20

In the morning, I started running. Too many thoughts careened through my head. As long as I was moving, I could pretend Elena was sleeping off a hangover and that Jack meant less to me than a good cup of green tea.

I veered away from the river—couldn't handle the memories—and toward the main road. I slowed down when I recognized the long silhouette coming toward me.

"Good morning," said Jefferson. I could see the faint outline of his breath in the air.

"Hi," I said. It didn't feel right to blast past him, so I jogged in place, warming up my muscles.

"You can bury Elena tonight," he said.

I felt like he'd pressed the air out of my lungs for a second. I hiccupped and recovered. "Thank you."

"I know you were closest to her and that it's important to you, so I wanted to let you know."

I nodded and swallowed before I changed the subject. "Did you stay up all night?"

He shrugged. "Not all night. I did the best I could with the evidence I had. For example, her clothes had been cut off."

"Because we needed to warm her up," I remembered.

"That's fine. First aid always comes first. But I could have gathered more information if her clothes hadn't been cut off and wadded up."

I couldn't even remember what had happened to her clothes. I guess someone must've grabbed them and tossed them in the van.

I kept running in place, but brought it down to a slow jog. "I'm sorry if we messed up the investigation."

He gave me a crooked smile that didn't touch his eyes. "It's not your resuscitation efforts that bother me so much as your little attempted CSI maneuvers the next day."

I licked my lips.

"We're very careful with crime scenes, you know. There's a reason we mark them off with police tape. Even the investigators are supposed to have only one path in and out of the scene so as to minimize damage. The worst thing is to have amateurs—even well-meaning junior police officers—lead parades through the crime scene."

I closed my eyes and waited for the earth to swallow me in shame. Jack and I had paraded through the scene using more than our feet. I knew it was wrong at the time, but somehow…

"I did some preliminary scene work after the sun rose. I've marked everything off. But from what I see, there was a large disturbance at the riverbank, close to an overhanging tree. I saw footprints leading to and from the tire tracks. And I saw the tracks from you and your… companion."

My jogging slowed to a stop. I lowered my head and averted my eyes.

"I'm asking you and Jack not to play Nancy Drew again. I realize this is not an investigation that will go to trial, but I'm conducting it as a homicide investigation until proven otherwise."

I nodded, still staring my mud-splattered Adidas running shoes.

"I'll ask you more questions later. But for now, I'll be concentrating on the scene, and the best thing you can do for me is to stay away."

"I will," I said. My hands tightened into fists. I couldn't explain or justify our lack of control, but I'd work as hard as I could to make sure it didn't happen again.

"Good." He smiled and his face lit up briefly, transforming it. I found myself leaning toward him, wishing I could making him look like that all the time. Then his eyes shuttered again and he nodded at me. "I'll speak to the others too. Good day to you."

"'Bye," I said.

His boots crunched on the gravel, back toward the camp. I heard someone's electric shaver buzz—probably Laurent—and realized I'd have only a few precious moments to myself.

I started running again.

Homicide investigation.

Had someone bashed Elena on the head? We'd assumed she'd fallen out of the tree, but maybe someone had smashed her head with a rock.

Was it possible Elena was going to meet someone at the river? She hadn't mentioned anyone, but I might've been too distracted by scum-sucking Jack. Even if she had said, "I met this axe-killer on Craigslist and he's going to camp with us!" I might've nodded and said, "Camping is fun."

I heard some noise behind me and glanced over my shoulder. Jack was standing on the main road, arguing with Jefferson. I almost laughed, but instead I kicked into high gear and left them to fight.

Even so, before I reached the main road, called the Sixth Concession, I heard more footsteps crunching in the gravel. I glanced over my shoulder and nodded at Jack.

He put on a burst of speed and then fell into pace beside me. "What an asshole."

I didn't answer.

"He thinks he's hot stuff because he collects debris from under her fingernails. And then he gives me shit about cutting her clothes. Like he knows anything about resus. I'd like to see him try to perform a pericardiocentesis in a ditch. He'd probably stick the needle in his own eye."

I lengthened my stride.

Jack matched it and kept on talking. "He even told me that sometimes he goes to hospitals and lectures them about how to deal with the evidence so it doesn't get messed up too much during codes."

I shrugged. It sounded like a good idea to me. I checked for cars—nada—and turned left at the road.

"Like anyone's going to take pictures or carefully lay the clothes out when you're trying to save a life! I told him to shove it."

In the distance, I could see a dairy farm. As we got closer, I noticed the wrought iron gates on either side of the driveway were shaped like two Jersey cows.

"Tasty," said Jack.

I laughed. "You mean, tasteful? As in, not?"

"I mean tasty. We're going to have to stay away from his barn during a full moon."

I winced. I could imagine one of us breaking down the barn door and ripping into the side of one or more of those cows. Say, Laurent.

"So what'd he say to you?" asked Jack, changing the subject back to Jefferson.

"That we could bury Elena today."

"That's a relief." Even though I kept a good pace, Jack had no trouble keeping up with me and talking at the same time. I liked that. I tried not to notice the muscular shape of his legs through his pants and the increasingly tangy smell of his sweat.

No Jack. No, no Jack.

"Although I'm a little concerned about burying her here," said Jack.

Clearly, he wasn't as distracted by the magnificence of my body. I sprinted a few steps to work off my annoyance, but Jack stayed with me the whole time, so I dropped back into my normal pace and asked, "Are you worried because the paperwork hasn't gone through for the land yet?"

"Of course. It's not officially ours. Then, if someone wanders on to the land and finds this freshly dug mound, and calls the cops…"

I shivered, despite our fast pace and the weak April sunshine. "We'd be fucked."

"Right. And how we're going to explain Elena's disappearance to everyone at home—"

I hadn't even thought about that. "Oh, dear God."

"—especially if someone remembers that she was camping, and her van comes back without her."

A black GMC truck whooshed past us in the oncoming lane, giving us wide berth. Even so, mud and gravel bits sprayed my legs.

I said, "We'd better get back to camp and make a plan." Before any more human witnesses, like the truck driver, noticed us in the area and spread the word.

"That's what I'm thinking." Jack gestured for me to take the lead, and we ran back to the campground in silence.

CHAPTER 21

"We have considered this, but I am glad you raised this matter," said Bernard after we assembled for breakfast and Jack brought up the Elena's-gone-AWOL problem. Bernard gestured for us to sit down at the picnic table graced with three different kinds of breakfast cereal. "The simplest thing would be to have Elena message all of her friends and tell them she has decided to leave the country from here. Does that seem likely?"

Laurent grunted a no.

I shook my head and said, "She wouldn't up and leave like that. First of all, I can't think of any major reason she'd go. She didn't have any big job opportunities."

"Why was that?" Sylvie wanted to know as she passed cereal bowls around the table.

I took a bowl even though I wouldn't touch a bite. "Well. She got downsized two months ago." Elena would have put it in a much fancier way, but I couldn't remember the latest euphemism. "She did marketing for a small company that went out of business. She had a couple of interviews, but nothing caught hold."

"Perhaps that could be the ticket," said Sylvie, glancing at Bernard. "A secret opportunity she was keeping under wraps, waiting for it to come to fruition. We have contacts in Europe."

He wrinkled his nose, and for a second, I could imagine him as a wolf. "Would her family be suspicious?" he asked me.

"I don't know. She didn't talk about her family much. Most of the them are in Czechoslovakia."

Bernard frowned some more. "Did she speak to them in Czech?"

"Yes." I'd walked in on a few conversations on the phone. "But mostly English with a little Czech thrown in."

"Still." He tented his hands.

I tried to remember what I could. "Her father died in some sort of construction accident, and a childless aunt and uncle sort of adopted Elena and brought her over to Canada."

"Is she still close to that aunt?"

"No. Well, sort of. Her aunt recently went into a nursing home, actually." Elena's exact words were "She drank too much and fried her brain. But forget that. Check out my new thigh-high boots." And of course I'd gotten distracted, especially when she showed me the new Union Jack leggings she was going to wear with them.

"What about her uncle?" asked Sylvie. She sipped from a large insulated mug of coffee.

I shook my head. "I never met him."

Mac said, "He's in Buenos Aires."

We all stared at him. He flushed. "I met him when he was trying to raise money for some 'get rich quick' scheme. He contacted Elena. She sent him away. I think he lives in the States now, but he's trying to set up a business in South America, especially Argentina."

Bernard and Sylvie exchanged a long look. Then Bernard said slowly, "What you are telling us is that Elena has almost no family in Canada and no job."

"She was doing temp work," I said.

"Regardless, this may be a blessing in disguise. Sylvie and I have discussed the safest way to have Elena disappear."

I rubbed my sweaty forehead. Jack pressed his thigh against mine, under the table. Despite myself, I felt comforted by his touch.

"We would like to falsify Elena's return," said Bernard. "We can't have witnesses that she left Montreal to come to this piece of land and never came home. There would be too many questions. It would be easier to have someone else take on her identity and then quietly disappear."

I gnawed on my bottom lip, peeling off cracked skin and tasting blood.

"It's a shame you two are so physically different," Bernard mused aloud, staring at me as if he could turn my hair blond. "Otherwise, you would be the obvious choice. You knew her the best. You know her apartment and her friends. You would be able to imitate her voice."

My throat locked up.

Up until that moment, I had been a trouper for Elena. But somehow, this seemed like the last straw. Bile rose in the back of my mouth. I swallowed it back down.

Jack jostled my arm with his. "I could find a friend who would do a good job."

"No need," said Bernard. "We have someone in mind. But Leila, you will need to tell her about Elena's background and her usual habits so she is as prepared as possible."

"Is she trustworthy?" said Jack.

Bernard flashed his teeth. "Absolutely. She is our daughter."

CHAPTER 22

At least Gisèle St-Hubert had the boots right: thigh-high chestnut leather boots.

Right in a manner of speaking, of course. Those boots were totally loserish for a campsite, especially in the spring. The girl lived in the country. Surely she'd heard of mud. But when she slammed the door of her Prius and strutted toward us in those boots, dark wash skinny jeans, a short khaki trench coat, wavy blond hair, and oversized sunglasses, Jack, Laurent, and Mac goggled at her so intently, it was a wonder they remembered to keep their tongues in their mouths.

I felt like kicking Jack in the back of his knees. Then he'd topple to the ground like the total jackass he was.

But Elena owned a pair of boots like that. And jeans like that. And even the sunglasses. So I crossed my arm and watched Gisèle.

She kissed her parents' cheeks and hugged them briefly. Then she held her hand out to me.

Up close, my first thought was that she was her mother pushed through a time machine. She had the same sensible bob grown past her shoulders. Under the trench coat, I spotted a basic beige tunic top, and her makeup was subtle.

What kind of psycho 20-something imitates her mother instead of rebelling against her? The only difference was that she had her father's strong jaw. If you knew who ex-Prime Minister Brian Mulroney is, or his son Ben, who hosted *Canadian Idol*, you'd know that kind of prominent, Mountie-gets-his-man kind of jaw, which she had tried to camouflage with foundation, concealer, and powder.

Despite the outer clothes, I couldn't picture this girl eating beef jerky and gunning a Honda van. But I had to admit, the dirty blonde hair was the right shade, and she had the same thin build as Elena, albeit a few inches shorter.

I shook hands. Hers were cold for a wer, and her grip was loose.

When we all introduced ourselves, her eyes lingered on Jack.

He held her hand way too long. She sidled her body closer to his and smiled up at him through her lashes.

My jaw clenched. My thighs tensed. As a wolf, I would've pounced on her and wrestled her to the ground.

As a human, I wanted to kick the ass she'd crammed into those skinny jeans.

Instead, I smiled as an excuse to bare my teeth. Jack and I were over. No more sex games with the Jackinator.

Sylvie said, "Would you like to meet Mac? He's Elena's ex-boyfriend."

After a beat, Gisèle withdrew her hand from Jack's. Mac told her he'd be happy to answer any of her questions. She nodded, but I noticed her gaze magnetize back to Jack.

Beeyotch. And I didn't mean it as a compliment.

She turned her bleached teeth smile on me in the semblance of a smile. "I need to know everything about this Elena. I want to play my role convincingly."

Her role? My smile widened into psychotic territory, but she didn't blink.

Bernard tucked his arm around her waist. "She's an actress. We're fortunate she was home visiting."

Oh, so fortunate. Since she'd returned home to the sticks, far from New York, LA, or even Toronto, with time to impersonate Elena, she must be between jobs. I tried to feel grateful.

Elena said, "I believe in doing my research." She tossed her hair. It cascaded, rippling down her back like a hair conditioner commercial. The way the guys stood hypnotized, it was as good as if she'd whipped out her diamond-encrusted breasts. "I'm part of a generation that believes in studying my craft."

As opposed to, I don't know, Meryl Streep, the well-known slacker?

Her red-lipsticked mouth continued to emit annoying sounds. "If you have pictures of her or, even better, some videos, I could get an idea of how she moved and interacted with people. I Googled her before I came."

Smart move, yet it felt creepy. In general, wers try to avoid pictures online, even though that's more and more impossible these days, what with satellites and Facebook. "You found pictures of her?"

She nodded. "Not easy. I found one of her from *Nuit Blanche*, on Photobucket."

Laurent said, "We'll have to delete that."

I nodded. Now that Elena was gone, we didn't need anyone comparing pictures to Gisèle and figuring out she was fake.

Laurent pulled out his phone. "I'm on it."

I relaxed a little. Finally, it felt like Laurent and I were on the same page.

Sylvie said, "But Gisèle will need full access to all your photos and videos, as she wisely mentioned. I also recommend that she read letters or e-mails, to see how she expressed herself."

"I don't have access to Elena's e-mail. And I think that would be... private," I said. I knew I should be more helpful, but Gisèle made me want to firebomb all of Elena's stuff to keep the impersonator's manicured nails away from it.

Sylvie's well-groomed eyebrows rose. "We'll have to obtain access. However, in the meantime, surely you have copies of her messages to you?"

"Yes, but I don't think *C U @ 3:30* would be relevant. I'll see what I can find," I forced myself to say. "I've got pictures on my computer, maybe a video or two where she's waving hi."

"Anything," said Gisèle. "After all, I want to help you as much as possible." She glanced at Jack from under her lashes again. Two more minutes and she'd undo his fly to demonstrate how much she could help him out.

"Thank you," said Jack, in a relatively neutral voice, but I still wanted to thump him.

Laurent made a noise. When we swiveled to stare at him, he said, "I found the pic. I've run a few search engines on Elena, but I haven't come up with any other images. I'll keep working on it."

"Very good," said Bernard. "However, I know most of the information online is cached. We'll have to contact the person who owns the picture and ask him or her to remove it."

"She's got her c.v. up in a few places," said Laurent.

Bernard nodded. "Let's keep it up there to maximize her visibility before she takes her new opportunity."

Gisèle licked her lips and glanced at Jack again.

His nostrils flared.

I noticed Mac's hands flexing and unflexing into fists.

And I thought, *No. No, it cannot be.*

But from the way the guys were acting, I suspected Gisèle and Elena had one more thing in common.

Gisèle was in heat.

Like Elena, she probably wasn't in full-blown heat. Maybe next full moon, she'd come into the full meal deal.

Which would make her irresistible to every hetero male werewolf in a four kilometre radius.

Including Jack.

CHAPTER 23

And she knew it. She sidled next to Jack. If she'd been a cat, she would have wound herself around his leg.

That just ain't right in a werewolf. We're related to dogs. We're straightforward. We like you, you know it. We run with you, try to knock you over, nudge you with our heads or ask you to rub our bellies.

We don't slink.

Well, this girl did. But I guess she was straightforward in a way. She breathed at Jack, "I've never been to this campsite before. Do you think you could give me a tour?"

I cleared my throat. "I don't think tours are a good idea. Jefferson Hollingsworth, the investigator, asked us to stay away from his investigation site."

"And we're staying away from that one place, out of courtesy," said Jack, smiling at Elena. "I could still show you the main building, the overhang, the showers—"

The showers. Could they *get* any more obvious?

"Oh, I like the sound of that," said Gisèle.

I guess they could. I glanced at Bernard and Sylvie to see if they'd reign their pup in. After all, they were the ones supposedly in charge. But Bernard crossed his arms and looked on like nothing was wrong, kind of like a cop watching traffic and trying to look important. Sylvie's lips quirked, but she made no move toward their daughter.

Why was I bothering? I'd sworn off Jack. He was a consenting adult. I should let them do the horizontal hula. They were going to do it anyway. None of my business.

But I felt like plucking all the hair out of her tail, sticking it in her eyeballs, and rubbing her eyelids up and down. And that was only the starter dish.

Gisèle placed her hand on Jack's arm like he was going to escort her into the prom. Her red talons shone against the black leather of his jacket.

I opened my mouth. I wanted to say, "I'll go with you." But I clicked my mouth shut again and averted my eyes. If they wanted to bounce, they would. No need for me to play witness.

A different male voice spoke up. Mac. "I know the area pretty well. I came here with Leila a few times when we were deciding what land to buy. I'll show you."

Laurent clicked off his phone and shoved it in his front pants pocket. He drew himself up to his full height. "No. I will."

Gisèle touched the tip of her pink tongue to the bow of her upper lip. She toed the ground with her shiny hooker boots. "Oh, my. You're all too wonderful. But I really only need one guide and Jack has already offered…" Her voice trailed off, somehow sounding even more suggestive. "However, you all certainly know how to make a girl feel welcome," Gisèle purred.

That did it. She sounded like a cat again. That was wrong-o. "I could guide you," I said, too loud.

Her head snapped up. Her eyes met mine. Even behind the sunglasses, I could tell the mockery had died in her gaze.

"I know this land better than anyone," I said. "I'm the one who's negotiating to buy it."

"I'm providing the legal counsel," said Laurent.

I took a step toward Gisèle, holding her eyes in mine. "I've trained as a tracker, too. Whatever kind of tour you want, I can give it to you. Let's go."

Sylvie cleared her throat gently.

I strode up to Gisèle so less than a foot of space remained between us. If we'd both been exceptionally well-endowed and perky, we might've been able to rub our bra cups together. I knew my eyes and nostrils were probably dilated and I looked less like a friendly tour guide than a warlord in Afghanistan. But one thing I'd learned as a wolf first and as a human second was that you must establish hierarchy immediately. And I wasn't about to roll over for this feline freak, no matter how easily she could twist the guys' members around her pinky.

Sylvie's voice broke into the blood rushing through my brain. "In all fairness, Leila, although you may know the site best, we'd prefer you didn't show Gisèle the sights. Jefferson informed us how you and Jack damaged the investigation site. We'd prefer you stay in the camping ground at all times until Jefferson is finished."

I whipped around to stare at Mama. She'd insulted me and declared me a camp prisoner, on top of everything else.

Jack held out his hand, resting it on my arm to calm me while he spoke. "That's ludicrous. We didn't cause any irreversible damage."

Bernard snorted. A soft noise, but the hairs rose at the back of my neck and Jack's feet swiveled in the gravel.

"It remains to be seen how much damage you have caused with your footprints and other…unusual activity," said Bernard. His grey eyes didn't blink.

Yes, he and Sylvie and Jefferson had all discussed me and Jack doing the wild thing at the "investigation site." No, I could not feel any more humiliated. The blood rose in my cheeks.

Bernard mused aloud, "No, neither of you have proved trustworthy and neither of you will play tour guide. Instead, Jack and Leila will remain here. You may clean up the campground area."

Grounded at age 27! With Jack-ass!

I could feel the rage floating off of Jack without even looking at him. But he clenched his fists and bit his tongue while Gisèle sighed and scuffed the gravel with the heel of her boot as if she were the one being inconvenienced.

Sylvie murmured and jerked her head toward the clearing.

That sobered me up. I nodded.

"I can handle it," said Jack.

I repressed a snort. Of course he could. He could handle anyone and anything. That was the problem.

Bernard said, "You two must learn to cooperate with self-control and self-restraint. Both of you, take the shovels from our car and go to the clearing."

Aye, aye, sir. I marched away from Jack, speed-walking toward the CRV. I didn't want to get stuck with him any more than he did with me. True, part of me gloated that they'd peeled him away from Miss Vixen, but I wasn't any booby prize.

Jack stayed behind to argue, so I only grabbed a spade for myself and stalked toward the clearing. But before I hit the trees, his footsteps crunched behind mine and he had the shovel tossed over his shoulder. When he caught up to me, he said, "Who do they think they are?"

"The alphas," I said.

"So what? Some hicks elected them? That doesn't make them my alphas."

"Watch yourself," I said. I know mavericks are all the rage these days. Hey, even the elderly Republican who ran against Barack Obama tried to cast himself as one. But one thing wers do better than humans is to listen to our older and wiser 'uns. Running down the St-Huberts right after Elena died? Not a good move. Especially when they might still be within earshot.

Jack kicked a rock like it was a soccer ball. Got pretty good lift, too. We both watched it soar into the distance before it landed with a thunk.

I said, "Don't worry. You'll have your chance to get into her pants later."

"What? That's not what I'm mad about."

"Yeah, right." I couldn't look at him. It hurt too much. So I kept my eyes trained on the trees and tried to take solace in the their dappled shadows.

"Look, she's pretty, I'm not denying that."

"Keep digging," I said.

"But I already told you. You're my mate. I don't care if another piece of tail shows up."

"Nice," I said. In some ways, I meant it. Jack knew how to say all the right things. Well, some of them. I'm not crazy about a girl being called a piece of tail, even though it's kind of a pun because we take wolf form once a month. But that girl knew how to work him up, and it was a matter of time before he succumbed. If nothing else, she'd play the estrus card.

Jack walked in front of me to cut me off. I dropped my spade on the ground with a clink and refused to meet his eyes while he said, "Look. If I wanted her, I would've gone for her and I would've tried to please her mommy and daddy. Instead, I'm hanging out with you."

"Because they ordered you to."

"Because I wanted to. I don't like being told what to do. I was going to work on the grave anyway. It's the last thing I can do for Elena."

I glanced at him sidelong. "You didn't even know her."

Was he blushing? No. Couldn't be. I'd never seen the guy get rattled. "I met her. I tried to save her life. Not to mention that she was your friend and one of us. I want to do right by her."

That, at least, we could agree on.

The air felt cooler and more humid. I slung the spade back over my shoulder and started walking again, but more slowly now.

"You like it here, don't you," he said.

I knew he meant the piece of land. "Love it," I admitted. "Or, I did, before Elena died."

"She wouldn't want that," he said.

I nodded. True story. She would've said, "Are you crazy? This place is perfect. I don't care if I died here. Well, okay, I would've rather kicked off when I was 102 with two well-oiled boys rubbing my feet. But since I did go, this place is where I'd want to end up anyway. In fact, you'd better hold on to this land so my bones get a chance to rest. Don't let the dick smacks get you down. And have a shot for me, okay? Coconut milk."

I found myself smiling. She liked coconut milk shots way more than I did. But I'd have one for her when I got home.

"You miss her," said Jack, shifting his shovel to his right shoulder so his left hip could swing closer to my right.

"For sure. She was the life of the party, you know?" While my other friends got married and/or popped out the babies (in Quebec, these events are not necessarily linked), Elena would text me stuff like, "Do you want to go to clown school with me? There's a free trial class!" or "I found the best hamburgers. Want one?" at 3 a.m.

In the end, I guess it didn't matter if she didn't give a hoot about the endangered right whale. She was still a great friend. I mouthed into the air, "I love you, Elena."

Jack glanced at me out of the corner of his eye, but he didn't say anything. He left me to my semi-private moment between me and E. And somehow, I didn't mind Jack being there.

I stumbled slightly over the uneven ground. Jack steadied my elbow. I let him, but I detached myself seconds later, when we came upon the grave we'd made in wolf form and expanded as a group.

I bit my lip. I remembered excavating a giant, deep tomb. It did reach six feet deep at the centre, but it was narrower than I'd like.

Jack reached his hand out for my spade. "I can handle this. Why don't you take five?"

I shook my head. "Goes faster with two," I said, swinging the spade off my shoulder and holding on to the handle.

I'd chosen the spade so it could bite into the earth, but Jack said the shovel was better for transferring the dirt. I saw what he meant. I had a tendency to dribble dirt off the pointy end.

Still, I fell into a rhythm of physical work. I jumped on the spade blade, occasionally muttering a little "Hi-*yah!*" that I thought Elena might appreciate before I tossed the dirt off to the side.

Jack was much less theatrical. He preferred to strike and shovel, pressing down with his heel if he needed the extra force. But he didn't make fun of me for doing it my way.

And I kind of liked his way, slow and steady. I've always been a sucker for a guy who knows how to use his hands for more than pushing paper and pumping iron in a gym. I could hear Jack's breath coming shorter and faster with exertion. His sweat sharpened the air.

Then I gave up and started sneaking peeks at him. Even under his jacket, I could make out the bulge of his biceps. I admired the contour of his back. And every time he bent over, I ogled his ass.

Guilt pinged my heart. I really shouldn't be lusting over forbidden fruit while digging my friend's grave. True, I probably worked faster than usual, trying to burn off my desire. But Miss Manners definitely wouldn't approve.

Then a smile broke across my face. Who cared? Elena would high-five me if she could.

Even with my secret salivating, we fell into an easy work rhythm. It was like our bodies synched up naturally, whether we were hitting it or walking down the road or even digging my friend's last home.

If only our heads and hearts synched up this well.

And if only he could stop synching up with every other woman in sight.

The pit widened and deepened. Jack jumped into it and started flinging dirt out. I followed suit, but it was harder than it looked, tossing dirt above shoulder height. My right shoulder protested and I slowed down, testing it through range of motion. I could keep going, but not at this pace.

Jack said, "You've got the spade. What if you clean up the edges? The shovel's better for throwing dirt out. We're almost done, anyway."

I shook my head, but he said, "Come on. We can switch after if you really want to."

"Okay." I pushed my toe into the moist, crumbly dirt, trying to get a toehold.

Jack boosted my butt. I would've protested except it really helped me thrust myself out of the pit. I grabbed the edge and hauled myself over, ignoring a thrust of pain in my shoulder until all fours were back on secure ground.

Jack noticed my grimace and handed me a water bottle. "Take five."

"No, thanks."

"Leila, you really think Elena would want you to bust up your shoulder making a perfect site? I'm almost done here. Anyway, I wanted to use your brain."

I pressed the cool stainless steel bottle against my shoulder and closed my eyes in relief. He was probably full of it, but whatever. "Shoot."

He started shoveling again. Between loads, he said, "I've been making notes. I want to bounce them off you."

I unscrewed the top of the water and took a sip. The water tasted metallic, but anything was a relief after digging. I dangled my legs into the pit and took another sip. "About Elena?"

He nodded and swiped his hand across his forehead, leaving a smear of dirt that hypnotized me. I had the bizarre urge to lick it off.

After a beat, I said, "Sure." I drank more water and averted my eyes so I could concentrate better. "I made some notes too. I started off with a timeline of events." It was the most detective-y thing I could think of doing.

"Me too." He touched his back pocket. "I've got mine on my iPhone."

I felt like a rube. "Mine are on paper. In my tent."

"That's cool. We can still compare after." He swung another shovelful of dirt on the opposite end of the pit. "I should wash my hands before I touch my phone anyway."

"Sure." I beamed at him. He looked taken aback for a second before he smiled back. I guess I'd been scowling at him, but now I felt cheered up that he was trying to solve Elena's murder. He didn't only care about punani. He had a brain, too.

He kept digging in silence. I started to twitch. I said, "I'd better give you a hand."

"Nah. Look. We're six foot deep, easy. I'm finishing the length. We don't want too big a hole or else it'll draw even more attention to the area. Give me another five."

After six, he tossed his shovel out of the hole, planted his hands less than a foot away from my left knee, and jumped. He sprang high and planted his knee next to mine. Within seconds, he'd plopped himself beside me and plucked the water bottle out of my hands.

"Please," I said.

"Right. Could I have my water back, please?"

"You're such a gentleman."

He dusted off his hands and poured a bit of water over them, working the worst of the dirt off. "You know it. Okay. Here we go." He downed some water. I watched the line of his throat and his Adam's apple bob up and down with each swallow. Then he handed me the bottle and slipped his iPhone out of his pocket.

"This is what I've got." He tapped a few buttons.

I pressed my shoulder to his in order to get the best look. He smelled like sweat and dirt and himself. I could have licked his biceps like an apple. I closed my eyes and inhaled deeply.

"Leila?"

My head snapped up. He was staring at me in amusement.

I straightened up, avoiding shoulder contact. "Right. Your timeline."

"Right here. Now, we got to the campsite at five—"

"Just after."

Together, we hammered out an agreement about the times.

5:07: Arrival
5:20: Laurent noticed Elena was missing, told Mac.
5:24: They told me and Jack
5:25: Running to the river
5:38: He finds her body in the river, carries her out, and starts resuscitation
5:49: Laurent and I run for the van
6:03: We bring the van, load Elena, start driving back to the campground

6:13: Elena's pulse back
6:14: pulse lost
6:21: moonrise

Jack saved this version. "I'll send it to you and the rest of the pack, encrypted. But you know what bothers me the most? In half an hour, she managed to disappear, run to the river, get a head injury, fall in the river, and basically drown. If someone killed her, he had to work very fast." He paused. "It might be someone professionally hunting werewolves."

CHAPTER 24

My heart felt like it broke open in my chest. "That can't be right."

"I'm not saying it's right, Leila, but we've got to work with the worst case scenario. And Mr. Slow might not have figured that out while he dicks around trying to lift fingerprints off the bark of trees."

It took me a minute to realize that he was talking about Jefferson. I opened my mouth to defend him. Obviously, someone needed to be methodical around here. I didn't pretend to know anything about detective work and, no matter how much he blustered, neither did Jack.

On the other hand, what if Jack was right and someone was hunting us? What if Elena's death was just the beginning? I pushed myself up to standing. The water bottle thunked on the ground. Jack snatched it. "Leila. Chill."

"How can you spring this on me and expect me to *chill?*"

He reached for my hand.

I retreated and slipped on a mound of fresh dirt. I wasn't hurt, but my cheeks flamed. Humans get embarrassed by clumsiness. As a wer, I find it utterly humiliating. I planted both feet firmly in the earth and changed the subject. "Okay. Let's play worst case scenario. What if your werewolf hunter isn't alone? What if it's a group of people?"

Jack glanced downward to make sure I was grounded before he answered. "Could happen. It wouldn't be the first time."

He knew as well as I did that we'd been the target of pogroms and "ethnic cleansing" before.

"This is Canada," I said. My voice rose plaintively. I closed my eyes and clenched my fists. What happened to my fairy tale ending, buying a beautiful piece of land for my pack? My friend was dead, my would-be boyfriend panted over other women, and a group of freaks might hunt us down.

Jack's eyebrows drew together, watching me. He held out his hand once more.

I didn't move away. His strong fingers cupped my elbow, electrifying the skin even through my clothes.

I rubbed my gritty hand against my forehead and resisted the urge to fall against his body. Now, more than ever, I should not seek consolation in his warm flesh. "We need more information to figure out if this was an—isolated incident or if someone is targeting us." I didn't want to talk about Elena like that, but it made it easier. "It's possible Elena was going to meet someone here and got caught by a random psycho from Singlewhitefemales.com or whatever. If that's the case, for sure she would've e-mailed the guy. The St-Huberts were asking me to break into her e-mail anyway. So I could try that. I'd know the answers to some of her security questions, so if I could reset her passwords, we'd get the ball rolling." I made a face. "She might've booked off for the weekend, but usually she's online or on her phone 24/7, so if I'm going to impersonate her I've got to move it."

"What about her phone? That might be easier." Jack's thumb and index finger started to draw circles on my elbow. You'd think I'd hardly feel it through my jacket, but my nipples rose in response. I licked my lips. Jack's gaze flew to my mouth.

I drew my arm away from him and tried to get back to business. "That's true." Elena used to make fun of my pay-as-you-go phone without camera or Internet connection, but hers wasn't much better. We might be able to unlock her phone and grab some messages. "Great. As soon as we get back to camp, I'll try her phone. I think she had it turned off to save on roaming charges, but I can at least see what kind of security she's got on it."

"Perfect. I'm sure Gisèle is curious."

I stiffened. We'd been having a great, goal-oriented conversation and he'd been caressing my elbow, but he had to bring up the big blonde. "Yeah. Great."

He glanced at me out of the corner of his eye. "I'm telling you, she's nothing to me."

Then why bring her up? I shrugged. "Makes no difference to me. We're talking business here."

Jack dipped his head a crucial two inches forward and kissed me.

CHAPTER 25

I closed my eyes and kissed him back, devouring his warm, firm lips. He tasted like coffee and smelled like fresh dirt and his own insanely good musk.

I wrapped my hands around his head, drawing him closer.

I knew I shouldn't. But at this exact moment, I couldn't recall why this man was verboten.

Jack's hands roamed down my back, squeezed my hips, and lifted me slightly in the air.

I protested, a muffled noise against his lips, but he plunged his tongue into my mouth while his hands urged my legs around his waist.

No. Yes. Yes. I wrapped my legs around his waist, which made me taller than him, so I bent my head and kept right on kissing him. Black stars swirled behind my closed eyelids. I'd kissed other guys, but none of them made me insane, intoxicated, almost addicted.

"Closer," muttered Jack.

That was the name of a Nine Inch Nails song that used to drive Jack crazy. I arched my chest against his, shoving my fingers through his sweaty hair.

He growled softly, maybe remembering what we used to do to that song. Or maybe my body alone inspired that kind of ferocity. Either way.

He tore his lips away from mine and nibbled my neck. I moaned aloud. It reminded me of Jack in wolf form as well as Jack in human form, both of them masterful and irresistible.

He reached a hand under my jacket.

I wasn't wearing a bra, but I didn't pull away. I waited for him to make that discovery.

He cupped a breast in each hand and closed his eyes. I almost laughed at the rapture on his face, except then he started making circles around the areolae with each thumb, and it felt so good, my body seemed to levitate for a second.

"You are so sexy," he said, before he claimed my mouth again.

I broke away from his hot, wet kiss and breathed, "Prove it."

He growled and tightened his grip on me before he started tipping me backward. I clamped my legs around him, but he laid me gently on the ground, cradling my head with his hand and slowly levering us down with one arm.

Still, fresh dirt trickled on my face.

I winced and raised my hand to brush it away. Then I froze, remembering where we were. We'd already defiled her investigation site.

Jack said, "Hold on to me. Keep your legs around my waist."

"Jack—"

"Around my waist!"

I threw my arms around him and squeezed him with my legs. He pressed one hand against my right thigh, silently asking me to tighten my embrace.

I did.

He levered on to his knees. Then he slowly rose to his feet and began striding deeper into the woods.

A ladybug buzzed by my ear before the shadows fell over us. Branches crunched under Jack's feet.

I clung to him and closed my eyes, giving myself over to the wilderness around me and throbbing inside my body. No more thinking. No more self-denial. With every beat of my heart, I was sure someone would discover us and tear us apart from each other. But in the meantime, I would relish every delectable moment with this man.

Jack missed a step. I started to turn my head, to see where we were headed, but he said "Uh uh" and pressed my back against something solid.

Bark poked into my scalp and roughed up the strip of my skin exposed between my jeans and my high-riding jacket. I could smell the tree he pressed me up against. Its sap was beginning to flow. But more than that, I could smell mud and moss and a sexually primed male.

I opened my eyes to see Jack's face staring into mine.

"You're mine," he said. He unzipped my jacket. The sound pierced the air and made me. The flaps fell open, revealing my purple microfiber dress shirt. He tried to unbutton it until he realized it was fastened with snaps. He popped the top one open.

He raised his eyebrows and snapped open the second. Third, fourth, fifth. Pop, pop, pop, pop. "I like this," he said. "When we get back, I want you to wear this shirt for me again and strip it off."

Already, he was making plans for the future. I closed my eyes instead of answering.

Underneath the shirt and jacket, I wore a raspberry fleece top. He pushed it up and said, "But don't wear this."

I giggled.

"Much as I like Mountain Equipment Co-op—"

I laughed out loud. He recognized the brand, which meant he loved to camp as much as I did.

"—it ain't sexy. Or, not very."

"Hey." I pretended to pout.

"But you are. So I guess you can wear granny pajamas if you want, but snap tops are much better."

He tickled my breastbone. I waited for him to stroke my breasts, but instead his hand slid south and unbuckled my jeans. He unzipped them slowly. I lifted my hips, trying to help him slide them off, until I realized he was watching me wiggle while wearing an ear-to-ear grin. "Bastard," I said.

"And proud of it. Wolves don't need marriage certificates."

I didn't bother following his train of thought. I shoved my nose into the tender skin between his neck and shoulder and inhaled the fresh air and his musk. How I loved being with Jack. I'd tried human guys. I'd wear perfume and short skirts. I ate vegetarian meals. I exorcised wolves from my vocabulary and even from my book shelves and web browsers after a few got too curious about my "obsession." But no matter how many guys I dated, not one could make me laugh or make my body sing the way Jack did.

At least, no one yet.

Jefferson's dark brown eyes and chicory skin flitted into my mind for a second.

I screwed my own eyes shut.

"Second thoughts?" asked Jack.

Uh oh. An unfortunate choice of words, given that I was momentarily considering another option. Another giggle bubbled up my throat. I tried to choke it down.

Jack peered at me. "Leila?"

I cleared my throat. "Yeah." My voice still sounded rusty.

"You all right?"

I nodded.

"Okay, then." He shimmied my jeans off my hips. My lilac underwear peeled off with them. I tried to yank them back up, but Jack stilled my hand and said, "Uh uh. That's the benefit of skinny jeans, God love 'em."

I laughed. "I wouldn't have thought you knew what skinny jeans were."

"I know what shows off your ass."

I laughed, pleased despite myself.

"I remember the boot cut jeans." He tugged my jeans and underwear down an inch. "And miniskirts." Another inch. "And the boots." Jeans and panties to my knees. "Do you still have those black leather boots?"

Even though I was half-naked and about to be ravished, I recalled those boots. Below-knee black leather boots, square toe, flat heel. Mildly sexy, but not slutty like the ones Gisèle wore now. So Jack had tripled his bonus points right there. I smiled and let him unlace my utilitarian hiking boots, marveling at how he could work so efficiently while keeping me propped against a tree.

"You can wear the tearaway shirt, some lacy bra and panties, and those boots when we get back to town." He pulled my boots off and let them thump to the ground.

"What about on the bottom? I'm not Lady Gaga."

"You're better," he growled. He lowered me down, shielding my back from the bark with his hands, until I was sitting on his bent knees. He was kneeling on the muddy forest floor.

He lifted my ass so he could slide my underwear and jeans off. At the last second, he said, "Do you want your socks on?"

I shook my head. Within seconds, my lower half was completely exposed to the wind and Jack's fierce gaze.

I could've hidden my goods, or at least my face.

Instead, I decided to spread my legs wide and let Jack have a good look.

His eyes blazed. "This is why I love you, Leila."

Whoa. Before I could react to that one, he spread his knees, letting my bottom fall on the moist ground. Or, not quite. He shoved my jeans under me, cushioning my fall.

While I giggled, he dove forward and planted his tongue directly on my hot spot. By that, I don't mean he landed on my clitoris. I mean he covered as much of my labia as possible with his long, thick tongue and waited, breathing in and out.

He felt good, but I wasn't sure what he was playing at. Maybe he remembered that I don't like being abraded immediately. A little foreplay within the foreplay, if you know what I mean.

Jack began tracing a figure eight with his tongue, sinuously brushing around my clit on the top loop and my vagina on the bottom loop. I bucked, both turned on and confused and—oh, yes. Oh, yes, Lord.

He slid his hands under my ass and held me open. That turned me on even more, that he was controlling me.

He glanced up at me and caught the delirium on my face, because he dug in and this time he concentrated more on my clit.

Just as I started to wiggle and moan, he clamped down on one leg with one hand. With the other, he inserted a long finger inside my vagina.

"Jack," I choked out.

In response, he hooked his finger north and tapped my G-spot.

I gasped.

He murmured in satisfaction and withdrew his hand so he could side one, two, three fingers inside my cunt. Then his tongue started doing tiny figure-eights around my clit while his fingers worked inside.

This time I screamed.

Jack nipped my leg. "Quiet," he said, but then he returned to his divine work, and the fever worked up inside me to such a pitch that I literally saw red and I started to yip. I bucked and jerked over the abyss, spasming into Jack's mouth.

CHAPTER 26

My heart beat in my chest and thrummed in my neck. My breathing slowed. I caught my breath and smiled at Jack, who was lying belly down in the dirt, watching my reaction.

He grinned and opened his mouth, clearly ready to deliver more lovin'. The man remembered that I liked to go multiple rounds.

That was what I loved about him.

Double whoa.

I shoved aside the L-word and arched toward his mouth. No woman thinks clearly after she comes, especially when she's about to go for a double header.

I watched him close his eyes and apply his tongue to my tender flesh. But before he could flick, I heard someone call from a distance.

"Lei-la."

I thought it was my post-Big O-hallucination until Jack's head jerked up. He listened with his body poised on alert.

"Jaaaaack." This time, it sounded like a woman. Gisèle, to be precise. And closer than the other voice.

Jack jumped to his feet and tossed me my socks. "I'll distract them. Don't worry."

I let the socks bounce off my chest. I had more important things to cover. I plucked my panties out of my inside-out jeans. As soon as my ass was covered, I felt a smidge better, but it took me a crucial thirty seconds to get the jean legs straightened out and a good minute to wedge into them. Now I rued the skinny jeans and the extra seconds they took to shimmy on. I was freezing and filthy from the cold, wet mud both inside my jeans and squelching between my toes.

Jack wiped off his face with his sleeve. Then he grabbed his bottle of water and offered me some. I shook my head while I shook out my socks and laced on my boots. I threw on my purple shirt and jacket last without bothering to fasten either one.

Jack gargled and drank some water. He splashed it over his face, too, before he offered it to me again.

"Jaaaaack," the woman's voice called, less than 20 feet away. I hated the way Gisèle called his name, flattening the A.

Jack shook the water bottle at me. "Take some. We both need it."

I wasn't exactly thirsty since I was riding an adrenaline wave. After a minute, I realized he was trying to cut my smell on him and wanted me to return the favor. As if Madame Gisèle wouldn't be able to smell the sex anyway.

I sipped the water and muttered, "Thanks."

Jack took my hand and started striding back toward the grave and away from the scene of our latest tryst. "We're over here! Taking a water break!"

Is that what the kids were calling it nowadays?

"Jaaaaack." Gisèle placed her hands on a maple trunk and peered around it adorably at him like she was in a Bollywood movie. "We've been looking all over for you. You didn't answer your phone."

"I've been right here. We just finished," said Jack. He squeezed my hand and I felt slightly comforted, even though that was pathetic.

Gisèle stepped around the tree. I felt childishly pleased to see the sprays of mud up and down her hooker boots. She didn't bother looking at me. Her grey eyes fixed on Jack while she said, "Jefferson has some news for us and wants us to gather around the campground."

Jack nodded, but he pulled his phone out of his pocket to see if they'd called us. I knew my little Rogers phone hadn't buzzed.

"Neither of you were answering," said Gisèle.

Jack said, "I guess I turned it off by accident."

Gisèle nodded, still not looking at me. I realized she was going to pretend I didn't exist, as if she could make me disappear by ignoring me. Her nostrils flared, though. I wondered if she'd detected my scent on Jack.

I smiled and took a swig of the water bottle.

She glanced at me then. "Jefferson was asking for you."

I coughed. I cleared my throat and did my best to fasten the bottle top one-handed.

Jack stiffened and let go of my hand.

Immediately, Gisèle pressed herself against his free side and slipped her arm through his. "Shall we?"

CHAPTER 27

It seemed childish to grab Jack's hand back. So I didn't.

And, to tell you the truth, I was kind of scared of what we'd done.

Not the sex, so much. That I could pass off as animal instinct or body gravity or something. Jack could probably make me come on my death bed.

No, it was more what he'd said.

This is why I love you, Leila.

He could've said, "This is what I love *about* you, Leila." My body. Sex. That was normal for us.

Instead, he'd slipped those three little words in.

Guys say anything in bed. We all know this. Elena and I once made a list of "It doesn't count if he's..." In bed, drunk, on drugs topped the list, although we added stupid stuff like "kidnapped" or "between another woman's (or man's) thighs."

So I should write it all off.

But somehow, I couldn't.

Even though another woman now clung to his arm and tried to set the pace so they were always two steps ahead of me.

Jack glanced over his shoulder at me, but he didn't say anything. That was okay. I was still reeling. And Gisèle chatted enough for triplets. When I tuned in, she was blabbing about Glengarry county in winter. "And it's so beautiful with all the snow! You'll have to try our snowmobiling trails."

I almost smiled. Jack preferred non-motorized sports. Like sex. And snowboarding. And more sex.

"Yeah, maybe," he finally broke in, before we entered the camp. "Do you have any idea what Jefferson has found?"

"He looked awfully serious," said Gisèle, "but he's always like that. I suppose that's natural, considering his own personal tragedy."

My human ears pricked up as well as they could.

She tossed her hair, nearly brushing Jack's shoulder with her locks. "My mother told me he's been like that since his wife died."

His wife?

Died?

Wife?

"Man," said Jack.

Gisèle squeezed his biceps and said, "I *know*."

For once, I barely noticed her flirting. No wonder Jefferson emitted such a hands-off vibe. He must've still been in mourning. How long ago had he lost his wife? And how?

I squinted into the sun. The man himself stood with his back to us, speaking to the rest of the group.

Mac glanced at me, raising his eyebrows in relief before he wrinkled his nose. If he'd been a wolf, he would've flattened his ears back. Whatever Jefferson was saying, he wasn't buying it.

Jefferson glanced over his shoulder at us. "Glad you could make it," he said.

I nodded and inserted myself into the circle between the Mac and Laurent, facing Jefferson but downwind of him. I didn't want to advertise Jack's and my latest interlude any more than I had to.

Gisèle towed Jack between her and her parents, stroking her hand up and down his arm. Jack gently moved his arm out of his grasp, but for someone who was "mine," I found him awfully slow to distance himself from the blond one.

Jefferson said, "So she managed to track you down." When he said "track," his eyes flicked toward the river. I knew he was thinking of us messing up the investigation site. I straightened my spine and gave him a curt nod.

"I have important news," said Jefferson.

Jack's hands tightened into fists. He noticed me noticing and crossed his arms over his front, trying to relax.

Bernard inclined his head, waiting.

Jefferson said, "I think Elena was lured down to the river. I found some chicken bones near the tree where she was found."

Chicken bones! I'd wrestled a chicken bone out of her mouth during the resus. How could I have forgotten to mention it to Jefferson?

Jack's eyes lasered on mine. He was thinking the same thing.

"You believe she was lured down to the river using a chicken?" asked Bernard.

Jefferson nodded. "The chicken bones appear to be fairly fresh, judging from the bits of meat still attached. Scavenger animals had moved them around, but the bones seemed to centre around the tree."

I put up my hand before we got any further. Bernard blinked permission for me to speak. Jefferson gazed at me, silently assessing me while I admitted, "I found a chicken bone in her mouth." I glanced at the rest of the group. "Remember when we were having trouble doing mouth-to-mouth because something was in her throat? I pulled out a bone and tossed it away."

"Why didn't you say anything?" asked Laurent.

"It didn't seem important at the time. I tossed it and kept trying to help. And then I kind of—" Forgot about it. Jumped Jack's bones instead of worrying about chicken bones. But they already knew that. "Elena was always hungry before she 'shifted. That's why she ate the beef jerky. I know the chicken bone part was weird, but..."

"It is not clear to me how someone could have lured Elena away from the safety of her pack to the river shortly before moonrise, chicken or no chicken," said Sylvie, in the tone of a woman who would choose famine in the name of fashion.

For once, I agreed with her. Elena was hungry, sometimes starving before 'shift change. But not enough to run away and certainly not toward the river. I said, "What if the chicken was poisoned?"

Everyone looked at me. I met Jefferson's steady brown eyes first. "Or what if it was baited or tampered somehow to make it irresistible? Or both?"

Laurent huffed, "Why didn't the rest of us respond to it, then?"

"I don't know," I admitted. But then I had another brainwave. "Elena had the best sense of smell of any werewolf I know. It was almost freaky. She wouldn't even go to certain districts in Montreal if the wind was blowing the wrong way. It was even more acute when she was about to 'shift. So maybe she picked up something the rest of us didn't."

Laurent shook his head, but Jack said, "We've got to consider the worst case scenario, which is that someone might be hunting werewolves."

Gisèle squeaked and grabbed his arm.

Mac bared his teeth. Laurent snarled.

Bernard held up his hand. "There is no evidence for this. Calm yourselves."

Jack gently shook off Gisèle's hand. "I'm not trying to scare anybody. I just want us to stay on alert."

Bernard said, "I understand. However, I believe there is no cause for raising a Code Orange without any evidence. Let us return to the findings to date. Jefferson, have you found any evidence that the chicken was tampered with, as has been suggested?" He waved a negligent hand at us.

Jefferson said, "We would need to test the bones for some sort of substance."

Jack cleared his throat. "I have access to a lab through my work. I could pull in some favours."

I glanced at him.

His cheeks reddened, but his eyes didn't deviate from Bernard's.

Great. Another lady friend. Jack was practically a walking billboard for those "You sleep with everyone your partner has ever slept with" ads.

Bernard said, "We will discuss this later. Dr. Flores has a laboratory, albeit a small one, and Jefferson has contacts as well."

I raised my eyebrows. Better not discuss it too much later, or the rain would wash away any useful traces of evidence. The bones might not still have anything on it, but the ground might.

Jack's eyes met mine and I knew he was thinking the same thing.

Jack narrowed his eyes, turning his gaze toward the river. Uh oh. If I could read the guy's mind—and, occasionally, I thought I could—if they tried to hold him back from the evidence, he'd steal it and bring it to the lab himself.

He liked to break the rules way more than I did. But once Jefferson took down his police tape, we'd have free access to the site. I might be able to figure out where I'd flung the bone lodged in Elena's mouth. We could dig up the earth around the site. And Jack could bring it to his lady friend for testing, with or without the alphas' permission.

CHAPTER 28

After a quick supper of sandwiches I barely tasted, Bernard said, "It is time."

Time to bury Elena.

Jack, Mac, and Laurent silently carried her body from the overhang. She was wrapped in a white sheet. Jack cradled her head and shoulders.

It reminded me of him stabilizing her neck during the resuscitation.

I closed my eyes for a second before I surveyed Mac, who kept his head lowered while he supported her body. Laurent came last, carrying her legs.

And me, her closest friend here? I wasn't doing anything. I was standing with Jefferson and the St-Hubert family. Strangers.

I rushed toward my friends and grabbed Elena's feet. Laurent didn't need my help, but he silently moved further up her legs, closer to Mac, so I could grasp one small part of her.

The sheet slipped. The toe of Elena's pink ballerina shoe poked toward me.

"No!" I cried out.

Laurent whipped the sheet back over the shoe. "It's all right," he muttered.

But it wasn't all right. It wouldn't be all right until I found out who did this.

Out of all the people here, I was the one who'd loved her. But I was also the one who'd fought for this piece of land that would now be her burial ground.

I hadn't noticed her slip away from the campsite. I hadn't been able to resuscitate her. I'd messed up her investigation site. I'd forgotten about the chicken bone.

So many ways I'd wronged her.

I felt like I'd killed her.

Inside, I was screaming. My cheeks felt cold. I touched them and realized tears streamed down my face, unchecked.

Then I gripped Elena's cold ankles even more tightly.

Elena was dead.

I couldn't bring her back. But I could solve her death.

Jack met my eyes across Elena's body. "We'll get him."

I shook my head. Jack couldn't have read my mind. And more importantly, I was going to do this myself. I was the responsible one. He hardly knew Elena.

"I don't know why she died, but we'll find out," said Jack. He'd stopped walking. He stood there, cradling Elena's head and shoulders while he spoke to me like I was the only person present. "This is a pack thing. We lost her together and we will avenge her together."

My heart hammered in my chest and in my throat. I shook my head. I couldn't speak.

"We'll do it together," Jack repeated. He glanced down at her body, still wrapped in the sheet. His jaw tightened.

"Count me in," said Mac. For some reason, I remembered how he and Elena used to read the newspaper together and argue over who got the sports page. Even though it hadn't worked out, they'd really loved each other in some ways.

Laurent bared his teeth. "You couldn't leave me out."

And so the four of us made a pact over Elena's cold body. In that instant, Jefferson and the St-Huberts might as well not have existed.

Vengeance is mine, saith the werewolves.

CHAPTER 29

The Accidental Murderer

Darryl didn't mean to kill anyone. He only wanted his land back.

He remembered visiting his grandparents when he was a kid. Grandad taught him how to milk by hand. Darryl remembered the feel of the soft, squishy teat in his hand. He remembered the smell of manure and the plink-plink of milk in the pail.

He remembered the way the barn cats would prowl around them, waiting for a squirt. Once in a while, Grandad let them have it. He'd try to hit them between the eyes, so it was a bit of a contest, see, between Grandad and the cats.

Darryl remembered Grandad scooping up a cup of milk from the pail. The milk tasted weirdly warm, but also so good and creamy that Grandad let him have two cups instead of one. Darryl and Grandad could sit in the barn, hay under their feet, the cows flicking their tails, and they wouldn't have to say a word. This was their place.

Even in those days, you didn't usually milk by hand anymore. But Grandad said it was important to know how. "In case the electricity or the equipment breaks down. And so you get the feel for the animal. Farming is about you and the animals and the land, and don't you forget it."

Darryl never forgot it.

Problem was, his father didn't, either. Dad got up at 5 a.m. to milk the cows before school and came back after school, grabbed a bite to eat, and had to milk them all again. Their family almost never went on vacation because Grandad didn't trust anyone else to look after his operation.

Dad hated it. He'd rather read. He dreamed of university. He wanted to wear a lab coat and never touch a cow again.

Grandad dropped dead of a heart attack when Darryl was ten. Dad sold the farm as soon as he could get a buyer.

Darryl begged his dad to leave him a part of it. "I want to be a farmer, Dad. Let me have it. I'll drop out of school when I'm 16—"

"The hell you will. You'll go to university like I did."

"Dad, I'm telling you—"

"There's no future in farming. It breaks your back and your bank account. I'm saving you, Son."

Yeah, right. But Darryl was only ten years old. All he could do was watch them kill his land. It changed hands a few times, but mainly, they started breaking up the hundred acres for houses. Except one old coot who set up a campground on 50 acres.

Darryl dropped out of school anyway to become a hired hand. He worked as hard as he could, but he never seemed to scrape enough pennies together for a barber, let alone his own land.

Until finally, the old man kicked off at 52. Heart attack, just like Grandad, despite his fancy pills and exercise bike. And Darryl finally had enough dough.

But not the land.

Darryl could've bought a hobby farm and worked his way up to a bigger holding, but he wanted his birthright: Grandad's land.

Darryl approached the campground owner, an Armenian city guy who'd gone out of business anyway. The guy said he'd already started negotiating with some environmental group who "needed a retreat away from the city."

Darryl could have spit. Farmers needed land to make food so city boys and girls could have milk for their double lattes. They could "retreat" to their gay bars or whatever they did for fun.

No one needed the land like Darryl.

And he was going to make sure he got it.

CHAPTER 30

Leila

After I placed the last boulder over Elena's grave, making a crude cairn, I crossed my arms over my chest, hugging myself.

Jack wrapped his arm around me. I wanted to press myself against his toasty body and forget everything else. But I'd done that too much already. I had sworn to find Elena's murderer.

My phone buzzed in my back pocket. Glad for the excuse, I pulled away from him and said, "Let me get that."

It was a text from Mr. Tabassian, the land owner. I clicked on it, expecting some eleventh-hour wrangling over the final paperwork. Instead, I found a rather formal note that he'd have to "delay negotiations for the foreseeable future."

No. No, no, no, no, no.

Not only did we need this land way more than any weekend cottager or hobby farmer, but we'd buried Elena's body here.

I texted him immediately. My first priority was to get back to Montreal.

Jack raised his eyebrows at me, but I was already calculating how to borrow a set of wheels without stranding the rest of the guys here.

"Is something wrong?" inquired Bernard.

"I'm sorry, Bernard, but I have to go." I showed him the message. "This is the man selling us this piece of land. I need to talk to him personally. I'm not sure what's going on, but Mr. Tabassian doesn't talk well on the phone." His English broke down a little. Plus I wanted to read his body language and his scent to figure out the real story. Mr. T's son was often in trouble. Maybe Mr. T wanted more money for the land, and this was his underhanded negotiation tactic. "I'll have to negotiate with him ASAP."

Bernard nodded. "That seems reasonable."

Sylvie added, "I have some contacts in the real estate industry. Would you like me to call them?"

I considered it for a split second. But this land was my baby. My passion. I didn't want to screw this one up, too. "I'll let you know if I need them. Thank you."

I glanced at Jack, Mac, and Laurent. "Who wants to come back with me? I completely understand if you want to stay longer. I'm leaving in an hour, though. If I have to, I'll take a taxi to the train station and leave the van here."

Bernard held up a finger while he and Sylvie conferred quickly in French. He said, "By no means. If necessary, we will drive you. However, it is probably best if you return en masse in exactly the way you came—with Gisèle at the wheel, acting as Elena."

I digested that. It made perfect sense, even though every cell in my body screamed against it. At last, I nodded. Whatever got me home quickest. That was the most important.

"We're coming with you," said Jack. "Just give us twenty minutes to take down the tents and load up the van."

"This is my card." Jefferson materialized behind me and held up a solid square of grey cardboard embossed with his name. No title, but multiple modes of contact, including Twitter. For some reason, that struck me as funny.

I smiled at him. "Thank you." I brushed his fingers with mine accidentally on purpose when I took the card. His skin felt cool and dry.

He didn't smile, but I saw something flicker in the depths of his caramel eyes.

"Let's move," said Jack.

Jefferson and I gazed at each other for another beat. Long enough for me to wonder how his hair might feel against my cheek or what he might do if I pressed the tip of my index finger against the tiny dent in the fullness of his bottom lip.

When I finally pulled my gaze away, I spotted Jack already stalking back toward the campground. I didn't think too much of it until I came across him yanking my tent pegs out of the ground.

"Hold on!" I leapt to his side. "That's not how I take it down."

"Look. I'm helping you."

"No, you're not. You're taking over. Why don't you take down your own tent?"

"I'm trying to help," he said. He still wouldn't look at me. He dropped the peg back in the hole and stomped it back into the ground. "Happy?"

"Extremely." That was one thing I hated about Jack—he was so friggin' bossy. Worse than my dad.

I collapsed my tent the normal way, but that tent peg he stomped was the last one to come out. He'd driven it in far enough that my hands slipped on the metal and got covered in wet, slippery mud. I couldn't get the effing thing out.

"Want help?" asked Jack, sliding his orgy tent back into its blue canvas bag and tossing it over his shoulder.

I gritted my teeth, prayed, and pried that sucker out so hard, I fell on my ass. But I held the peg up in victory.

"Good work," said Jack. He cracked a smile.

I didn't smile back. Gisèle practically gave him lap dances, and he found that perfectly kosher. But if Jefferson handed me his business card, Jack acted like we'd crossed the line.

And Jefferson had disappeared without formally saying good-bye. He'd probably headed back down to the river, trying to collect every last chicken bone. I missed him even as I shoved my tent in the back and slammed the trunk shut. Thanks to Jack, I was the last one on board.

And Gisèle was already drumming her red acrylic nails on the dashboard with her skinny white tuchus firmly ensconced in the driver's seat.

Chapter 31

Gisèle signaled left and accelerated to 130 clicks an hour, easily passing a Passat. "So was Elena involved with anyone?"

"Not officially," I said from the front passenger seat. "But by the way, she tried not to go above 120."

Gisèle pursed her lips as she decelerated.

We'd passed the *Bienvenue au Québec* sign, so I explained, "Too many cops around." Quebec may lack decent roads, library, or funding for health care and schools, but by gum, we have a lot of cops. Even 120 clicks was pushing it. Cops didn't hand out as many tickets at 9 p.m., but you seriously never knew.

"Wasn't she at her limit for points, too?" Laurent called from the rear right seat. "I remember the time we had to chip in for the speeding ticket—"

"Only the one time?" said Mac, from beside him, and we all laughed.

Gisèle glanced at Jack in the rear view mirror. "How did you know her?"

I'd called the shotgun seat to throw some distance between Jack and Gisèle, forcing him to sit behind me. I dropped down my makeup mirror to watch him talk to her. "I met her through Leila," he said. After a minute, he added, "She used to cook all the time."

I laughed. I'd forgotten about that. Elena had gone through this huge cooking phase.

Mac said, "One time I came over and found a giant beef tongue on her counter."

"Remember those dinner parties?" asked Laurent. "She would invite complete strangers to dinner parties and ask them to bring wine."

"Isn't that how we met you?" I asked.

Laurent grinned. He was walking home from the metro and Elena buttonholed him for one of her parties. At first, she'd make a roast or something fancy, but she got sick of all the vegetarians and cheap losers who inhaled her food and destroyed her bathroom. I think Laurent came to one of the last parties. She made spaghetti sprinkled with olive oil, Parmesan cheese, and parsley, and drank Laurent's wine.

"The pasta was terrible," said Laurent, "but the company was worth keeping."

I nodded and smiled. I cracked open the window and let some fresh night air blast through my hair. This felt like more of a wake than the bonfire.

Until Gisèle spoke again. "She seemed extremely...social."

I swiveled in my chair to look at her. She gave a Gallic shrug, a tiny, insouciant movement of both shoulders. "Was she seeing more than one man?"

"Sometimes," I said. In general, Elena dated as many guys as she could get. But I did not like where this was heading.

Gisèle smiled and lowered her head. "She liked company. Male company especially. Am I right?"

"Are you saying what I think you're saying?" I said softly. Werewolves work in packs. You don't often see us backstabbing or gossiping about each other the way humans do. So part of me could not believe Gisèle might consider Elena a slut.

Gisèle braked for a construction sign that showed her lane ending. She cut off a transport truck while merging into the right lane. Its headlights blinded me for a second, but it managed to slow down in time. She said, "It was merely an observation. I know Jack has proposed his theory of poisoned chicken, but it is also possible that someone from Elena's past wanted to harm her."

"No way," I said, on two counts. That was my theory about the poisoned chicken. And Elena never mentioned any big bad from her past.

"I heard she gave her phone number to complete strangers," Gisèle continued.

"Once in a while," I said. "Who doesn't?" Actually, I didn't, too much, but that was beside the point.

"Calm down, Leila," said Laurent.

"She's calling Elena a ho and you're telling *me* to calm down?"

"We could all be more tactful," said Jack. I'd rather he had told Gisèle to bite herself, but at least he was nominally on my side.

I took a deep breath. "Look," I said to Gisèle. "I take your point. We need to investigate all the possibilities. Fine. You think Elena might have brought this on herself. Fine. When we get back to town, I'll probably be able to get into her accounts. I think I might know where she wrote down her passwords. We can go through all her personal messages and see if anyone was stalking her. But in the meantime, I don't want anyone talking trash about her."

Gisèle chuckled, but before she could say anything, Jack cut in, "That sounds fair. I, for one, promise not to talk about the time she went on a spicy food diet. Oh, wait. That was Leila."

"Elena did it too, until she thought it was giving her an ulcer," put in Mac.

I smiled reluctantly. "Hey. That wasn't a diet. That was a way of life. I got so tired of bland cafeteria food—"

"You used to carry around a hip flask of hot sauce!" said Jack. "And then you'd whip it out at the restaurant and start seasoning everything."

He had such a good memory. Painfully so. "Um. I guess that could've been slightly embarrassing."

"Slightly," said Jack.

"I wouldn't talk if I were you, though," I said. "What about the time you dressed up like M.C. Hammer at Hallowe'en? They put on 'Hammer time' and you actually got up and did the dance, with those pants?"

"*T'es pas sérieuse,*" Laurent called from the back. Mac guffawed.

"That's not embarrassing," cooed Gisèle. "That's amazing. I'd love a man who was that disinhibited—and could dance that well." She shook out her hair. "I've always had a weakness for men who could dance."

"You should go out with Laurent, then," I said. "He's the best dancer here." Now that Elena was gone.

Laurent called, "The check is in the mail."

"I'm serious. Elena thought it was because he was in touch with his animal side."

Mac howled and Laurent whacked him to make him shut up. But it got me thinking. I remembered Elena saying that and smiling at herself in the mirror while she combed her hair. A small, self-satisfied smile. Had she and Laurent hooked up? And if so, how many guys had she done?

The more we thought about it, the more confusing it got. I just wanted to help solve Elena's death.

The simplest thing would be a poisoned chicken. But Jack, Jefferson, and Dr. Flores would handle the lab work. My job was to protect the land and show Gisèle how to fake Elena's identity and then disappear.

I glanced at Gisèle out of the corner of my eye as if I could make her disappear Right Now.

She bared her teeth at me in a facsimile of a smile.

CHAPTER 32

I rose at dawn and donned my most conservative suit. By 9 a.m., I was meeting with Mr. Tabassian while Laurent glowered by my side.

"Mr. Tabassian, I don't understand." I folded my hands, tilted my head, and smiled my most charming smile. This was the man who used to tell me my hair was as dark as his daughter's. This was the man who told me he was relieved the land would pass into good hands. This was the man who was supposed to sign the final papers in two weeks. This was the man who'd agreed to meet me on Monday morning to clarify his message.

He shrugged and wouldn't meet my eyes. "You understand. It's business."

"We agreed on a price. You agreed to do a title search for us," I said.

"We drafted a deposit check for you," said Laurent, sliding it across the rickety black desk covered in file folders.

Mr. Tabassian folded his hands on his belly. "I can't accept it."

"Why on earth not?" I asked, ignoring a glance from Laurent. I'd always been direct with Mr. Tabassian. I brought him baklava, for heaven's sake. I didn't care if he was fat and his office smelled like cigar smoke. We were pals.

"I've had another offer," he said.

"A higher offer?" asked Laurent. He sounded calm, but I heard the growl underneath.

Mr. Tabassian met Laurent's eyes, the first time he'd managed to make eye contact with either of us so far. I breathed a little easier while he said, "Of course higher."

"Then tell us what it is and we'll see if we can match it. We have the prior claim."

Mr. Tabassian shook his head sadly. "I don't think so."

My guts clenched. We weren't rich. Werewolves tend to fall into middle class at best, and Côte-des-Neiges was a relatively poor neighborhood. But I said as softly as I could, "Try us."

"He tripled it."

Even while my head whirled, I seized on to that clue. It was a guy. "He" could be a lawyer representing a corporation. But somehow, I didn't think so. Our nemesis was a man. A rich man, no less.

But why would a rich man want this old campground in the middle of nowhere? Why now, right as we were about to close on it and after we'd buried Elena's body on it?

"Sorry, kids," said Mr. Tabassian. "You know I like you, but business is business."

"It's more than business," I managed to push out. I laid my pen down on his desk.

Laurent placed a warning hand on my knee. I wasn't going to say anything more, but he never trusted me. Laurent said, "I understand business, Mr. Tabassian. I also understand that you are reneging on our prior agreement. I will be in touch with your lawyer."

Mr. Tabassian spread his hands. "Hey, now. There's no need to get lawyers involved."

Laurent bared his teeth. "Too late. I am already a member of the bar. You seem to have forgotten that, along with your prior agreements. Good day, Mr. Tabassian."

I snatched the check back and placed it in my folder. Wasted money.

I stalked down the stairs instead of waiting for the elevator. The metal steps rang under my feet and reverberated in my ears, but I didn't feel safe talking until we'd hopped a bus and made it to the Crémazie metro station.

"Can we force him to sell to us?" I asked, strong-arming the station door open.

Laurent shrugged and followed me in. "I'll do my best. But he hadn't signed the papers or accepted the deposit, so he's not obligated."

I shook my head and stomped on to the escalator. "You work on that."

He'd shaved his face clean, but he hiked his still-bushy black eyebrows at me, reminding me of his wolf roots. "Got it, Leila. The question is, what are you going to do?"

124

We descended into the bowels of the Montreal subway system. The darkness and musty air seemed particularly appropriate right now. "Two things. One, find what happened to our friend, and two, figure out who wants our land. If we can get rid of both…"

"It's a two-for-one," agreed Laurent. He checked his watch. "You heading back to work?"

I reached for my Opus transit pass. I knew I should hit my desk. But my petitions and fundraising dinners could wait a few days, even weeks, if need be. Green Belt Montreal's highest priority had to be finding Elena's killer and securing this piece of land.

Now, if I were a detective, what would be the best way to accomplish both?

I followed Laurent through the turnstiles and down the steps to the Côte Vertu line, pondering my options. I said out loud, "I need a car."

Laurent frowned at me over his shoulder and led me to a relatively isolated part of the platform. "Do you want to borrow Elena's van?" It was at her apartment, but I could swing by and borrow it if I asked the blond one's permission.

I shook my head. The van was too conspicuous for what I had in mind, which was heading right back up to Mr. Tabassian's office. "I'm pretty sure I can find one." I checked my phone, but I didn't have any signal. "Does your phone work down here? I need to check a few things online."

Laurent sighed. "I don't like the sound of this." But he tossed me his phone anyway.

CHAPTER 33

Within an hour, I'd borrowed Mac's beloved blue VW Jetta and driven right back to Mr. Tabassian's office.

Mac had grimaced. "Why do you need a car?"

"Surveillance," I said. I would've called it a stakeout, but my cursory online search had already taught me something.

"How long do you need it?"

I made a face. "I can get it back to you tonight."

"But then you want it again tomorrow?"

I shrugged. It really depended on the rich man making contact with Mr. T.

Mac sighed. "I have to go out of town in a few days. Can't you borrow anyone else's?"

"Elena's wouldn't fit in. Laurent takes the metro. I don't have my own car." I cocked my head. "I suppose I could talk to Jack…."

Mac pitched me the keys. "Use it in good health. But I have to go to Boston on Thursday."

"Bon voyage," I said.

Montreal is not a big van town. A bright red passenger van like Elena's sticks out like a lollipop. Maybe I could get away with it on the West Island, where the yuppies go to procreate, but not in the garment district north of Highway 40.

Even though the VW would stick out a bit amongst the sedans lining the streets around Parc and Chabanel, most people were working too hard to pay much attention to me, as long as I didn't violate one of Montreal's many street parking injunctions like "No parking from 8:30 to 9:30 on Wednesdays in winter."

I crawled west on Sherbrooke, past indifferent businesspeople and cheery McGill students sunning themselves on the lawn behind the university gates. At last, I managed to navigate north on Parc and head back to Mr. T's office area. I always forgot how annoying it was to drive in the city, bumping over potholes and braking for vans stopped in the right-hand lane to make a delivery.

North of Highway 40, I started cruising for a parking space. Chabanel Street used to be the heart of Montreal's manufacturing industry. The stores still held out, but more and more, it seemed to be the home of old ethnic guys who missed the days of yore rather than a shopaholic's dream.

Still, Mr. Tabassian's seven-story white brick building bordered two streets. I decided to drive up Verveille, since Mr. T's office on the second floor overlooked that street. If nothing else, I could amuse myself by staring at the correct windowpane.

I didn't kid myself. I knew less than Encyclopedia Brown, the fictional kid detective, about "surveillance." But I couldn't sit in my office and lobby against wolf hunts when I thought I might be able to do something. The other wers were locked into their jobs. I was the only one with the flexibility—and the determination—to sit here for ten hours if I had to.

I also felt too twitchy to sit and wait in my office, tapping my foot while Jack dug up lab results or Jefferson hunted for clues. I'd rather run around with a rifle (figuratively). I'm pro-gun control, although I support some limited hunting. After all, both as a human and a wolf, I'm a predator myself.

Still, while Jack and Jefferson and Dr. Flores tried to ID the killer, I'd track down the rich man. Our competitor. And since Mr. T wasn't about to release his identity, I was going to have to figure it out by stealth.

I glanced around Mac's car to make sure I had everything I needed. Trail mix to satisfy my hunger. Ice water. One guy had recommended eating ice chips all day, to minimize the need to pee, but I wasn't that restrained. I'd packed an empty milk carton and a funnel in case nature called. And some spy stuff.

I folded up my suit jacket and tucked it in a bag. Underneath, I wore a plain long-sleeved white shirt. The black pants from my suit were well-cut but not flashy. Basically, I didn't want to look memorable in any way, whether that meant too dressed up or down. The articles I'd read had suggested layering clothes.

I lowered my seat back and dropped a straw hat over my face, barely covering my eyes. The idea was to look like I was taking a nap, when in fact I was watching everyone come and go down the street.

Wolves are very good at stalking. That's how we survive.

I tried to slow my heartbeat and my breathing and zone out. A man in a pinstriped shirt climbed into a Hyundai a block away and drove north. A car oozed past me, searching for parking, while a red car rode its tail.

Well. This was boring.

I wished we could've tapped Mr. T's phone or put a keylogger on his computer. That way, if Mr. Tabassian even typed the rich guy's name, we'd have it made in the shade. But Laurent the uptight lawyer insisted we play by the rules. "We do not want to break the law if we don't have to," he told me last night.

I looked at him. The law wouldn't look too kindly on us burying Elena.

He had the grace to redden. "Any more than is absolutely necessary," he said. "The district heads will be in touch with us soon."

Somehow, I couldn't place my faith in the district heads. The Côte-des-Neiges group was always fighting over their tiny scraps of power, and the St-Huberts—well, let's just say they had different priorities.

Like keeping their daughter safe. I didn't blame them. If I ever have fruit spring from my loins, you bet I'll be the biggest mama wolf around. So maybe I shouldn't have been surprised when Bernard handed Gisèle a farewell present: a pocket-sized GPS tracker.

"I don't want my daughter going unprotected," he said in a low voice, but we all heard it. She argued with him for a bit before she shoved it the box in her oversized Prada purse and we took off.

That was her only complaint on the ride back. "My father treats me like a little girl. We used to live in Montreal, and now he wants to babysit me. I swear, he would come with me if he could!" She scooped out the "Master Tracker" and handed it to Jack. "Could you use this?"

He demurred. "I don't think your father would be too interested in where I go."

She shrugged. "I'll tell him it broke."

"I'll take it," I said. I spent the rest of the ride puzzling out the instructions. As far as I could tell, this device, smaller than the palm of my hand but over an inch thick, ran on two AA batteries and let you track someone in real time online. Bernard meant for Gisèle to stick it on the underside of Elena's van. If the car wasn't moving, it would shut into

128

snooze mode and save battery power. It could last up to six weeks if you only used it an hour a day.

"I don't know why he bothered. I have GPS software in my phone," she complained.

While Jack soothed her, I slipped the Master Tracker into my own purse. That was Bond gadget number one on my present-day stakeout.

In real time, a woman shepherded her two little boys down the street. I couldn't make out her words, but her tone made it clear that mama ain't happy. The two boys ran away and she shouted after them before she gave up, muttering to herself and plodding down Verveille.

If this were a reality TV show, we'd have to do some serious editing for boredom. We'd have to throw in some young hot things baring their abs, maybe a hick to break things up, plus some no-good-niks to drag everyone down and sleep with each other.

I resisted the urge to check my phone. Jack hadn't called or texted or e-mailed me since we dropped him off. He'd put a hand on my shoulder and said, "Call me." And then he'd jumped out of the van, grabbed his tent and bag, and sailed into his apartment.

If he really luuuurved me, could he be that blasé?

I thought not. More likely, out of sight, out of mind. On to the next girl who wiggled her ass at him.

Gisèle wouldn't start up the van until Jack had closed the door behind himself. Then she sighed and said, "He's hot." She gunned the engine a few times to make her point before she reversed out of the driveway. She would've run down a kid on his tricycle if Mac and Laurent hadn't screamed a warning.

So no, I wasn't going to call Jack. I wasn't even going to think about him. I was going to sit outside of Mr. T's office until the rich man walked into the building.

Sooner or later, the guy should show up. Mr. Tabassian does e-mail, text, and fax, but he's an old-fashioned dude. He likes to shake hands and maybe have a drink together. No way he'd let a big land deal go down with no face-to-face contact. Especially after he basically chased us away.

So I had to wait and watch.

Now, I know what anyone sane would think.

How would I recognize a guy I'd never met? I had no idea what he looked, sounded, or smelled like.

Answer: I'd tail anyone who entered Mr. T's office.

In fact, if the day was this slow, I might tail anyone who entered the building, period. Greg Fallis, the guru whose articles I read, was a PI who actually preferred following people on foot because it kept him awake and gave him a challenge.

Of course, he actually knew what he was doing.

I had a few technological advantages, though. Fallis's books seemed to date from the '80s or '90s. Some things hadn't changed. Like I'd asked Laurent to search for abandoned offices or offices for rent around the area. Then some younger wers could apply for odd jobs. If someone could get hired on as cleaning staff, we'd have a better in. But all this was going to take time. So in the meantime, I was doing the stakeout the old-fashioned way.

But I bet in Mr. Fallis's day, he didn't get to play with a camera hidden in a pen: Bond gizmo number two.

On our drive back, Mac had gone online and found a spy camera pen through Kijiji. We swung by and paid cash. No record of our transaction. He even walked a block from where we'd parked our van to try and discourage anyone from linking our van and the camera pen. Very cloak and dagger for a businessman.

I'd already tried out the pen, taking discreet photos and videos of Mr. T during our meeting so everyone would know what Mr. Tabassian looked and sounded like. Then I e-mailed them from Mac's office. Done.

My stomach growled. I pressed my arm across it. And then I smiled. It reminded me of Elena. She was the only girl I knew who loved to eat as much as I did. More, even.

As if that was a sign, I glanced out the window and eyeballed a big black GMC truck rolling up the street at about 25 clicks an hour, clearly searching for a parking space.

I sat up slightly in order to watch it attempt to seesaw into a space on the left-hand side of the road, about a block up. The driver clearly wasn't used to parallel parking, especially in a big monster vehicle unsuited to city streets with cars parked on either side of the road.

My eyes focused on the blue letters on the license plate.

An Ontario plate. Not Quebec.

Bingo.

CHAPTER 34

Now, we get a fair number of visitors to *la belle province*, but April was a little early for tourists, and the garment district doesn't draw them in the same way St-Catherine Street does with its cheap beer and T-shirts that say "Good girls go to heaven. Bad girls go to Montreal." Sure, you can bring your cash for sales on Chabanel, but mostly on Saturdays. And mostly for locals, not tourists.

Especially not for tourists who couldn't parallel park.

And, now that I thought about it, I'd spotted a black GMC truck pulled over on the land next our campground on the night Elena died. Okay, there had to be thousands of GMC trucks cutting through the back roads. But my gut told me otherwise.

I pulled my pen camera out of my pants pocket instead. My heart thumped in my chest.

Up 'til now, we'd worked as a pack around Elena's death.

Up 'til now, other people had a say in what I was doing.

Now it was show time for me.

The car finally gunned its motor and took off north up Verveille.

I turned my keys in the ignition. A plan formed in my mind. I'd parked in a nice big spot so that I could make a quick getaway. But now I had a better use for my parking spot.

I reversed out of my space, taking my time, and slipped Mac's VW into the spot where the truck had failed to insert itself.

It was a gamble. I could lose the black truck to another parking space down the street. Maybe I should've flat out followed the truck. But if he was here to see Mr. Tabassian, he'd be back on foot, if nothing else. I should be able to spot him even if he parked a few blocks away and crossed back to the building.

Unless he entered from the door on the parallel street.

This must be why the police like to work in teams.

While I shifted in the seat, second-guessing myself, the black truck nosed back up rue Verveille, behind me. He'd looped around the other one-way streets and ended up back in the same place again.

He hit the brakes. As I suspected, my newly liberated parking spot was the only one big enough for his truck.

He reversed into it, pulling tight to the curb with more finesse than I'd shown with the VW. I revised my estimation of his driving.

He slammed his truck door shut and I got my first good look at the driver. Probably six feet tall or thereabouts. Shaggy brown hair threaded with grey, partly hidden by a baseball cap. When he turned his head, I figured he was probably in his forties from the wrinkles around his mouth, but it was hard to tell because, holy smokes, he had a moustache. I hadn't seen one of those since some of the guys decided to hold a moustache contest last year.

Just my luck. The one guy I was trying to ID had masked himself with facial hair. Between that, the ball cap, and sunglasses, he reminded me of the Beastie Boys in their old video parodying the '70s, but I snapped a few quick pictures anyway.

Next, I made sure to shoot his body. Broad shoulders, lean torso and legs. A working build, I found myself thinking. Not the usual gym body. I clicked a few more full-body photos and switched the pen to video. Most wers recognize body language and movement, so we like to see what the target looks like moving.

The target glanced both ways across the street. A red Ford whooshed by him. The target swore—I saw his lips move—before he crossed the street. From the way he hunched his shoulders and kept glancing around, and from the real mud splattered on his truck, he wasn't from around here.

Which meant he was suspicious, or at least already on alert, because he was out of his territory.

I considered waiting by the car. I'd gotten pictures of him. I could stay here and watch Mr. Tabassian's window.

Instead, I pulled my own baseball cap low on my forehead and climbed out of the car to follow him.

132

CHAPTER 35

First, I sniffed the air carefully. I detected a light touch of manure and hay. No, this guy wasn't from around here.

Then I backtracked to get a full-on view of his truck. I glanced at the license plate, memorized it, and took a quick shot of it too.

Finally, I slipped in through the back door of Mr. Tabassian's building that faced Verveille Street, saving me time while the target walked around to the front entry. I'd noticed they kept this back entrance propped open with a pebble so they could come and go to smoke. The door lifted open with hardly a sound.

I snuck up a flight of metal stairs and paused on the landing in front of the door marked EMPLOYEES ONLY. I could smell my own sweat. It was one thing to fancy myself Nancy Drew and another to take the risk of trespassing and imprisonment.

The second I pushed open the door, the target might spot me. Thinking about it made my spine tingle.

Mr. Tabassian's office lay at the end of the hall. How could I spy on the target without being identified?

I glanced through the stairwell window and spotted one of those round mirrors that help you see around corners. Perfect. I kept my eyes trained on that. Sure enough, I soon spotted the target knocking on Mr. Tabassian's door. Mr. T ushered him into the office.

I wished I could eavesdrop. I would've settled for a glass pressed against the wall, like a kid spying on her parents. Would it be safe to venture down the hall, now that they were both inside? They'd probably spend five minutes on chat and over fifteen on paperwork.

If only Laurent had let me sneak a bug into Mr. T's office as Bond gizmo number three. That would've solved everything.

Suddenly, I heard a squeak of metal from one of the upper floors. The hairs shot up on the back of my neck.

Get out, snapped my wolf instincts.

I flew down the flight of stairs and pushed the outside door open before I heard another stairway door clink open and women's voices echo down the stairs.

I shoved a cigarette in my mouth and lit it as I sauntered toward my car, disguising myself as a carefree smoker. As soon as I clinked the door shut, I stubbed the cig out and plugged the camera pen into my laptop with a USB port. Then, using *Île Sans Fil,* this great wireless setup across Montreal, I e-mailed the pictures and video to the pack.

If anything happened to me, I wanted them to have those pictures.

That done, I cautiously relaxed into Mac's microfiber seats and tried to figure out my next move.

Good news: I'd found the rich man.

Bad news: my instincts told me he was as dangerous as a pack of werewolves. But I still had to try and get the Master Tracker on his truck.

CHAPTER 36

I replaced my laptop in my knapsack and grabbed my most unlikely weapon: a bunch of leaflets for a local tanning salon. Real ones. I'd swiped them from a guy handing them out next to Mac's office. (He'd looked stunned and then said, "God bless you.")

I shrugged on a jean jacket, pushed a pair of Dollar Store sunglasses over my nose, and swapped my ball cap for the straw hat to hide as much of my face as possible.

Then I walked south on Verveille, shoving tanning salon leaflets under everyone's wiper blades.

I had to work fast. The target didn't look like someone to linger over the doughnuts. He might sign the papers and fly before I had a chance to plant the tracker.

Still, I worked my way down my car's side of the street before I switched to his. It would look too suspicious if I started weaving back and forth. I also pretended to chew gum and slouched as much as I walked, as if I couldn't wait to get to my lunch break.

I sighed elaborately when reached the GMC truck. Its windshield was about a foot out of reach for a petite girl. While I strained over the hood, reaching for the wiper, I managed to spew my last bunch of leaflets on the ground.

I swore and kicked them before I crawled on my knees to grab a few. While I was under there, flailing and saying, "What is all this garbage? Does anyone ever pick up around here?"—trust me, it wasn't only cigarette butts in the gutters. I even saw a pink plastic doll's leg hanging out in there and it ain't pretty—I smacked the Master Tracker on the underside of the truck on the passenger's side.

Then I used the last of my leaflets to cover another block of cars.

When I worked my way back on the west side of the street, where Mac's car awaited me, the target reappeared.

He slowed down when he saw something under his windshield. It obviously wasn't a ticket, but he still surveyed the area.

His eyes lit on me.

I ignored him. Fortunately, I still had two leaflets left. I hoisted the windshield wiper of a station wagon to place another flyer.

He yanked the flyer and stood there, glaring at me. For a second, I thought he might shove it in my face and give me what-for.

For a rich guy, he sure carted a lot of rage.

He swore to himself, loud enough that I could hear, but I moved on to the next Volvo.

Then he hopped into his truck and fired up his motor. He barely tapped the brakes at the stop sign at the end of the street before he took a hard right around the corner, belching grey exhaust.

If I was lucky, the police would pick him up on a traffic violation. Rich man would lose his temper. Cop would book him, and Mr. T wouldn't be able to sell the land to a prisoner.

Unfortunately, breaking the traffic laws and swearing for no reason only meant he fit into Montreal better than the average tourist.

I sauntered over to Mac's car. I kept the hat and sunglasses. If I changed too many times, I'd raise a few eyebrows. From the safety of the vehicle, I glanced up at Mr. Tabassian's window. No movement. Either they'd concluded their business in record time, or the rich man had strangled him and taken off.

Before I fired up my own motor, I pulled out my phone and texted a group message:

MT's on the trail.

MT. Master Tracker.

Just like the Mounties, we'd get our man.

CHAPTER 37

I couldn't concentrate at work, despite the papers piled on my desk and the keyboards tapping and phone convos murmuring in the cubicles around me. I needed to tell someone about my detective work.

First, I texted Jefferson. No answer.

Twice I started to dial Elena before I remembered that she was dead and I couldn't stand her replacement.

So, after approximately fifteen minutes, I broke down and called Jack.

It rang four times before I got "Hey, it's Jack. Leave a message."

I left a quickie. Then I sighed, toyed with the idea of calling Mac, and opened my latest PowerPoint presentation. We had a major fundraising banquet coming up in June. But I mainly counted down the minutes until my phone buzzed and showed JACK MENG.

"Hey, you," said Jack. His voice cracked, not from emotion but from poor reception. Someone was talking in the background.

"Hey." I lowered my voice in case anyone in my office was eavesdropping. At least one girl walking toward the water cooler glanced my way. I spun away from her so my chair faced the door.

Jack said, "Are you coming to Elena's party tonight? You know she's taking off to Prague, right?"

He played his part well. I injected some enthusiasm into my tone. "Yep. Seven p.m."

He mumbled something and then said, "Sorry, I'm at work."

"I figured." But it meant I couldn't brag about my exploits. Well, maybe I could, but co-workers on either end would hear a little too much. But if I called him without actually talking, that was even more loser-clingy-girlfriendish. I tried to figure out a code way to tell him he was talking to the newest amateur detective.

"Did your meeting go well?" he asked.

"No," I said, "but I learned some useful things afterward."

"Yeah. I saw your messages. Good work."

Of course. He'd checked his e-mail and already gotten pictures of the target and my note about the Master Tracker. Now I really felt like a desperate dolt. "Yeah. Okay. I was only checking to make sure you got my messages. Thanks."

"Sure did. You're the woman."

I smiled for the first time and propped my feet up on my wastebasket. "How about you? Any news?"

"Not that much. Some of the lab results came back, including the toxicology screen. That's checking if the patient had any drugs on board."

"Did she?" My skin electrified. My poisoned chicken theory, put to the test.

"Nothing major. It came back positive for marijuana, but nothing else. Not even aspirin or Tylenol."

I slumped in my chair and accidentally knocked over the waste can. Luckily, it was empty.

"But the lab sends out fancy stuff like GHB. It can take up to two weeks."

"Two weeks!"

He sighed through his phone. "They'll do it as fast as they can."

I bet they would. I remembered my suspicion that Jack knew a lab girl or two, in the carnal sense.

"And actually, one other lab test was abnormal. Her venous gas was acidotic. I know that doesn't mean that much to you, and it might be normal because she was, uh, down for so long. But it's a pretty pronounced acidosis."

"Does that have something to do with taking acid?" I asked. I knew it was a stupid question, but maybe if Elena was having an acid flashback, it would explain her running down to the river.

He laughed. "No, like I said, the drug screen was negative except weed. And I don't remember too much about blood gases myself, to be honest. One of the docs explained it to me like, the blood is supposed to be not too acidic and not too basic, but hers was way too much on the acid side. And sometimes that comes from drugs or diabetes or stuff like that. So we'll keep looking."

I cheered up. Another clue, and one in line with my theory. Ha. "Does Dr. Flores know?"

"She's doing a lot of the work."

"Awesome! Thanks for keeping me in the loop."

"Yeah. I should go." Instead, he paused. "Have you heard from... anyone else?"

I smiled. I had a pretty good idea who he was asking about. "I borrowed Mac's car. And Laurent and I met Mr. Tabassian together."

"No word on the investigation?"

"Not yet," I said. I didn't mention my text to Jefferson. "See you at seven. I'll send you the directions to Elena's apartment."

"I already Googled them. She lived—lives—across from the cemetery, right?"

"Yup." That made it sound creepy, but the Notre-Dames-des-Neiges cemetery is actually quite beautiful. It covers over 300 acres on top of Mount Royal, and people run and bike through it and even take wedding photos there. They have a life-sized marble reproduction of Michelangelo's Pietà, which is a statue in the Vatican. More importantly to me and Elena, it's full of groundhogs, rabbits, and other tasty treats. Nearly all full moons, we'd get out of the city, but if we were stuck, we could always hit the cemetery.

"See you there," said Jack, before he broke the connection.

Now we were cooking with gas. I'd sighted the target and Jack was closing in on a possible bait/poison.

No way I could concentrate on work now.

I minimized my PowerPoint so I could log on to the Master Tracker website.

Gisèle's papa had sprung for the top-of-the-line model so I could track the target in real time, up to every ten seconds. The target had paused at a truck stop off Highway 40 for the last ten minutes, so the Master Tracker had stopped sending updates in order to conserve its battery.

But when I blew up the map, it was obvious he was making his way west, back toward Ontario, with a pit stop. "I'll get you and your little truck, too," I muttered to myself.

My phone rang. Elena's number. My heart fluttered for a second before I steeled myself and I picked it up. "Hello?"

"Hi, Leila?"

"Hey, Elena, what's shaking?" I said, trying to change Gisèle's tone. The real Elena never asked if it was me. We recognized each other's voices instantly.

"My dad called me and asked why I was driving back to Ontario. Did you leave town without telling me?"

I closed my eyes. Some actress. "Her" father was supposed to be deceased. "I'll explain tonight."

"Okay. But he's really worried—"

"It's kind of weird to talk about it over the phone, *Elena*," I said, trying to place some emphasis in my tone without shouting, *Remember who you're supposed to be, dimwit.* "I know you might be getting *flashbacks* about your dad in *Czechoslovakia*, and that's rough. I'll see you at seven, okay? We're supposed to be celebrating your new job."

It took her a split second to process that. "Oh. Yeah. Right."

"Great. So I'll meet you at your place. Jack is coming too."

"He is?" Her voice warmed up twenty degrees. "Wonderful."

"Scum-sucking motherfucker," I reminded her. Papers rustled at another cubicle. I'd better get back to work. Too many phone calls after taking the morning off.

"Yeah. That bastard," Gisèle said, after a slight hesitation and not enough heat.

But she was learning. "Great. Later." I hung up and checked the Master Tracker map online again.

No change.

I bent my head over my presentation, adding some wolf howls and some graphs showing wolf vs. prey populations, showing how the wolves followed the curve of the population, plus the usual explanations of how wolves keep the ecosystem in balance by culling the sick and the weak.

I answered some e-mails from Defenders of Wildlife, an organization based in the States that started a "Save America's Wolves" campaign. Since the Bush administration took wolves off the endangered list, Idaho and Montana have started killing wolves for sport. Corporate sponsors make it into a game, offering three points per dead wolf. In Alaska, gunmen in low-flying planes have chased and shot more than a thousand wolves with their high-powered rifles. It's enough to make a girl cry, let alone a werewolf.

By the time I checked the MT website again, I realized the target truck hadn't moved for the past half an hour.

It was possible the guy was having lunch or a major dump or both, but the little hairs rose on the back of my neck.

If this guy could pay triple for the land, he wasn't dumb. And he'd seen me and my flyers. He knew I'd passed by his car.

Maybe he'd found the tracker.

CHAPTER 38

If he found the tracker and tossed it into the bushes, it wouldn't send a signal. It would sit there, conserving its battery until it got tossed into a garbage truck and got reactivated.

I needed a way to triangulate around this guy. The tracker alone might not cut it.

I decided to run his license plate. I had no idea how to do that, of course, so I hit the Internet once more.

My cell phone screeched. Literally. I jumped. I'd forgotten about my new red-tailed hawk ring tone when I switched it back to audio mode.

First I checked the caller ID. The name came up as "Unknown," but I answered it anyway.

Jefferson's baritone poured down my ear. "I need to speak to you."

"When?" I glanced at the Master Tracker screen. My little yellow dot still hadn't stirred. But of all the people I knew, Jefferson might have some ideas of how to track the target down.

"As soon as possible. Are you in town?"

"Yes. I'm at work until five."

"Great. Give me your coordinates and I'll meet you afterward. I prefer not to meet in public."

My pulse picked up. I tried to ignore it and concentrate on his words. He said coordinates, like a true Montrealer. "Okay. Would you rather come to my place? I live down the road, on 1678 Chevalier, south of the Metro supermarket. Côte-Ste-Catherine metro station."

"I know where you live. I'll see you in at 5:15." He hung up.

I frowned. The guy was borderline rude. Did he not know how to say good-bye?

My eyes flicked back to the computer screen. The truck still hadn't moved. I paged through the Master Tracker website. Was it possible the battery had died already? It only seemed to last twelve hours on continuous mode if you bought an extended battery. Since the tracker was so small, I doubted it contained an extra battery.

But if the battery died, would it no longer show up on the map? It seemed to work fine on the way out of Montreal.

I was working my way through a bunch of web reviews of Master Tracker when the clock struck five.

The yellow dot still hadn't moved.

I jogged home, combed my hair, and barely had time to bolt down a glass of water before my buzzer went off at 5:09.

I pulled my black blazer on before I buzzed him in. This wasn't a social call, and I wanted to look as formal as possible.

When I opened the door, Jefferson seemed to fill the whole doorway. It wasn't only his size, although he was tall and broad enough. It was his presence. You know how some guys seem to fill your whole vision and suck the air out of your lungs? Like that.

I did my best to ignore that, too. I held my hand out. "Hi. I'm glad you found the place."

He took my hand. A miniature thrill zapped along my skin from the seconds of contact.

I dropped his hand while he nodded at me. "Thanks for meeting me on short notice, Leila. I've got a few loose ends I need to tie up."

Hello to you too, I thought, but I liked his confidence and his goal-orientedness, if that's a word. Plus he smelled so good, I swear my nostrils dilated for a second.

He gave me a strange look. I realized that I was standing too close to him instead of letting him into the apartment. The man was human, no matter how attractive he smelled.

I backed up and gestured him in. "I want to help any way I can. And actually, I have a few questions for you, too."

He noticed my shoes on the boot tray and slid off his leather lace-ups. I liked that I didn't have to ask him to take off his shoes. For Chinese people, it's a given, not to mention my apartment gets dusty enough without having to sweep up extra street dirt. I had to train Elena.

"This is a nice place," he said, glancing at the sitting room.

"Um, thanks." My university futon doubled as a sofa, and the bookshelves and desk were a mix of Ikea and junk my parents had picked up at various auctions. Not exactly high-end style.

He pointed at a photo of a wolf pack I'd hung above my desk. "I like that."

I nodded slowly. Not everyone got that photo. The usual wolf picture nowadays is either Jacob Black and company, meaning werewolf Stephanie Meyer style, or the prototypical lone wolf howling at the moon.

I'd chosen an aerial photo of an entire pack in Yellowstone Park, a mix of grey wolves and black wolves, some sitting, some standing, all of them having made tracks in the snow. It's not a classic photo. There's not a lot of cohesion, and it doesn't show their faces the way humans like. But it shows wolves as they are, doing their best in the remnant of land they've got left.

So I liked that Jefferson liked the picture. And that he was belatedly trying to make a bit of small talk. I said, "Could I get you a drink?"

He shook his head and pulled a notebook out of his back pocket. Spiral bound. The whole bit. Retro, compact, and much cheaper than an iPhone. I was charmed even though the social niceties were clearly over. He sat on the office chair and swung it around to face me. "I've been reviewing my notes. I'm interviewing everyone separately."

That made sense. "Who else have you interviewed?"

He pursed his lips for a millisecond and tilted his head. He didn't want to tell me. But then he said, "Jack."

I nodded.

"I have a few questions about how Elena went missing at the campground."

"I didn't see her go."

"I know that. But you did see Jack finding her. Describe exactly what you saw."

I closed my eyes. "It was dusk. I didn't see well. But he had his arms hooked under her arms and he was trying to drag her out of the river and still hold her head steady."

"And when did he start CPR?"

I frowned. "As soon as he got to flat ground, away from the river. He was howling for help."

"Did he start CPR on his own?"

"Yes. He's a paramedic," I added, which Jefferson already knew. I didn't understand where he was going with this.

Jefferson didn't blink. He made a note in his book.

144

I said, "What's the big deal."

He sighed. I could tell he was deciding whether or not to answer me. Finally, he said, "What you're saying is, he initiated CPR instead of waiting for someone to help steady her neck."

"I guess so."

"Even though three of you were right there to help."

I had to unstick my tongue from the roof of my mouth. "Why are you asking this?"

"Leila, if you could answer the questions, it would help the investigation a good deal."

I tried to remember. So much chaos. I couldn't believe it was Elena, couldn't believe she'd fallen in the river like that. "He did ask me to take over the airway. He knew I'd done first aid before." It's a good skill if you're going to protests. "He had to help me open her jaw."

"And that's when you found the chicken bone in her mouth."

"Right."

He made another note and flipped the page. "Did she have blood around her mouth?"

I frowned. "I guess she might have cut her lip."

He shook his head and leaned forward. His eyes hypnotized me. "I'm not asking you to guess. I want you to remember. Did she have traces of blood around or inside her mouth?"

I closed my eyes and inhaled, trying to take myself back. The adrenaline had run so high, I hadn't noticed as much as I ordinarily would have. "Not so much on her face, but I think yes, inside her mouth."

"Chicken blood?"

I furrowed my brow. This was not a question a human would probably be able to answer, but I'd been on the cusp of 'shifting. Dead chicken blood and fresh human blood do not smell or taste the same, even when you're trying to save your friend's life. "A bit of both. But mostly chicken blood."

"On her teeth?"

I nodded slowly. "I think on her front teeth and canines. Maybe her molars, too." I glanced at him. "But surely the autopsy—and your own investigation—you would have been able to figure that out."

"I'm trying to put the whole story together," he said.

"Jack found her. And it does look like she choked on a chicken, for whatever reason. Jack told me some of the blood work came back abnormal, too, so you might want to ask him about that." I paused. The real question was what Jefferson was doing in my living room. "You seem to be implying that Jack didn't run the code right."

Jefferson shook his head. "I'm gathering the facts. I'm not a paramedic or a doctor."

"Yes, but the way you're asking..." I didn't bother to pursue it. He wouldn't admit anything. I decided to change tacks. "I guess Jack could've left her in the water and yelled at us to help get her out, but Jack is a man of action. He pulled her out himself."

"And let you do the airway. So you found the chicken bone."

"Yes." I stopped short. "Is that strange?"

He shrugged again. "I have no idea. I'm trying to assess the pattern."

He asked more questions, but mostly he centered on Jack's code. Finally, I asked, "Aren't you going to ask me about Elena?"

"I'm trying to gather information about the circumstances of her death before I move on."

The guy was thorough, no doubt about it. But he moved about as fast as a dog turd in January. I could see why Jack wanted to kick him in the ass. I made a face. "Okay, now I'd like to ask you something unrelated. Or sort of related."

The corner of his mouth turned up in a not-quite-smile. "I suppose that's fair."

"Do you put tracers on people's cars?"

He raised his eyebrows and shifted in the chair. It squeaked under his weight, but somehow that didn't detract from his dignity when he replied, "Do you have a particular reason for asking?"

"Of course! Did you get the e-mail I sent showing pictures of the guy who met with Mr. Tabassian?"

He nodded.

"So you know I put a tracker on his car. And I can follow him in real time on their website. May I?" He stood up, allowing me to sit at my desk and boot up the Master Tracker website.

I entered the ID number. Yellow dot still sat off Highway 40, at that same stupid rest stop. I jabbed my finger at the screen. "That tracker hasn't moved in an hour an a half. I'm wondering if the battery died or—"

My hands fluttered to my sides.

The target now trailed along Highway 40. It was moving.
Only problem was, it was heading east. Back to Montreal.

CHAPTER 39

"Two choices," said Jefferson, once he'd understood the whole story and lectured me about the foolishness and illegality of my actions. "Either the guy's decided to pull a U-ie, or he's moved the tracer on to another vehicle."

I pressed my fist to my forehead and started pacing the living room as best I could, around the furniture. I had to move. "You think he's that smart?"

Jefferson watched me stomp around the coffee table. "Do you have any idea who this 'target' is?"

"I'm pretty sure he's ursurping our land."

"But do you know what his name or background is? You have the license plate. You could have checked his ID that way. It's a lot easier and more legal than placing a tracker on his car."

I lifted my chin. "As a matter of fact, I did that too. I found the Canadian Police Information Centre and entered his plates in the database for lost or stolen vehicles." I showed him the page, re-entered the information, made a big show of clicking on "ON" (Ontario) for the province. "No records found."

"That's the tip of the iceberg," he said.

"I'm sure. But since you're busy cross-checking the details of the resuscitation from last Friday, I'm the one who's keeping up with today."

He rolled his eyes slightly. "You saw an Ontario truck park around Mr. Tabassian's building and a man enter his office. That's not evidence."

"Look. I'm sure it wouldn't hold up in a court of law. However, this would never get to a court of law. I need to know who the guy is."

"So you can scare him off? Don't play the vigilante, Leila. That's why we have the police and the legal system."

I smiled at him a little sadly. I could tell he wasn't one of us. "We" didn't have the police or the justice system. They existed, and sometimes they might help us if our goals were in line. But we have to look after ourselves. Always have, always will.

I didn't bother arguing with him, though. Nod and smile. That's how it works with humans, no matter how good they smelled or how much you felt like intertwining your hand with their strong, slim fingers.

"I'll have to tell Bernard about this," he added.

That made me grit my teeth. "He's my leader. Not yours. I'll tell him."

"He's my employer."

I couldn't quite manage the nod and smile this time. Instead, I stood up. "You know what, Jefferson? I hope you got what you needed during this interview. Because I've got things to do and places to go and I'm sure you do, too."

He glanced pointedly at the computer screen and the little yellow dot showing a truck moving eastward. "Don't do anything foolish, Leila."

"Never," I said, as sincerely as I could. I didn't look at the screen, but my peripheral vision noted the truck growing closer and closer.

CHAPTER 40

After Jefferson finally moved his sweet (but annoying) ass out the door, I checked the screen again.

The yellow dot wasn't transmitting every ten seconds. More like every thirty. And then it seemed to bump along infinitesimally, even when I blew up the map.

Rush hour traffic.

Since I lived in the city and took the transit system, I avoided the worst gridlock unless our full moon journeys got off to a late start, but I clearly remembered the stop-and-go.

The target must really have a hard on to get back to the city if he was braving the 4:45 influx of commuters cursing their way back to their cute downtown condos.

Was the target throwing me on a wild goose chase? Had he moved the Master Tracker onto another unsuspecting schlub's vehicle?

Had he forgotten something?

Was I in danger?

Wolves are predators, but we know better than humans how life is balanced on a razor's edge. For example, wolves can and will eat a bear cub, but Mama Bear's claws can slash open a wolf's belly the next instant.

One thing for sure. I didn't want to sit in my apartment and wait for the guy to come to me. I wanted to do something. Anything.

I seized my cell phone and paged through my contacts before I caught myself. My first instinct was to call Jack.

No. First of all, I wasn't Cinderella waiting for my prince. I booted that player out of my life two years ago. Today, after approximately six minutes (or so it felt), I leaned on him like a right-hand man? Forget it.

Also, I'd already called him. He had my number. As my mother told me a million times, if the guy wanted me, he'd make the effort.

I still had Mac's VW. I'd planned to return it at Elena's tonight.

I'd go and chase the target down.

But first, I needed to let someone know where I was going. Not backup, exactly, but prudence. I dialed Mac and explained what I was doing.

"Leila, what?"

"I'm going to make sure the MT is on the right car. That's all. I should be back in time for Elena's party."

"If your MT is working, why go looking for it? He's coming here. Just watch him online."

I paused. That was logical. But I couldn't bear to sit still now. Maybe it was what happened to Elena. Maybe it was Jefferson telling me I was a dough head. But I could no more passively wait, filing my nails and staring at this screen, than I could trust Jack around any female aged 18 to 50. I changed the subject. "He's on the 40. He can't get too far. I'll head west of him, switch to the eastbound lane, and then come up behind him. He won't have any idea I'm there."

"Leila, no offense, but you don't drive that much—"

"So? It's not that hard."

"—and I've seen you with road rage. Not pretty."

"That was Elena."

"That was you passing the Mustang at 140 and giving him the finger."

I vaguely remembered that. "That was a long time ago."

"It's my car, Leila. I'm going to Boston, remember?"

"I'll treat it better than my non-existent children. I don't have time to go vigilante on him." Jefferson's word popped out of my mouth. I hesitated for a second. "Thanks for the loan."

"I'll come with you."

"No. You're at work." That was one reason I'd chosen to call him. Mac was some sort of business dude that I didn't understand, but it made him a slave to the desk late into the night. Plus Mac was the least likely to give me a hard time.

He sighed. "Be careful."

That was how I knew I'd won.

CHAPTER 41

I plopped my laptop into the passenger seat. I felt a twinge of conscience. You're not supposed to use your iPad when you drive, let alone a full-blown computer. But honestly, all I needed was to track that little yellow dot every few minutes, to know the target hadn't pulled another U-turn.

I hit every red light one Côte-Ste-Catherine before I hooked north on Décarie, heading for Highway 40. "I'm a good driver," I scoffed to myself.

Until I tried to merge on to Décarie. No one wanted to let me in, and my lane was ending. I finally cut off a blonde who was, FYI, chatting on her cell phone. I don't care that she was using a headset. She was much more dangerous than my laptop.

And then we basically pulled to a halt. At 5 p.m., everyone in Montreal wanted to get to the suburbs and vice versa, and with still more people jockeying on and off Décarie, a major north-south artery, nobody was going nowhere.

I drummed my fingers on the steering wheel. If I kept up the detective life, I'd buy a motorcycle. I'd weave in and out of traffic and pull into the tightest parking spots.

I glanced at my laptop. The target hadn't moved, either. He was at the corner of Highway 40, a.k.a. the Metropolitan, and Boulevard des Sources, squarely in the West Island.

I curled my lower lip and blew my bangs off my forehead. I flipped on CBC Radio's Homerun show and learned that a truck had stalled in the right-hand lane on the 40 east of Sources. So that was slowing my target down significantly. But by the time he cleared the accident, he might zoom into the city while I was stuck south of the Orange Julep.

Two people cut me off. I gritted my teeth, chanting, "Not my car, not my car," while I slowly made my way into the left-hand lane. I remembered that the exit for the 40 was on the left.

I kept an eye out for the Orange Julep. It's a Montreal icon, a gigantic orange ball of a restaurant. Elena wanted to go, but I always blew her off. "You said the food's not that great."

"The orange julep is good. It's kind of like orange juice and milk— no, like a Creamsicle—"

"Don't make me gag."

"C'mon. Waitresses on roller skates. How can you resist?"

"Watch me," I'd said. And now she was gone. I closed my eyes and shook my head. I didn't want to cry. Maybe I could persuade the gang to hit the Orange Julep tonight, in her honor.

The 40 West sign came up without a sign of the three-story high fiberglass orange. I belatedly realized you could only see it coming south instead of going north. Maybe that was what life was like. I kind of assumed Elena would be around forever, and now she was six feet under. I blew a kiss at the sky. "Miss ya, babe."

Then I had to hit the brakes. More traffic. I glanced at the yellow dot on the website and sent another silent prayer sunward.

If I could make the 40. If I could know that, at the very least, the beast and I would cross paths once more, and I'd see with my own eyes.

I realized that part of my hang-up was not trusting computer/ satellite/GPS technology as much as your average 21st-century gal. I wanted to stare that GMC truck in the face one more time. Whether he recognized me or not, I wanted to let him know that he'd met his match. Not only would I take the land, I'd grind him under the heels of my non-slutty boots.

That was the idea, anyway.

At long last, I swooped on to the ramp westbound. I had to dodge over to the middle lane to avoid going back to rue St-Laurent. And then I was literally heading into the sunset, closing in on my target.

Who was weaving his way toward me in the eastbound lane, faster now that he'd made it past the accident. Past the exit for the 15.

If I didn't make it in time to exit, switch directions, and merge behind him, I'd have to make sure I could spot him from across the barrier.

I hadn't realized how big the 40 was. They're always doing construction on it, and I guess I'd focused more on cool tunes than tracking traffic when we drove out of town. The westbound and eastbound highway seemed to have three lanes, separated by a jersey barriers topped by a metal screen.

If I was stuck going west while he whipped east, I could easily pass this guy and never know the difference.

Calme-toi, I ordered myself. You didn't drive out here for nothing. There's going to be something and it's going to be good.

Shortly after Cavendish, the major barriers dropped, and I could get a good look at the oncoming cars.

And, according to the website, the Master Tracker headed right toward me.

Okay. I wouldn't have time to exit and follow the guy. But I should be able to eyeball him, especially since they'd slowed down.

I stayed in the left-hand lane at 100 clicks. I wanted to stay as close as possible to the oncoming traffic, and this was as slow as I dared go. A few people zoomed around me, passing on the right in a pissed-off way, but I ignored them.

And then I spotted it.

Black GMC truck. Ontario plates. The way the sunlight reflected off the windshield, I couldn't get a good look inside, but there was only the driver, and he was heading in to Montreal.

Master Tracker was still on the target.

Now all I had to do was figure out what he was doing back in Montreal.

CHAPTER 42

"What happened to you?" Jack asked, yanking open Elena's door.

I bowed at him. "Hello. Nice to see you, too." I was 20 minutes late, but it still annoyed me that Jack had beat me to Elena's apartment. No doubt Gisèle had draped herself all over him. I glanced past him, but she had yet to make her appearance, so I shucked off my shoes and placed them on the boot tray.

Mac materialized and frowned at me. "You made it."

"Wow, everyone's in such a party mood today," I said. "Don't worry. Your car baby is safe. You'll make it to the airport on Thursday." Mac shook his head and gave me a careful once-over before he hugged me. He felt like a big, soft teddy and smelled like bread. "You're going to get it one of these days," he growled, but I knew he wasn't really mad at me.

Jack slammed the door behind me. He ran his hand through his black hair, which made it stand up even more, but I tried to ignore the urge to smooth it back down. "What did you do, Leila? Mac was telling us you decided to follow the guy."

"I did. No harm done."

"And what did you find out?"

"He's back in the city. The Master Tracker works. We'll follow him online. I'll give you guys the codes, and we can track him tonight while we're partying." I grinned at him.

Jack shook his head. "You suck."

"No. I rock." I kissed him hello. Real kisses, not air kisses. I could smell the aftershave on his newly-shorn cheeks. Compared to most Asian guys, he was a hairy bear. Not so surprising in a wolf man so close to the full moon. But no human-made product could cover up the raw male smell that made me close my eyes and inhale for one illegal second.

Jack nosed me back before his back stiffened and he pulled away from me. "We need to set some ground rules. You can't go off half-cocked like that. You should have someone with you at all times."

"Bullshit," I said. "First of all, I think only guys go off half-cocked."

Mac laughed.

Gisèle's slightly nasal voice cut our love-in short. "You're half an hour late."

"Sorry," I said, not bothering to correct her on the time. "What did I miss?"

She twirled a lock of hair around her finger. Without the sunglasses, she didn't look so much like Elena. Not only were her eyes grey instead of green, her face was too round and her lips too pouty, although she'd applied Elena's grey eye shadow and favourite wine-coloured lipstick. "I showed them whatever messages and e-mail I could. The passwords in the file you found only worked on some of her accounts."

Gisèle rubbed me like sandpaper. I loathed the image of her rummaging through Elena's accounts and makeup only slightly less than I despised covering up for the real murderer. I took a deep breath. "Did you find anything?"

Gisèle made a face. "Well, she kept profiles on a lot of dating sites, even ones I'd never heard of. Did you know there was a site for French-speaking athletes?"

I shrugged, not mentioning that I'd tried that site out myself. A girl's gotta do what a girl's gotta do. My gaze slid over to Jack. His eyes met mine and moved south to my mouth. After a beat, I realized I was licking my lips, and his eyes were riveted to the tip of my tongue.

"Do you want something to drink?" asked Gisèle, too sharply.

I glanced up. "Sorry." I didn't mean it. Jack's eyes crinkled and we both had to stifle a laugh.

Mac patted Gisèle on the back. "I bet you did a great job. Was she dating anyone suspicious?"

"Not that I could tell. She was dating a lot of people, though."

"We've covered this," I said.

Mac started rubbing Gisèle's shoulders. He has big, baseball mitt-type hands, and I've heard he knows how to use them. Certainly Gisèle leaned into his touch and closed her eyes. "That feels good," she cooed.

I raised my eyebrows. Werewolves are more touchy-feely than most humans, because we don't have the same body hang-ups, but this was friendlier than I liked. "Did anyone else find anything today?"

Jack made a face. "That investigator came and harassed me at the station. He should know better than to come to my work."

That did seem strange. I would have pegged Jefferson as more discreet than that. "Were you working a twelve-hour shift?"

Jack shook his head. "I got called in for a few hours to cover a guy who got the flu. The 'detective' could've waited."

I filed that away for future reference while I updated them on Laurent's and my meeting. "You've probably already seen these, but—" I uploaded the photos and videos of the target and his truck. "I followed him to make sure the Master Tracker was working. I saw him myself on the 40. He's back in town."

Jack whistled under his breath. "You be careful, Leila."

I stood up very straight. "I'm as careful as you are."

He snorted.

Gisèle jabbed her finger at the screen. "From what you're saying, you're not certain this is the man. And you can hardly see his face. What use are these pictures?"

Mac started rubbing her shoulders. She relaxed visibly until he said, "This could be our murderer. Memorize that face and build as best you can." He glanced at me. "Or, if you're Leila, try to track him down on your own."

Jack's eyes narrowed.

I explained about the tracker, avoiding Jack's gaze.

"So that's why Papa thought I was driving back to Glengarry!" exclaimed Gisèle. "He's going to be very angry." She shook Mac off and picked up her cell phone.

"Wait," I said. "Let's think about this. We need the tracker on that truck. That's our ace in the hole. He won't go anywhere without us knowing about it. If your father freaks out and tries to repossess it, we lose. Especially if Jack's right and this guy actually hunts werewolves."

"All the more reason for Papa to know."

Jack said, "Good idea."

I crossed my arms and glowered at him.

"No, seriously, Leila. He's the district head of the area and he should know. But you're right, too. We've got to leave that tracker in place and have someone on him at all times. Do you think you can persuade him of that?" he asked Gisèle.

"But of course," she said, standing up straight and thrusting out her boobs at him.

Jack turned his dark brown eyes on me while she dug out her cell phone. "You said you'd give us the codes."

So I showed him and Mac the Master Tracker website and the ID codes they had to enter. They uploaded the information to their phones while Gisèle called her papa and spoke rapid-fire French.

Jack said, "We need everyone on this. Let's alert all the CDN wers. I'd like to tell my guys too, in Mile End. Is that all right?"

I nodded. All the CDN, or Côte-des-Neiges wers, would be affected anyway. And Jack was as knee-deep in this as any of us, so if he wanted to tell his Mile End posse, I didn't mind.

Mac said, "How about my downtown gang?"

I nodded, a little more reluctantly. This could get out of hand. The downtown pack is much larger. But we should probably err on the side of alerting more people rather than less.

"Let's talk to the district heads and maybe we can release a bulletin to all Montreal wers," said Jack. "I know you don't want anyone to blow our cover, but this is a person of interest. The more hands on deck, the better."

Jack was already taking it to the next level. I honestly didn't like it to leave my hands, but this was bigger than any of us. "Okay."

They started calling and texting their people while I browsed Elena's e-mail. It felt weird, scanning all her messages, but I figured, better me than the substitute blond bimbo. Elena had told me about most of the guys she'd found online and offline, although mostly by description instead of by name, i.e., "talked too much about himself. A total egomaniac. I guess that makes sense in a school principal" or "a guitarist but he had a really small dick. You'd think that'd be illegal."

I relaxed. Despite Gisèle's "slut who brought it on herself" theories, I thought it was far more likely that a poisoned chicken brought Elena down. And whether or not the rich target was involved with her death, he had to be stopped too.

When the guys looked up from their mobiles, almost simultaneously, I checked my watch. Getting close to eight o'clock. "We need to get out and promote our cover story soon. Hey, do we have details about Elena's big offer, in case anyone asks?"

Mac nodded. "Josh e-mailed the job offer details this afternoon."

I vaguely remembered Josh, one of the few overweight wers I'd ever met, but an alpha geek who could handle any computer chicanery, which is a definite asset, especially in a case like this.

"One more thing," said Jack. "We need to pay off her bills so the creditors don't come after her. Did you get the password to her credit card and her bank account?"

Gisèle nodded. "It was all in that encrypted file."

The one I'd unencrypted when we got back from Glengarry. So Jack took a few minutes to pay off and shut down all of her accounts. A few places needed Gisèle to answer some skill-testing, verify-your-ID questions. I got stumped on favourite food because Elena had so many, but Gisèle eventually giggled her way through that one. "OMG. Steak? Chocolate? I have soooo many" until the guy gave her a free pass because she knew all the other ones.

At long last, we set off for drinks. I convinced Gisèle to wear a pair of lace gloves in case she left fingerprints. "Paranoid," she muttered, but when Jack joined in, she slipped them on and pouted that no one could see her nails.

Mac insisted on driving, I think so he could eyeball his car baby and make sure I hadn't totaled it.

"See? Not so much as a seagull dropping," I assured him. "I even filled up the tank."

Meanwhile, Gisèle slid into the back seat. It took me a second to realize that made her cozy with Jack. I shrugged and buckled myself beside Mac while Gisèle squealed, "I'm so excited about my new job! I can't wait to get back to my hometown." So she'd entered her "character."

"Congratulations," said Jack, playing the role with her.

She kissed him full on the lips. Just for a second, but still enough to leave his lips stained and his cheeks flushed. She said, "You're so sweet! I'm going to miss you."

"You're from Hradec Králové, not Prague," I reminded her, bringing her back to her "hometown" crack.

Gisèle shook out her blonde hair and gave a throaty laugh. "Homeland, I mean. What are you being so picky for? Are you going to come visit me?"

Jack swiped his lips against his hand a few times, but still came up looking like he'd been eating raspberries. Gisèle giggled. "Sorry. I forgot I was wearing the long-lasting kind."

Long-wearing lipstick isn't supposed to come off when you kiss. But I'd decided to ignore her hard-core flirting. I said, "Sure. Are you inviting me to the Czech Republic? I wouldn't pass up the chance for a free crash pad."

Gisèle giggled and dug through her purse. "*Mi casa, su casa.* Hey, Jack, I have some powder on me somewhere. Or maybe some concealer."

"Are you talking about more makeup on me? No way!" said Jack, leaning away from her.

She snapped her compact at him like it was Pac Man. "Real men wear blush."

"Guess I'm not a real man, then," said Jack, refusing to rise to the bait.

I exhaled slowly. It was going to be a long night.

CHAPTER 43

We started out on Crescent Street, which I find overrated, but everyone agreed it was the best place to see and be seen. Gisèle had texted Elena's entire address book to join us: *OMG! I've got a job in Prague! Leaving this week! Come celebr8!*

Not quite Elena's style, but everyone was too happy to care. Gisèle showed us a bunch of replies, mostly "Awesome!" and "WTG!" mostly as an excuse to press her body up against Jack's.

He ended up taking a few calls from the Mile End wers, partly to explain the deal with the target, but I think also so he'd have an excuse to lean away from Elena and hunch over his phone.

Mac answered a call or two using his Bluetooth. So only I stuck my head out the window, feeling the spring breeze on my face while I watched cars parallel park. Women wiggled out of passenger doors in heels and tight dresses.

"Look at this one!" Gisèle exclaimed. "This guy actually sent a picture of 'me' in bed and said 'I'll miss you.'"

She flashed it at me. Elena was in bed, true, with her hair tumbling over her bare shoulders, but she was covered up with a sheet. It was a Hollywood type of pose, except she was delivering her "Give me coffee, or I'll give you death" scowl.

Even I had to laugh at that one.

Mac finally pulled into a parking lot. I bit my lip. Elena and I hated paying for parking, but Mac didn't want anyone to scratch his car.

Jack pulled out his wallet. "It's on me."

"Hey. It's my wheels," said Mac.

"Right. Your gas and your mileage. Let me chip in."

They jockeyed a bit before Jack finally gave the attendant a ten. I flashed him a smile. Gisèle cooed, "Thank you," and linked her arm in his.

He said, "So where are we going first?" and gently detached himself. I gave him points for trying to get rid of her, but she giggled and tapped him on the nose. "I get to choose! It's my party!"

We started off at the Mad Hatter, which bills itself as a dive bar but has really given itself a facelift. Still, the drinks are cheap, and I grudgingly awarded Gisèle a point for picking one of our least trendy old haunts.

"We should've come tomorrow. They have all-you-can-eat chili and beer," mourned Mac.

Gisèle slapped his thigh. "We can come tomorrow too!"

She led us up and down through Crescent's greatest hits, from les 3 Brasseurs to Thursday's to Newtown for a drink here, a flirt there.

Mac bought the first round of drinks, and we all did shots. I hated that they came in translucent white plastic cups, even though this was one of those high-end poser bars that charged enough money for real glass. Environmentally incorrect.

I hesitated while everyone else downed them.

"*T'es pas sérieuse*," chided Gisèle. "I'm going to Prague! Bottoms up!" She jabbed her nail at the cup. "Or else I'm going to buy you something much worse."

One shot. Just one. To take the edge off the night. Hell, off the week.

The peppermint liquor burned my throat. I blinked. A minute later, the hazy lights of the bar seemed much more benign. Elena always used to tease me about my lightweight liquor status. I blamed it on my Asian genes, but Jack still looked pretty sober. Since Mac planned to drive his car o' love home, he stuck to Coke sans rum.

After two more shots, Gisèle pulled me on to the dance floor. I lagged for a minute. "This is not the place," I said, nodding at the elegant blondes and middle-aged suits looking on.

"I'm going to Prague!" she screamed. Even behind her sunglasses, she looked a little cock-eyed, so I decided to shake it to "Mony, Mony" with her. But when she screeched "Hey, motherfucker..." I didn't join in.

"Party booper. I mean pooper!" she giggled, spraying my face with spit.

Uh oh. Gisèle made a worse drunk than me. As in, irritable and out of control.

A dangerous drunk might spill our wer secrets. My spine stiffened even as I pasted a smile on my face. The music switched over to "Sexy Bitch," and after a minute, Gisèle gestured that she needed another drink.

"Eighties music is better! I hope they have it in Prague!" Gisèle yelled, weaving off the dance floor.

"I think they've got Cindi Lauper in Botswana," I said. "Hey. I'm going to grab us some water, okay?" They'd left a pitcher and some glasses at the side of the bar. It might slow Gisèle down a little.

Four guys waved at us from the doorway. For one heart-stopping second, I didn't recognize them, but Mac yelled out their names and said, "What're you having?"

"Who cares what we're having. It's what we won't be having. As in this beautiful blond beast who's leaving us," said the tallest one, a skinny one wearing a Habs shirt.

Gisèle laughed and lowered her sunglasses to flutter her eyelashes at him. "I'll miss you too. Could you get me a white Russian?"

"A Russian? I thought you were going to Prague. Forget those guys. Are you going to take me with you?"

"Would you fit in my luggage?"

I relaxed a little. Gisèle knew how to flirt, so it didn't really matter whether she recognized anyone or not. Also, if she messed up, she could blame it on the alcohol. Still, I didn't dare leave her side until all the humans vamoosed.

"Do you think you could fit this in your luggage?" A dark-skinned, Arabic type guy with acne scars, but somehow still lean and sexy, leaned close and whispered something elaborate in her ear.

She swatted his arm. "Hey. I'm leaving to get away from all that."

He shrugged. "What about one for the road?"

"How about this for the road?" She showed him one dainty fist.

The Arabic guy laughed pulled her hand toward his lips so he could kiss each knuckle. I honestly didn't remember him, but he was obviously a smooth operator, letting the Habs guy get the drinks while he worked "Elena." "I'm going to miss your spicy little ass." He opened her fingers and kissed her palm. "Do me one last favour. Take off your sunglasses."

"Why?"

"Because I want to see your gorgeous green eyes one last time," he said.

My heart thudded. Even in the relative dim light of the club, Gisèle didn't look enough like Elena to fool an attentive former lover. And unless she'd bought some coloured contacts, her eyes were grey.

Gisèle pushed him away gently. "I wouldn't have invited you if I'd known you were going to get so sentimental. Come on, dude! Let's party."

"Yeah! I'll get the next round," I said.

"No, I will," a third guy insisted.

By the time I bought a round, we'd ended up at a little hole in the wall that served excellent Indian food at the bar and pumped dance music throughout the restaurant. I bought beers all around, except for Mac, who'd switched to coffee. I held my pint aloft and called, "To Elena, who always drinks beer with Chicken Tikka Masala!"

We cheered. "Elena" chugged her beer and hauled us on to the dance floor. Pretty soon she was undulating on one of the speakers to Timbaland and Katy Perry's "If We Ever Meet Again."

I checked for Jack and realized he'd silently slipped away, as he had most of the night. Eventually I spotted him back at our table, chowing down on some beef biryani.

When Gisèle soared off the speaker in a stage dive, one of the guys caught her, but she could've poked my eye out with one of her stilettos. I pulled up a chair beside Jack.

He glanced up when he saw me. "Eat this."

He held a forkful of beef to my mouth. My nose twitched. It smelled good.

He said, "You've got no tolerance for alcohol. Come on."

I pointed at his all-over-red face. "Takes one to know one."

He bowed his head in acknowledgement, and I plucked the fork from his hand. "Thank you, sir." Then I started to eat. And eat. I hadn't had a proper meal yet tonight and I was starving.

"Hey," said Jack, after a minute.

"Hey, yourself," I said. I held the fork in the air and when he reached for it, I scooped more food into my mouth. "I'm not that easy."

I polished off another piece of beef. Okay, two. "I'll buy the next one," I mumbled around a mouthful of rice.

"It's all right. I like a girl who eats," said Jack. He dropped his hand on to my thigh and squeezed it.

164

Was he saying I was fat? I chewed a bit more slowly. But then I decided, screw it. He always knew Elena and I could eat him under the table. If he preferred blondes who drank their calories instead, he knew where to find at least one.

Jack's hand drifted north. On my inner thigh. When I glanced up at him, he smiled at me semi-innocently.

I nearly choked on a grain of rice.

Okay. I knew the game he was playing. Tit for tat. Sexual tension vs. beef biryani.

I could win both if I played my cards right.

I said, "You're pretty good at that."

"What?" Although his fingers didn't stir, they seemed to burn through the denim into my skin.

"Whatever you want to call it. Playing the game. Seduction. Making a girl lose control—or at least drop her biryani."

"It's my biryani," he said. His thumb drew a circle on my thigh, so high up that he'd brush the hem of my boy shorts if he'd pulled off the denim.

"Details, details," I said, which was all I could think of with his hand on my skin. This might be harder than I thought. I chewed faster, but I hardly tasted it until I bit into a peppercorn.

I choked.

"Is something wrong?" Jack passed me a glass of water with a bland expression.

"Nothing I can't handle," I said.

He smiled slightly. "Glad to hear it."

"Are you drunk?" I wanted to know.

"A bit."

"Does that give me a free pass?" They'd started playing Ricky Martin's "Livin' La Vida Loca." Gisèle screamed in delight. Involuntarily, I smiled. In some ways, she really was like Elena.

"Do you need one?" He casually covered the V of my jeans with his hand.

I tried to remember what we were talking about while all the blood in my brain drained south. And then I decided turnabout was fair play. I dropped the fork in order to cup his rigid cock through his jeans.

He jumped.

"See? Nothing I can't handle," I said sweetly, giving him a squeeze.

Jack's eyebrows drew together and he leaned close to me. "Leila…"

"Yes?" The lights of the room spun. His gorgeous face hovered close to mine. I could smell beer and arousal on him. I moved the palm of my hand up and down in a gentle stroke, testing his length and his resolve.

His nostrils flared. His eyes dilated even more. He was two seconds from ripping off my clothes and we both knew it.

"Get a room!"

"Get a room!"

"Get a room!" a skinny blond guy hollered directly in my ear.

Eventually, I exited enough from my drunken sexual biryani haze and realized we'd attracted the wrong attention from a good chunk of Gisèle's dancing troupe.

I pulled my hand off Jack's lap in order to show off my middle fingers on both hands.

Jack stood up, facing all of them. His chair clattered to the floor. He didn't say a word, but he stood in fighting stance. Even though he wasn't the biggest guy there, I knew he could kick some serious ass if he wanted to.

I faced them too, now with my fists clenched.

Gisèle draped her arms around two guys at the back. "What's going on back here?" she called over the music, a Great Big Sea song unfortunately titled "When I'm Up I Can't Get Down."

"Your friend here's about to get a lap dance," said the blond guy. "We want to watch."

"Have some biryani instead," I said, pointing at the plate.

"I'd rather have a lap dance," said the Habs giant.

Gisèle tinkled a laugh. "I know you horny boys would. But then I'd be too tired for my flight to Prague. I can do the lambada, though. How many girls can do *the forbidden dance?*" She tugged the Habs guy on to the dance floor. "It's just one-two-three…" When I glimpsed them behind the gang, they looked semi-ridiculous. He was so tall, his pelvis pressed against her stomach. "Crouch down!" she urged him.

A few guys laughed and went to the bar. The blond guy looked from Gisèle to me and back again.

Trouble.

Our unofficial pub/club crawl farewell party had climbed to a party of ten, but aside from a girl named Alison who wore glasses and looked like she'd rather pierce another hole in her upper lip than get it on with a guy, we were in a mass of men. Horny, drunk men.

Excess single male wolves often get driven out of the pack. That's where the lone wolf stereotype comes from. That SWM (single wolf male) tries to stake out his own territory and locate his own, rare, single wolf female. Or maybe he'll find another pack that might accept him. Possibly he could band with other single males to form a new pack. In general, though, they live a shorter, harder life.

Sounds harsh, and it is. But wolves understand that single guys are an unstable force. They pick fights; they try to sneak around with the alpha female even if she's sending clear "not interested" signs. If they could, they'd get drunk and demand lap dances too.

I cased the room. Jack was still standing, facing down four guys, although he'd cracked a joke and at least two of them smiled. Mac stood by the bar, flushed and bellowing about hockey with another guy who was three inches taller and about thirty pounds heavier. Mac shouldn't be drunk, but at 2 a.m., chaos starts to reign.

Time to break up the love-in.

I followed Gisèle on to the dance floor. To her credit, she was trying to give lambada lessons to about three guys at once.

She seized my arm. "Thank God you're here. You can partner with Pete. You can't have Steve, he's too tall…"

"Elena," I shouted, emphasizing the name, trying to snap her back to her role. "You know what we should do? We should go to a gay bar."

"What?" Gisèle swiveled toward me. Her lipstick had smeared above the bow of her lip, probably from all the kissing. She really did need long-lasting lip colour.

"A gay bar!" I shrieked over the music, which had turned into some Latin rhythm to match her dancing. "Remember? All those hot, oiled bodies and great music? You promised me you'd go to Campus and now you're leaving!"

The blond guy said, "What the fuck?"

Gisèle said, "But I'm having fun here!"

I glanced at my watch. "We've got to go now or else we'll have to pay a cover charge." Total lie. I had no idea which gay bars charged covers when, or what might even be open on Monday night. But I needed to shut the party down and take Gisèle away from here.

"I'm out," said the Arabic guy.

Mac, who'd wandered over to our group, said, "I'd rather shoot some pool."

The blond guy shook his head. Finally, he said, "What about a titty bar?"

I relaxed. The party was breaking up.

Pretty soon, Jack held open the door for me and Gisèle, and the rest of the gang filtered into the night, after multiple kisses, hugs, and at least one ass grab for the going away girl.

"You sure you don't want a ride home?" asked Mac, jingling his car keys.

"You sure you don't want to check out a gay club?" I asked.

He waved his keys at me. "Later."

Out on the street, my ears rang, recuperating from the music, and I shivered slightly from the wind. In Montreal in April, the days might heat up if you're lucky, but the nights can drop to freezing again.

"What did you do that for?" pouted Gisèle.

"Your party was getting out of control," I said. "All those guys wanting a lap dance? Hello."

"Only because you initiated it," she said, glancing me up and down.

I flushed. Nice. As if Jack had nothing to do with it. He stood by us, staying out of it. I felt pissed off at both of them. "You want to go to a gay bar or not?"

She put her hands on her hips. "I'd rather wrestle naked in Jell-O."

Jack stifled a laugh. Personally, I didn't think it was funny. "Sorry, *Elena*. It's just, we always talked about going. And now that you're heading to Prague, it's our last chance." Secretly, though, I hoped she'd kibosh the whole thing and split a taxi home.

"You think you know everything," she said suddenly. She pulled off her sunglasses and narrowed her eyes.

"Excuse me?" The buzzing in my head stopped. I stared into her cold grey irises. I didn't feel drunk at all. At this moment, Gisèle did not resemble Elena in any way. I didn't know this woman.

"Hey," said Jack. "Let me get that cab—"

"You think you run the show," Gisèle spat at me. She didn't acknowledge Jack. Her hatred homed in on me like a laser. "You tell me what I can or can't tell my father."

I tried to take her hand. "*Elena*, your father's gone—"

She shook me off and took a step forward, invading my space. She smelled like beer and old perfume and rage. "You always tell me what to say. You break up my going away party so you can get into Jack's pants."

"Whoa, whoa, whoa," I said. "That's not it. You had about ten drunk guys hanging off of you, ready to explode. It wasn't safe. We agreed it'd be a short night. I suggested a change of venue—"

"Fuck you. You…know-it-all Chinese bitch!" she snapped. She spun on her stilettos and tottered back toward the Hard Rock Café.

I stood there frozen for a second. Elena and I had fought plenty, but she'd never played the race card. Not once.

But after approximately two days, Miss Gisèle displayed her true colours. I only hoped Jack was taking notes.

Then I started to race after Gisèle. I was wearing peek-a-boo flats. I could catch her in five strides.

Jack matched my pace. "Let her go."

"But what if she blows—" our cover, I almost said. I bit my lip. Maybe I wasn't as sober as I thought.

He turned on the sidewalk to block me with his body. "Let her go."

For a second, I almost pressed my hands against his chest and shoved him out of the way. And then I understood how Gisèle felt. Jack was a know-it-all Chinese bastard. I would've been pissed if he'd broken up my going away party too. But shouldn't we kiss and make up, or at least shove her in a pre-paid taxi to make sure she didn't babble on about werewolves, Elena, Chinese bitches, etc.?

I jogged in place. I didn't manhandle Jack out of the way. I looked into his eyes, black and shadowed under the streetlights, and admitted to myself how much I wanted him—to the detriment of all thought.

"She could blow everything," I told him.

"She probably will," he said.

After a minute, I realized he meant blowing in another way. I laughed reluctantly. "I want to help."

"You antagonize the woman. Let me do it."

I swore under my breath, but I ground to a halt and let him chase her down. Of course, within approximately two minutes, Jack managed to bundle her into a taxi. He handed the driver some bills. She rolled down the window, and Jack leaned his head into talk to her far longer than I liked, but in the end, the taxi's tail lights faded into the distance and it was just me and Jack standing on Crescent Street in the wee hours of the morning.

"*Na zdravi*," I muttered under my breath, which means "cheers" in Czech.

And then I walked toward him to give him his reward.

CHAPTER 44

Jack placed a hand on my arm. Even with traffic whooshing and the occasional girls giggling and clattering by in their high heels, the night air seemed to hush. The darkness cloaked us. I could see his chest move in and out with his breathing.

I closed my eyes, all the better to relish the warmth of his palm resting on my biceps. That's how bad I had it.

"You still want to go to a gay bar?" asked Jack in a low voice.

"Um." I tried to think. His hand lay so close to my breast. If I pressed my arm toward my chest, I could bring him even closer. I tried to concentrate. Right. Gay bars. "I don't actually know any. I guess we could go to Unity II. Elena wanted to go to a strip one, but it turned out they didn't let women in except on Sunday nights—"

Jack covered my mouth with his. I threw my arms around him and kissed him back, relishing his firm lips and even the sour tang of beer and coriander on his tongue because it was him, him, him and I could not stay away. He was my Achilles heel, my Romeo, my Batman while I played Catwoman.

When he finally broke off the kiss, the streetlights spun around our heads, and I barely knew where I was. I wouldn't have been surprised if I glanced down to discover I'd wound my legs around his waist or my shirt had started to peel off. Or both.

This time, they hadn't. But I lost it around him. My brain, my self-control, my inhibitions. Everything.

"Your place," said Jack.

It wasn't exactly a question. For a second, I wondered why he hadn't offered his apartment as an option. But then I imagined one of his chiquitas bursting in on us and I rubbed my nose against his, a quick Eskimo kiss. If all we had was tonight, I'd take it.

Jack chuckled and nuzzled my nose too. Then he lifted his hand off my back, signaling a taxi. Seconds later, one eased up beside us.

"Smooth," I said.

"It's all done with mirrors," he answered. He opened the door and gestured me in first. I slid all the way to the driver's side and buckled up while giving the driver my address.

"You're still at the same place," said Jack.

I nodded, obscurely pleased that he remembered.

The bench seat sagged under his weight while he shifted closer to me. I kissed him on the cheek while he dug for his seat belt. He'd shaved, so his skin felt surprisingly smooth under my lips. I smiled and kissed him again. He turned toward me, and somehow my innocent cheek brush turned into full-blown snogging.

I'd never made out in a taxi cab before. Maybe that sounds ridiculously old-fashioned, but when I was in university, we couldn't afford cabs. We'd run from the McGill ghetto up the mountain in our T-shirts, drunk and yelling all the way. So making out in the street, yes. Yes, sir. Many sirs, even.

But not in a cab. Once my men and I could afford cabs, I'd grown up enough to realize that drivers were human and probably got sick of over-amorous drunk couples in their back seats. Like right now. I pushed Jack away. "Later."

He hummed and kissed my neck. All my nerve endings vibrated from my nape down to my breasts. He muttered, "Now."

I said, "No. We're..." My brain faded when his tongue snaked forward and licked and slithered along my collarbone. Not only did he know exactly how to work it, but it reminded me of many other illegal sex moves in his repertoire.

So I counted to twenty. Okay, fifty. I clung to the numbers while he somehow managed to spin me in my seat even though I was still wearing my seat belt. Now he was facing me and making full body contact while his tongue explored my shoulder and neck and back up to my lips again.

I opened my eyes. I was panting like a wolf.

I managed to twist my head to the side. The cab driver's dark eyes watched us in the rear-view mirror from beneath his turban.

I half-muttered, half-gasped, "We've got an audience."

Jack buried his head between my neck and my shoulder and inhaled. He was smelling me. One step away from taxi sex.

172

I pushed his head away. "Jack. Listen. Wait."

I wasn't too coherent, but he heard me. His entire body stiffened. His head jerked up to check my face: are you serious?

I nodded.

Jack sighed and threw himself back into his seat. He faced forward and crossed his arms like he was in school.

I touched his arm. "I know I sound medieval, but it's not my bag. PDA, I mean."

He glanced at me out of the corner of his eyes. I knew what he was thinking. With his wolf nose, he could probably smell how sexed up I felt, no matter how much I crossed my legs and pretended propriety. If he wanted to, he could make me do whatever he wanted. Inside the cab, on a street corner, any time of day or night.

I glanced out the window while we swished north on Parc Avenue. We should hit my place in 15 minutes, maybe less if the lights on Côte-Ste-Catherine didn't stop us at every block.

The taxi driver adjusted the volume on his radio. It crackled. He'd lost interest in us.

I took Jack's hand. He let me, but he kept his face and the rest of his body turned toward his window, like he was fascinated by the drummers by the statue at the base of the park statue.

I squeezed his hand. He squeezed back with a small smile.

"It's not cool to pout," I said.

"Just thinking." He gave me a crooked smile that accelerated my heart.

I glanced out my own window. We paused at the traffic lights of Côte-Ste-Catherine. I missed the heat of Jack's attention, but I felt proud of my self-control, too. I wanted to prove I wasn't a mere sack of hormones around him. If I could change history, I would move our sex fests away from Elena's tree and her grave. But I couldn't rewind. The least I could do was start here and now.

I thought you were going to give Jack up, whispered a little voice at the back of my brain.

Jack started drawing circles on the underside of my wrist with his thumb.

I am, I told the voice. *Real soon.* Just…after one last time. Or like one of my little cousins put it when I tried to take his video game, one last-last-last-LAST time.

In private. Like a lady. Not like a wolf or a careless friend.

We'd do it once and do it right.

Jack released my hand and brushed his fingers against my knee. "Is this okay?"

The taxi driver upped some Indian music. His radio crackled again. Somehow, that extended the illusion of privacy.

I relaxed a little and met Jack's impenetrable gaze. "So far."

"Okay. This is what I'm thinking. Clearly you've got limits and I respect that, except I don't know what your limits are. Why don't we play red light-green light?"

I frowned and pointed to the red light where our driver coasted to yet another stop. I've heard that in some places they synchronize the traffic lights or put a detector on them so that if there's no traffic, you can drive through. No such luxury in our town. "We're kind of playing that already. Or at least red light."

He shook his head. "You remember that game in school?"

"Not really." Especially not when his index finger started drawing circles on my knee. I know it sounds like a high school move, but not with Mr. Meng's fingertips.

"It's very simple. You're the traffic light." He kissed my ear and traced his tongue around its edge. "I'm the race car driver. When I'm doing something legit—" His hand slid south, down my inner calf.

I closed my eyes and clamped my legs together.

"You say 'Green light.' Or nothing. Or moan. That's all good." He nipped my earlobe, a gentle prick with his teeth, but enough to make my eyes pop open and my breath draw between my clenched teeth.

"But if I do something that makes you uncomfortable, no problem. You say, 'Red light.' And I'll stop. Deal?"

I knew this had to be a trap. But such a sweet one, I kind of lolled my head in a yes. "Red light," I managed.

"Good." He withdrew his hand from my leg and kissed my cheek. Sweet little butterfly kisses, the brush of his lips on my skin. Innocent enough to plant on a newborn babe.

I relaxed. Green light, baby.

He dipped his head and nipped the area where my neck meets my shoulder.

I shuddered and shook my head.

He kept his head there and licked his tongue in a slowly widening circle.

"Stop," I said weakly.

Instead, he slid his hand under my shirt, climbed under my underwire, and cupped my right breast.

I slapped his hand and gripped his wrist like a cop before I dragged it out from under my shirt. "What the fuck do you think you're doing?" I tried to keep my voice low in case Jack's antics hadn't already turned us into a peekaboo show.

"You didn't say red light," he pointed out.

I gritted my teeth and released his wrist. "You motherfucker. Go sit on your side."

"Yes, ma'am." He shifted his ass a critical three inches away and stared out the window. If the tent in his pants hadn't given him away, I might've been fooled by his indifferent expression.

Might've. But the tension in his shoulders and hands, the muscle working in his jaw, the way he shifted his legs back and forth, all gave him away.

I grinned.

Jack caught the movement in his peripheral vision and glowered at me, which made me laugh. So much of the time, it felt like he held the power in our relationship. Payback time.

Since I live almost at the corner of Côte-Ste-Catherine and my street is one-way south, I told the cabbie, "Don't bother going north and cutting across Van Horne. You can stop at the corner of Chevalier and that's good enough. Thanks."

"No problem," the driver replied. He barely made eye contact with me either.

So I feigned interest in the grand old homes looming on the mountain side of the road. By the time we neared the Université de Québec à Montréal (UQAM) buildings, their columns lit up by spotlights, the silence in the cab had grown oppressive, but at least the sexual tension had ebbed and I could think straight again.

"It's the next block," I said to the driver.

Since the traffic light was turning yellow anyway, he pulled over at the curb. I reached in my back pocket, but Jack was faster. He handed the taxi driver a twenty and said, "Keep the change." Then Jack opened his door and braced it wide open for me. "You coming?"

I unbuckled my seat belt and slid across the seat toward him. I smiled at his inadvertent double-entendre. Coming. Heh heh heh. "I hope so," I said, looking up at him from under my eyelashes.

He got it. He laughed a little and took my elbow to help me out. "Me too. But not in a taxi?"

"Right,"

"Red light," he said, straight-faced.

"Yeah." We started to walk. His hip bumped against mine. I laughed and slung my arm around his waist. "It's not like I'm a prude, but I don't like to be watched. It makes me feel—"

Jack stopped in the middle of the sidewalk.

I paused, too. I scanned the area in case he'd spotted something. Like the target. I live in a pretty safe neighborhood, mostly students and immigrants, but it was entirely possible a black GMC truck had snuck into a parking space around me.

No truck.

I glanced at Jack, raising my eyebrows in a question.

In response, he swung around to face me, planted his hands around my waist and lifted me up in the air.

I gasped even as I instinctively straightened my torso and reached for his shoulders in order to make it easier for him. My body knew what to do even if my head had no clue what was going on.

He lifted me higher in the air than I expected. I said, "Jack?" and stretched my toes toward the ground.

He bent my head and shoulders over his shoulders, draping me over his own shoulders so that he was carrying me fireman style.

The blood rushed to my head. I hate having my feet off the ground. I hammered on his back with my fists. "You asshole! What are you doing?" I kicked with my legs, too, but I was afraid he'd dump me on my skull, so I didn't try too hard, especially when he started striding toward my apartment building.

"Carrying you over the threshold," he said, barely out of breath. He must've aced the paramedics' physical exam.

"What?" I stopped slamming his back.

"You were going—" He grunted and adjusted me closer to his neck, but didn't break his stride. "—old-fashioned on me in the taxi. So I thought you wanted to go all the way. I'm carrying you. Over. The threshold." He slowed down, picking his way on the uneven paving stones making a path toward my apartment building.

"Put me down," I said.

"Nuh uh." He stumbled.

I grabbed his shoulder. "C'mon. The landlord doesn't maintain these stones very well and those little lamps are a joke. I can hardly see, and I'm not carrying a full-grown woman!"

"Over the threshold," he repeated. And, to my amazement, I saw we'd reached the pots of gardenias beside my front door.

"You need my key to get in!" I said.

"Right." He patted my back jeans pocket and dug them out, getting a good feel of my ass in the process.

"Chivalry is dead," I sputtered.

He gave my ass a reassuring pat. "Not dead. Just disguised a little." He unlocked the door, propped it open with his foot, and stuck his keys back into my pocket.

"Dude, more than a little. You're supposed to carry me in your *arms*, not like a sack of potatoes!"

"All you had to do was ask." He spun me around and caught me in his arms.

I looped my wrists around the back of his neck. He was breathing hard and his face glistened with sweat under the fluorescent light, but he looked—and smelled, and felt—hawt. Then he lightly stepped over the threshold of my apartment building. And my heart gave a queer double-thump, like a dream I'd never articulated had suddenly come true.

One night, I reminded myself. One night only.

CHAPTER 45

I glanced up the stairs directly ahead of the entrance way, not knowing if he remembered my exact apartment location. But before I could give him the number, he headed for the stairs and even took them two at a time.

Show off, I thought, but I buried a smile in his chest because, God help me, his wolf strength turned me on.

Fortunately, my apartment stood to the left of that landing, so we didn't have to test that wolf strength any more. He pulled up in front of my door like he had a built-in GPS. He said, "Hang on," and supported me with one arm while he eased the keys out of my back pocket again.

I clasped my arms around his neck like I could carry all my weight off of him while he unlocked the lock. He carted me over that threshold, too, before he set me gently on my feet on the opposite site of the door.

It took me a minute to balance myself and catch my breath. Even though he'd been doing the heavy lifting, I'd unconsciously held my breath. I flicked on the light.

He locked the door behind us and handed me the keys.

I placed them on the bookshelf beside the door and said, "The threshold thing is nice. But as an FYI, the romance book carry is much better than the caveman hold."

"Ug," he said.

I laughed. It rang a little hollow down my hallway. I realized that for the first time in two years, we were going to do it on terra firma in an actual building. Maybe on a genuine bed. For us, this was staking out new territory. This was deliberate act.

And now, thanks to my prudery, the taxi had forced a lag in our prolonged flirting, so we had to start all over again.

We looked at each other for a long moment.

I broke eye contact first when my foot made contact with a piece of paper. I glanced down at the mint green flyer on my welcome mat. Someone had shoved it under my door. Normally, people left ads in our mailboxes in the front entryway.

I picked up the ad to throw it in the recycling. It advertised home security systems. I laughed and showed it to Jack, trying to break the tension. "Check this out. Who would buy an alarm system for a rented apartment?"

He looked at me silently. His nose twitched.

Mine, too. A musky odor rose between us. My heart squeezed.

His eyes dilated.

I dropped the flyer.

And without a word, our lips cemented together. Not a polite, hello again kiss but a devouring, "I want to eat you up right now" demand.

No more foreplay, I thought with the part of my brain that still functioned. We'd spent the entire night on foreplay, including the push-pull in the taxi.

I grabbed his belt and yanked him toward me. He shoved my shirt up around my around my armpits and yanked my jeans down to my knees. My jeans were tight enough that my panties came right with them.

Within a minute of closing my apartment door, I was exposed. If someone had glanced through the peephole, they would have seen me.

Silently, I counterattacked. I worked his belt off and pulled off his jeans. He kicked off his shoes, but his boxer shorts stayed on until I clawed them off, exposing his arousal to my greedy eyes. His cock stood straight up already with a drop of precum on his tip. I smiled to myself, trying to decide what exactly to do with that monster first.

"Bend over," he said, indicating the wall to his right. The wall my apartment shared with a piano teacher, but at this moment, I didn't care if she was teaching arpeggios to triplets. I pressed my hands against the rippled plaster and bent over.

He didn't touch me for a long moment. I felt exposed. I glanced over my shoulder at him before he pulled a condom out of his wallet.

He glowered at me. "Don't move."

I faced the wall again and exulted to myself. All this and a guy who wore condoms, too. Sometimes, the universe rained happiness.

Over the beating of my heart, I heard a tiny rip while he opened the package. My legs tensed. I wished I could stroke the latex down his hard length, using my teeth or tongue, but he'd commanded me not to move.

He was taking over after the episode in the taxi.

I smiled to myself. There'd be plenty of time to show him my moves later.

He took his time cupping my ass with one hand.

I shifted and parted my legs to grant him greater access.

"Did I say you could move?" he asked.

I shook my head.

"Then don't."

No man had tried to dominate me before, including Jack himself. I closed my eyes and tried to deny it, but I knew my wetness might trickle down my thighs any moment.

All at once, he pressed the length of his body against mine, imprisoning me against the cool plaster. At the last second, I turned my face to the left, but my breasts were painfully compressed against the wall. The coolness made me shiver while the hot, hard length of his body awakened every nerve ending in my back, ass, and legs.

"This is your last warning," he breathed against my neck.

He slipped his hands between my breasts and the wall, to pinch my nipples.

I bit my lip instead of crying out. I didn't move a muscle.

He backed away and used his foot to separate my legs hips-width. Then he just watched me. I closed my eyes, knowing how exposed I looked.

"It's always push-pull with you, Leila," he said. "You're always pulling me with one hand and pushing me away with the other. That's going to stop now."

Of course, I remembered my vow that this was our last night together. But tonight and tonight only, I could agree to let him in.

He traced the lips of my labia from behind. I bit my lip to stop a moan. The iron taste of blood exploded in my mouth. I bit that hard.

But I didn't move. And I didn't make a sound.

"Very nice," he said.

I didn't know if he meant my body, my self-control, or both. Probably both.

Was this what his crazy ex had taught him?

180

If so, she had taught him well.

He traced down my thighs, chuckling at my wetness. He brought his fingers to my face for me to smell.

I didn't move. I inhaled my scent.

"Good girl," he said.

He moved his hands back to my mound of Venus and traced each fold, each hill and valley, brushing my clitoris in passing. I tried to suppress a shudder.

He passed over my clit a few more times, as if he was testing me. Then he massaged it full on, bringing tears to my eyes—of want, of frustration—

and when I nearly exploded, he stopped.

I waited on the precipice, a high-pitched noise locked in my throat.

A delicious sort of torture.

He touched me again, brought me to the point where stars obliterated my vision—

And stopped.

I screamed and ground my clit down hard on his fingers until the stars shot across the darkness of my eyelids and I cried out loud enough to wake the my piano teacher neighbor and the two potheads across the hall as well as nameless people living on the next floor up or down.

Much better.

I caught my breath as best as I could. Even without glimpsing myself in the hallway mirror, I knew I was grinning wolfishly.

That is, until Jack slapped my ass.

I sucked my breath between my teeth and glared at him over my shoulder.

He delivered three more sharp smacks, hard enough to bring tears to my eyes if I hadn't recently triggered an ocean of endorphins.

I bared my teeth at him and growled.

He backhanded me across both ass cheeks.

"I'm not going to apologize," I said. "It was too awesome."

His lips quirked for a second before he spanked my rear end hard enough to heat up the flesh and make me lose some of my high.

"Stay here," he said.

Then he prowled into my bedroom, immediately to the left of the entrance. He was still wearing the condom, his shaft proudly pointing near-north and somehow managing not to look ridiculous although it bobbed as he walked.

I turned around and faced the wall. I'd gotten what I needed. I could let him win this round.

I strained my ears. I could hear him click on the bedside table light. The hardwood floors creaked under his feet occasionally, but that was about it. I didn't hear any drawers slide open or my hangers bang together. What was he looking for?

The target again? The murderer was my default thought. Elena called it a "screensaver," the thought that I kept boomeranging back to. But I doubted Jack would have taken off and left me alone if he thought an intruder had invaded the apartment.

"What's this?" Jack re-materialized in the doorway, holding a red and blue embroidered book bound with thread.

"Give me that!" I lunged toward him.

He held it above his head.

I leapt for it. "Did you open it, you bastard?"

"Of course. It was on your bedside table."

"It was private!"

"I remembered that you kept a diary," he said. "I thought…"

"Thought what, buttwipe?" I jumped again. I noticed the way he watched my tits bounce, but I was too angry to care. "Thought you'd invade my privacy?"

"I don't know what I was thinking. I wanted to get back at you somehow," he admitted. "So I glanced inside the cover. What's the big deal?"

"That's my pillow book!" I snarled, finally managing to snatch the edge of it and tear it away from him.

"What does that mean? I remember hearing about a book or a movie."

He sounded so clueless, and his anatomy had deflated a bit. I smiled more kindly at him now that I had the book safely tucked under my armpit. "It was a book of thoughts by a Japanese court lady and they made it into a movie. But that's what Elena called her, um, porn collection, so um…"

"That's your porn collection."

"Erotica," I said, nose in the air.

"Huh." He sat on the bed, still naked, without bothering to cover himself. "So, want to go through it? I'm always up for a good 'pillow book.'"

"Well." I'd never shown it to anyone before, but he'd already seen the first picture. And he'd stopped spanking me, which was a plus. I sat on the bed beside him, leaving an inch between our naked bodies. "I guess you already saw the first picture. This is a painting by Rafal Olbinski."

He silently surveyed the portrait of a naked woman twisted to face the viewer with her arms bent and her hands on top of her head. Her breast was caught precisely in profile so that her nipple jutted straight out to the side. The full cheeks of her ass thrust toward the camera. She stared at you fearlessly, black hair tumbling down her back, sexual and unashamed. But on the black background, four red-gloved hands reached toward the woman. The sleeves were empty, but one hand tangled itself in her rich curls. A second pointed directly at her nipple. A third tested the soft skin of her ass with a thumb and her hip with an index finger. The fourth hand scooped forward, extending for and nearly caressing her vulva.

Jack said nothing, but at least one part of him stood back at attention.

I swallowed even though my mouth was dry.

"What do you like about this?" Jack asked. "The woman? The hands?"

"Everything," I admitted in a tiny voice. "Her body. Her face. Her attitude."

"Strangers touching you?"

I nodded, unable to meet his eye.

"Disembodied hands touching you?"

"They don't have to be disembodied," I whispered. "Or wear red gloves."

"Hm. I'll see what I can do." He shut the book and set it on the table. "Lie down, Leila."

I lay on my side, watching him. Jack always surprised me. When I expected him to dominate, he gentled himself.

"Lie on your back."

I did. The light seemed awfully bright, even though it was a 15-watt fluorescent bulb covered with a shade.

"Close your eyes."

I did. After a long moment, I felt his hand stroke my hip. And a feather touch on one breast. The other breast. My neck. My little toe. The inside of my thigh. My belly button.

I gasped.

He didn't speak. I heard his steps cross to the side of the bed and the lamp click off. Now we were shrouded in darkness.

His hands took over, playing my body. Testing me. Earlobes. Labia. Anywhere and everywhere. Until his butterfly touch drove me mad and I reached for his cock.

He blocked me with his thigh.

I moaned in frustration, lifting my hips. Was this how Carmen, the woman in the painting felt? Sexual and constantly aroused, but never allowed to peak?

"Please," I whispered. I stroked the hard muscles of his thigh and his wiry hair, climbing closer and closer.

He seized my wrist, brought it to his mouth, and kissed the back of it. Then he climbed on the bed.

I exhaled. For no good reason, tears welled up in my eyes.

He kissed my mouth and entered me. Gently but thoroughly opening me up, making sure to ride me high and grind against my clit while he was at it. This time, my orgasm built slowly, rising and falling like ocean waves. This time, I gripped his biceps and buried my head in his chest, smelling him, feeling him, until it finally I crashed somewhere on the shore and he landed somewhere beside me.

We lay in the darkness, listening to each other's breath. He touched my cheek, silently brushing away the tears still streaming out of my eyes.

"Did I hurt you?" he asked. "Sorry."

I shook my head and rubbed my tears away. Just when I should be high on afterglow, I'd fallen apart. Could I blame this on PMS?

He stroked my hair and kissed my cheek. Then he pulled his torso away. I reached for him, missing his warmth.

He laughed. "Give me a second to get rid of the evidence."

Oh. The condom. I heard it hit the trash can a minute later.

He enveloped me in his arms and kissed the top of my head. "You are fantastic, Leila."

"Um, thanks. You too."

His breathing grew deep and even. He'd fallen asleep.

I rolled on my back. He hugged me tighter. I wished we could stay wrapped up together forever like a burrito of love.

A burrito of love?

I squeezed my eyes. Uh oh. Slowly, I realized why I'd cried all over him. Not only because I was drunk. Not only because I'd flipped out over Elena's death.

Worse.

I'd lost it on him earlier when he found my pillow book because, if he'd flipped to the last page, he would've found one of his own pictures smiling back at him. Bare-chested. When I pasted it in, it wasn't that I was mooning over him, just that he made a nice addition to my jerk-off collection.

But now I had an even worse secret. My body had figured it out before my brain had fully admitted the truth.

I'd fallen in love with Jack again. For real.

CHAPTER 46

The Accidental Murderer

He watched the light switch off in the front bedroom. Through the trees and the translucent window blinds, he'd hardly glimpsed a thing, but he knew what they'd been doing.

Were probably still doing.

Fucking animals.

Deserved to die.

He shook his head. All Darryl had meant to do was attract some wolves, or at least some coyotes, onto the area and scare off these city slickers.

Then he remembered that blond woman tearing into the raw chicken with her teeth. He could hear chicken bones snapping. He could hear her smack and chew.

Darryl wanted to puke. Worse than animals. Beasts. Eating and fucking and fucking and eating.

They didn't deserve his land.

Hell, they hardly deserved the oxygen they used up.

He reached for the keys in his truck's ignition. Time to crash somewhere, anywhere before the sun rose again.

Instead, he sat in his truck on Chevalier. Waiting. Waiting for the light to turn on. Waiting for the shade to go up.

Waiting.

CHAPTER 47

Leila

"I have to go," said Jack.

I covered my head with my pillow. I'd hardly slept. As the sun rose, I'd watched his closed eyelids and his chest rise and fall. Stalker-ish, I know. But I kept thinking that this night was all we had.

If I paid for it in the morning, what the hell. A werewolf is used to pulling a few all-nighters.

Now that Jack had sat up on the edge of the bed, though, I regretted my vigil. Not because I'd probably smeared the last of my lipstick over my pillow case and added ten years to my looks with some eye bags, but because I was so tired, he could probably read the emotion on my face. Or my hands. Or my body.

He laughed and kissed my lips and my nose. "You sleep. I'll go make us some coffee."

Us. I liked the sound of that.

He padded out of bed and got as far as the front door. He paused.

I peeked from behind the pillow. He'd donned his boxers, but I could still admire the muscles in his back. He scooped up that flyer from the door mat, I guess to drop it in the recycling, but his back stiffened and his hands flexed.

I could feel the change in electricity in the air.

I kept watching.

He wheeled around. Dropped the flyer. Stormed at me. His eyes flashed and his hands nearly formed claws.

I licked my lips. "Jack?"

He looked furious, but it wasn't anger driving him. Not the way he was looking at me with his morning glory trying to fight its way out of his boxer shorts.

He ripped his shorts off. Tore them. The waistband held for another second before he launched them across the room.

He threw his weight down on me. Not gentle. Hungry. Devouring.

I opened my mouth, my legs. I lifted my hips. His mouth descended on my neck. My eyes rolled up to the ceiling. I thought, *Thank you. Anyone up there, thank you for this. For any extra time with this love god.*

And then Jack drove all sentient thought out of my head.

CHAPTER 48

"I'm late," said Jack.

"Me too."

"I should get dressed."

"Me too."

"I'm fucked."

I yawned. "That I definitely am. You made sure of that."

"This is nuts, Leila. I mean, even for us. I'm never late for work. The night shift is counting on me to be there."

"Uh huh."

"So I've really got to book it."

"Right."

Neither of us moved.

"Unless I call in sick."

I rolled toward him and traced around his belly button. "That would be bad."

"Right. I'm leaving now."

"But it's kind of true, right? I mean, what happened to Elena and all. We're all heartsick. Sick at heart. Something."

He rolled on top of me. "Very."

I undulated my hips under him. "Contagious."

"Very."

And then we stopped talking.

CHAPTER 49

The Accidental Murderer

He should leave now.

He'd watched the front door all morning.

The man and the woman stayed holed up in the apartment with the shades drawn.

He should talk to Mr. Tabassian about the paper he'd found mixed in with his own. Darryl had sat at the truck stop, gloating over his coffee and his near-done deal, when he'd found a nearly identical contract drafted for Green Belt Montreal, awaiting signatures by one Leila Fan and Laurent Laforest.

Their contract predated his own.

What was the old man playing at?

Darryl had taken advantage of the truck stop's free high-speed Internet and tracked down both of them.

Leila Fan first. Easy. The Green Belt Montreal boasted several pictures of its staff members at various workshops and even a close-up of Leila speaking at some fundraiser.

Two things hit him right away.

She was one of the kids at the campsite. She helped drag the blond girl out of the river, did mouth-to-mouth on her, the whole shebang. So not only was this group trying to buy that land, they could turn him if they figured out his role.

And then they'd have the land.

His land. Darryl's land, by rights.

He found some stuff on Laurent Laforest, too. A lawyer. An environmental lawyer, whatever that meant, but still.

Darryl swore to himself until his coffee got cold.

But then he turned his truck around and pointed it back toward Montreal. He didn't have a plan, exactly, but he couldn't lose the land.

He had to talk to Mr. Tabassian. He'd bring up Green Belt Montreal and pressure him into speeding up the process. Once the land was safely under Darryl's name, he could forget about this mess.

For a second, the blond girl flashed back into Darryl's head. Snarling.

He pushed the thought away.

The image got replaced by Leila Fan's face. She wasn't that good-looking. Flat-chested. Too skinny in general. He liked blond girls with more meat on their bones, and that was the truth.

But somehow, the thought Leila Fan wrapping her long, brown legs around that Chinese guy bothered Darryl.

A lot.

He checked his messages. Nothing from the Armenian. He'd better drive up in person, kick the old guy's ass. Make sure he wasn't getting cold feet.

But somehow, Darryl kept staring at the white slats of Leila Fan's vinyl blinds. Trying to see in.

He grabbed a stack of flyers and followed a guy into the building. The guy even nodded at Darryl as if he was a regular. These people practically begged to get ripped off. Darryl pulled his hat down low on his forehead and carried on to apartment number nine.

He shoved two flyers under their door. The second was the same tanning salon flyer someone had left on his truck yesterday, but with a little something special added to it.

From behind wooden door, Darryl heard a thump. Furniture screeched across the floor. What the heck were they doing in there?

He heard the slap of flesh on flesh. A woman gasped. A man groaned like a moose.

Darryl turned on his heel and strode out of the building. His heart beat so hard, he thought he might black out. He climbed into his truck.

Sitting in the sun, the heat was stifling. He rolled down both windows and opened a map so it would look like he was doing something when while he regained his cool.

Okay. So they were still going at it. That was what he wanted, right? He was lucky that they were so easily manipulated. Animals.

Nothing wrong with animals. He liked deer fine, for example. But they got to be pests and then you got a permit and got rid of them.

Not that he wanted to get rid of Leila Fan or the other guy. Just—out of the way. Away from his land.

He thought of that gasp, that little noise she made. He wondered what made her sound like that.

He shifted in his seat. None of his business.

Nothing to do with real estate.

But what the hell were they doing in there? Exactly?

Something enthusiastic, anyway.

A word flitted through his head: insatiable. Hell, he didn't even know where that word came from. But that stupid woman's face and body came up again like he was watching her on a movie screen. And now he knew what she sounded like, too.

He refused to think of the man with her. The man didn't matter. Darryl could track him down later.

Darryl couldn't lose sight of the real prize.

The land.

A woman pushed a stroller on the sidewalk. Darryl rolled up his windows, feeling a little calmer.

Leila Fan was an impediment.

Darryl knew how to manipulate her. That was all.

He fired up his engine and checked the map one last time, tracking the best way to the Armenian's. He could use the GPS on his phone, but Darryl still liked to trace a route with his finger and lay out the path in his mind.

Darryl checked his messages and found he'd missed one from the Armenian. He called back right away. "Hello, Mr. Tabassian. I'm glad you got my message."

The Armenian didn't mince any words. "There's a problem with your application."

Darryl's stomach dropped. His free hand tightened on the steering wheel. "What are you talking about?"

"You didn't fill out the paperwork right. You come by, I'll explain it to you. But more important, your check—"

"What about it?"

"Didn't process."

Darryl slammed his hand on the dashboard. He barely noticed the pain shooting up through his elbow. "What?"

"Got rejected by my bank. So I'm going to need a certified check or cash."

Darryl said, "There's some mistake. That's my inheritance. No way that money didn't come through." Unless the old man was screwing with him from the grave. But no. He'd seen the zeros in the bank account with his own eyes.

Mr. Tabassian sighed. "Listen. I already turned away this nice environmental group. I'm going to call them again."

"No!" Darryl roared. It rang through the truck cab loud enough that a passing jogger glanced over his shoulder. Darryl glared at him until the guy ran out of sight.

Mr. Tabassian's voice turned chilly. "Listen. Where I come from, you don't tell me how to do business. They might not have been as rich as you, but their money was good. And they're from right here in Montreal. Sometimes that's easier than dealing with people from outside."

Darryl snorted. "I'm from Ontario. The province right next door."

"That's what I said," the Armenian said. "From outside. It gets messy. So listen to me. I'm calling the environmental group. If they can get me the money by next week, I'm going with them. But you can come by and pick up your papers and do whatever you need to do with your bank, and I'll make my decision."

Darryl turned off his phone. For a minute, pain enclosed his chest. Hot, searing, burning pain that made his vision black out and his teeth grind together.

He glanced at Leila Fan's building one last time before he peeled out of his parking space on the way to Mr. Tabassian's office.

CHAPTER 50

Leila

"Mr. Tabassian, I don't want to get disappointed again," I warned him, even though my heart was doing somersaults in my chest.

Jack walked back in the room with a white towel wrapped around his waist and his hair a messy black cap from the shower. My heart skipped a beat. Oh, yes, I had it bad. Lust *and* love. A double shooter.

Jack raised a questioning eyebrow. I raised a finger in response: give me a minute.

Mr. Tabassian said, "No tricks, Leila. I feel bad about the whole thing. You were right, we had a deal. And that stupid 'millionaire,' his check bounced on me. So I got stuck with the NSF fee. I want you to put your application back in again."

"I can do that," I said. "Let me get my papers together. I'll be there in half an hour. How does that sound?"

He paused. "How about next Tuesday? Tuesdays are good for me."

"Do you already have an appointment?"

"Something like that." For the first time, his voice dropped like he was embarrassed.

"Sure. Nine o'clock at your office?"

"Perfect." His voice warmed. "Leila. It's always a pleasure doing business with you. I want you to know that if you and the millionaire come up with the same money, I'd choose you. No contest."

I knew there had to be a catch. "And if we don't come up with the same money?" I asked sweetly, even though my hands tightened on my pillow.

"Well." He sighed. "No matter how much it hurts me, you know, business is business."

194

I sure did. "Can you send me the millionaire's exact bid?"

"Sure, sure, Leila. You're my number one girl. You know that."

"Same to you, Mr. Tabassian," I lied before we both hung up.

I'd hate to see how he treated his number two girl. But at least we were back in the game. I only had to raise the cash and get Mr. T the money in, oh, less than a week.

My mind buzzed. I'd have to talk to the bank and see if they'd agree to a higher mortgage. They'd balked at first, since we were a non-profit organization. Tripling the mortgage would be a hard sell.

Maybe I could negotiate with another bank?

No chance of getting a grant, especially on the fly like this.

Jack wrapped his arms around me from behind and nuzzled the back of my neck. "Good news from Mr. T?"

"He wants to sell the land to us again." I paused. "At least, if we can match the highest bidder."

Jack's muscles stilled. "Why would he want to do that?"

"He claimed the check for the other guy didn't go through."

I felt Jack smile. His cheek bunched against mine and he hugged me a little tighter. I drew back to look at his face. "Do you know something I don't?"

"Well. Not officially. But our community's got a lot of connections. We put the word out about this deal. Maybe somebody made something happen."

I started to smile. "I like that." Werewolf power. Whenever I read books about vampires, they're supposed to have so much money and power sequestered over the centuries. Why shouldn't wers have a little of that, too? Especially since, unlike vamps, we know how to play well with others.

"You know it." He lifted my hair into a loose knot on the back of my head and kissed his way down my neck, vertebrae by vertebrae. Then he blew on my skin.

"Hey!" I said, shivering.

"I'm getting rid of a stray hair," he said.

"Well, stop it." I pulled my hair out of his grasp. "I've got to get Laurent on the horn, see if he'll be able to make it to the meeting tomorrow."

Jack kissed my cheek. "Game over for us, huh?"

"For now." I kissed him back on the lips, long and lingering. He smelled like soap. His towel fell on the floor with a wet plop, and we both laughed. I said, "Is that done with mirrors, too?"

Jack framed his pertinent bits with his hands. "Nope. This is the real thing."

"Splendid. Jaw-dropping. But I've got to make a phone call. Business. Life and death. You know the drill."

"Who's stopping you?"

I reached for the phone on the bedside table. Jack tackled me across the bed. I kicked him off, gently, while I secured the phone to my ear.

Jack massaged my feet, kissed his way up my thighs, and generally made me gasp and twist so much, Laurent asked if I was all right.

"Totally great!" I squeaked before I hung up and launched myself on Jack. One last-last-last-LAST time.

CHAPTER 51

"Drive me to the airport," said Gisèle, over the phone.

I yawned. I'd passed out on the bed. I could hear and smell something in the kitchen. Bacon. I sniffed again. Hash browns. Mmm. "Why? You're going next week. We don't need to do a practice run."

"I got a red eye ticket to Prague. Great deal."

Jack started humming in the kitchen. Something tuneless, but he was happy. I stretched my arms over my head. "When do you leave?"

"Three hours. I need a drive, stat. You can take me in the van and then keep it."

I sat up in bed. "Geez. I'm supposed to be working, you know."

"I know. I called there first. Since you're 'sick,' you should be able to take me to the airport."

My stomach rumbled. I eyeballed the clock. After 2 p.m. "You're going to get me stuck in rush hour again. Do you want to take a cab?"

"I want you."

I cast a longing glance at the kitchen. But if this was what it took to get the great imposter across the Atlantic, I'd do it. "See you in twenty."

I checked the Master Tracker while I pulled an organic cotton tunic dress over a pair of leggings. The target had parked right next to Mr. Tabassian's office. When Jack wandered in with a plate of bacon and hash browns, I said, "You're a godsend." While I devoured them, still standing, Jack pointed at the screen. "That where you're off to?"

"Maybe. I've got to take 'Elena' to the airport first. She's booking it." I explained about the last-minute ticket.

Jack frowned. "I don't like this. A ticket for next week cost enough. Why are they stepping it up?"

I shrugged. "I guess as soon as 'Elena's out of here, she can get on with her life. And, to be fair, sometimes really last-minute tickets cost less."

Jack shook his head without answering while I chewed two strips of bacon. Then he handed me a glass of water. "I couldn't find any juice."

"I drink milk and water." Juice was mostly a waste of calories to me. Not that I was paranoid about my weight or anything.

Jack said, "I'll come with you."

"Nah. She asked me. Girl time. I think." I resisted checking out the Master Tracker screen. Part of me itched to get back on the road and check out the target. Even if I missed him, I wanted to know what Mr. T was up to. A pleasure doing business with me, my ass. "And I really have to move it if I'm going to triple our payment in a week. I'll have to hit the office, make a few calls to the banks, that sort of thing."

"Okay," he said.

I glanced at him. He'd given in way too easily.

He held his hands up. "I can't complain, right? We got to play hooky."

"Is that what the kids are calling it nowadays?" I kissed him, pressing the length of my body against his. "I wish I didn't have to go. See you tonight?"

He shook his head. "I couldn't leave them short-staffed, so I traded for a night shift. I'll see you the day after."

I frowned. Now I remembered how Jack's twelve-hour shifts could throw him completely out of synch with my schedule. He'd have to crash Wednesday to make up for the night shift. "Are you back to days on Thursday?"

"Yes. And then working straight through the weekend. But then I get three days off. Don't be a stranger, okay?"

I kissed him again and biked over to Elena's apartment.

Gisèle was already waiting in the van's driver seat. She tapped her horn at me in greeting. I popped the rear hatch and shouldered my bike into the back after shoving her luggage out of the way and lowering the back seat.

Gisèle offered no assistance aside from tapping her still-impeccable red nails on the steering wheel in time to "Apologize" by Timbaland and One Republic.

She didn't speak, either, until we hit Décarie traffic. "You're late."

"I wasn't expecting a royal summons," I said before I could bite it back.

She nodded. She started to swerve into a left-hand lane, but a silver Ford Focus cut her off. She gave it the finger and then tailgated it for a few metres while I flipped the radio away from commercials and finally settled on a poppy French song, "Lever l'Ancre."

At last, Gisèle broke the silence. "Papa thinks Jack is correct."

"In what way?" I asked. As a wolf, my hackles would've shot straight up. As a woman, I tried to keep my voice and hand position neutral, even though I hated her even speaking his name.

"Papa thinks this is not an isolated incident." It took me a minute to realize she meant Elena's death. Nice. "He thinks someone is trying to undermine us. There have been other problems in the area. At a town meeting, someone wanted to set out wolf bait."

I tensed. Bait. Just like I thought, that chicken was baited. "Do we know who that person is?"

"Yes. Papa checked him out. He was a local eighteen-year-old, not very bright. Someone else may have put him up to it."

I nodded, although I liked this less and less. The more people involved, the bigger the conspiracy, the harder it would be for us to prove or to neutralize all the players.

She continued, "There have been flyers about hunting in the area. One of them even mentioned trying to hunt big predators like wolves."

"But there aren't any wolves in the area," I said. Our group had scouted the perimeters of the property and encountered nothing but coyote. In our jaunts around the countryside, also nada. We would've welcomed real wolves, even if we would've had to negotiate territory with them. But they simply didn't exist anymore.

"Yes. That's what Papa thinks, too. He's a hunter and he's explored Glengarry quite thoroughly over the years. He's never encountered a wolf. In the past, of course, there might have been. And we do have a few wolf-dogs and wolf-coyotes because occasionally a male wolf will mate with other breeds." Her voice dipped with disdain. She accelerated on to the Metropolitan ahead of a transport truck. "But so far, this is a campaign with no clear reason." She paused. "Last week, we received flyers in our mailbox specifically about hunting wolves."

Something about flyers pinged in my brain, but I couldn't quite figure it out. I pushed the thought aside for now. "So what do you plan on doing about it?" I asked.

199

"Well. It's up to Papa," she said. She hesitated and added, "He is the district head."

"That's true," I said, but the whole conversation made me uneasy.

She took over the radio, flicking from station to station until she found "Paralyzer" by Finger Eleven. She tapped on the wheel in time to the beat.

The subject was closed. For now.

At the airport, I wished I could drop her off at the departures door and wave sayonara, but she looked a little pale when she said, "Coming in?" so I signaled for short-term parking.

Of course, it meant that I struggled with Elena's zebra luggage and carry-on while she said, "Thanks, Leila. You're the best friend ever."

After she checked in at Air France, she pushed her sunglasses up her head and surveyed the airport while she tightened the carry-on strap on her shoulder. "I'll miss this dump."

"Prague should rock," I assured her, eager to get her on her way.

She rolled her eyes. "I know that, dummy. I'm the one who's from there, remember? But I'll miss you guys. You're my best friend."

I smiled. She did sound a little like Elena, finally. I hugged her. Her bones felt brittle under her new beige travel suit.

She air-kissed my cheeks and I returned the favour, pressing my lips firmly against her cheeks. Elena and I used to really kiss, not fake kiss. Because when all was said and done, we cared about each other more than our lipstick.

"Write me," she said.

"You know I will." Mac's friend had rigged up an e-mail account for her that would seem to route from Prague. Same with Skype.

"You'd better. And if I were here…" She paused and pursed her scarlet lips before smiling at me. "I might give scum-sucking motherfucker a run for your money."

My jaw dropped open. Wrong on so many levels. First of all, I was the only one who called Jack SSMF. It was like my trademark. Secondly, Elena and I never went after each other's men.

Thirdly, Jack was mine.

"See you on the other side," said Gisèle, striding toward security. I watched her go, a tall, long-legged blonde with a zebra-striped roller suitcase. She fit right in.

And she never looked back.

CHAPTER 52

The next three weeks passed in a whirlwind. When Laurent and I met with Mr. Tabassian, he spoke of "outsiders" and how he wanted to sell his land to a group who would "do it right." But he stopped short of signing any final contract until we got the money. I met nonstop with banks and tapped all our fundraising sources, from Green Belt Montreal supporters to wers in and out of the closet.

We finally came up ten grand short on Wednesday.

Mr. Tabassian regarded us sorrowfully when I gave him the news. His jowls hung down like an English bulldog. "I like you young people. But business is business. You understand."

Never mind that he'd nearly tripled the asking price as it was. I bit back my response and nodded. I'd have to come up with another ten thousand or Elena's bones would go to her murderer.

Jack stopped by my apartment while I paced and called people and paced some more. "You're doing your best," said Jack, pulling me down on the futon and stroking my hair.

"But what if my best sucks?" I said. I sat up and grabbed my laptop. "Close only counts in horseshoes and hand grenades. Hey. That reminds me. You know how you thought there was a werewolf mafia? Do they have money?"

Jack sighed. "You talked to Bernard, right? If they could get money, they would."

Screw Bernard. He could have liquidated some of his assets if he'd wanted to. He just didn't want to enough.

What kind of leader was he? As far as I could tell, the only thing he'd really contributed was Jefferson, who'd pinged me: *Coming over tonight. I've got more information.* Jefferson was good. But right now, we needed cash.

While Jack rubbed my arms, I stared out my window and, for the first time, wished I'd chosen something more lucrative than environmental activism. I would've mortgaged my house if I'd owned one. But heck, I didn't even have a car.

Actually, that wasn't quite true. Elena had sort of passed on her van to me.

How much could I get for Elena's van? I started Googling. The numbers that popped up made me smile. "Hey. We might be able to do this."

Jack leaned over my shoulder to read the listings. "That one has less than 100K on it. Plus leather seats. That's why they priced it at almost 20 grand. How much mileage on Elena's van?"

"I don't know. A lot." I tried to think. "At least 130K."

"You get more for lower mileage. And has she ever been in an accident?"

"She scraped the door on a parking meter once. No big deal." I pointed at the screen. "Come on. This is amazing. Even the low end is just under 10K. By George. I think I've got it."

Jack nodded slowly. "You're amazing. No doubt about it." He lifted me into his lap and started kissing my neck. It felt good enough that I leaned into him for a minute. He smiled.

Then I sat up again. "Sorry, Jack. I'm going to need to do some research on this. I'm pretty excited."

He sighed and kissed the top of my head. "Okay. I'll play devil's advocate. We still need a way to get out there. Not much good having land if we can't access it."

"We could take two cars. Or rent one. The most important thing is that this land is ours, and I mow that millionaire's ass."

Jack cupped my ass and squeezed. I wiggled against him, but kept on typing. He said, "Remember, we'd have to get 'Elena' back to sign any paperwork before it goes through."

"You're killing my buzz," I said. I'd so enjoyed her stuck in Prague, where all I had to do was reply "Awesome!" every so often to her updates. "When's she coming back?"

Jack checked his watch. "Her plane lands tomorrow at 5:30 p.m."

"But she's in Czechoslovakia," I said. "Right? She posted a bunch of pictures on Facebook." I cut myself off. That was the whole point, duping everyone else. But why hadn't she told me she was returning?

And how closely did she and Jack keep in touch?

"Maybe she's still there. I'm not sure about the time change," said Jack. He grinned down at me. "You didn't think she was going to stay there forever, did you?"

A girl could dream.

"She's got a passport under another name. She'll leave her luggage there and bring a few trinkets back. She already took a boatload of pictures that she'll post sporadically. Mission accomplished."

I licked my lips. "Well, good for her."

"Yeah. It hasn't been easy for her. It's one thing to pick up a script and act for even eight hours a day, but when you have to take on a real human, 3D identity and convince everyone around you, 24/7, that's who you are, that's pretty rough, especially when your entire community is counting on you."

I nodded. I got the feeling he was quoting Gisèle. She had a point. I'd considered her a charming little faker who enjoyed every minute, but now I admitted the downside. I still had to ask, "What's her plan after she touches down?"

"She's buying a train ticket—cash—and hopping back to her parents' place for a debriefing. To relax, you know?"

"Right," I said slowly. Much as I sympathized, it meant she was sticking around close enough to hurt. Not to mention Bernard's suspicions about a wolf hunter in the area. I didn't like any of it. "How are you guys keeping in touch?"

"Mostly texting. I hear about her through Mac, too. I think they Skype sometimes. You know."

I felt completely out of the loop. Okay, I'd been working the financial end, but everyone had kept radio silence on me. I said, "I wonder if those texts can be traced. You didn't call her Gisèle in them, did you?"

"Come on, Leila, Give me some credit." He placed both hands on my shoulders and rubbed them, starting a slow massage.

I leaned into him a little. "Which phone is she using? Hers or Elena's?"

"A new pay-as-you-go phone, using phone cards. We closed down Elena's accounts when she left the country, remember?"

I remembered. But, maybe infected by everyone else's paranoia, I'd come up with an even worse conspiracy theory centering around Elena and the reason Mr. T might sell us the land now.

What if the target had turned around and backed off of the land deal in order to trap us?

We were the ones taking on the job of hiding Elena's disappearance. What if the target watched us and pulled all the evidence together, leaving just enough rope to hang us all?

We figured he'd let it go because he wanted Elena to disappear even more than we did. On the other hand, maybe he'd try to put a final nail in the wer coffin by blaming her death on us. After all, we'd cut up her body, buried her, impersonated her, and were desperately trying to buy the land containing her bones.

Was this how he really meant to hunt werewolves?

Was this his whole new order of wolf bait?

CHAPTER 53

Jack felt me stiffen. "What's up?" He dug his fingers harder into my neck, breaking down the muscles, but he hit a nerve ending, and I yelped.

"Sorry," I said. I pulled away. I couldn't tell Jack my suspicions just yet. Too many things on tap: Elena's murder. The land deal. Fundraising. Gisèle. Elena. And the man currently trying to massage away all my stress.

I needed more evidence. So when he raised his hands for another massage, I shook my head. "Jack, you know, I'm zonked. I think I'll take a rain check tonight."

He frowned. I'd never turned down the wild thing since we'd hooked back up. He said, "I've got two night shifts coming up, and we'll be missing each other the rest of the week. I could just crash here if you like."

"Uh." I weighed the distraction vs. the security of his presence. Gisèle's imminent return tipped the balance. "Sure. See you in the bedroom."

But not for long, because in the middle of the night, someone rapped on my apartment door instead of buzzing like a normal person.

I checked the peephole. Through the distorted viewer, Jefferson stared back at me like he could see my deepest secrets. Sexy and discomfiting in one. I bit my lip and reached for the door latch.

"Who is it?" Jack appeared on my right and covered the door lock before I could turn it.

"Jefferson." I pushed his hand aside.

He let me, but barely backed up enough to let me swing the door open, so the first thing Jefferson saw was an overprotective werewolf glaring at him over the threshold. "Sorry," I said, from behind Jack's shoulder. "Personal guards these days. You know how it is."

Jack didn't move. Jefferson didn't, either. They glared at each other.

I took Jack's hand and drew him further into the apartment, giving Jefferson some space. "Thanks for making the trip down," I said, like it was perfectly normal for Jack to play bouncer in my apartment at midnight. I had to tow Jack about six feet back before Jefferson would enter.

He nodded stiffly at both of us. "No problem."

I ushered everyone into the living room, tidying pillows. "Want something to drink? Water?"

"No, thanks." He regarded me steadily, blocking Jack out. "Leila. Have you been tracking the target?"

I nodded. Somehow, it didn't surprise me that he called him "the target" too. "As best I can. The Master Tracker's battery died, but only after I pinned him at an apartment-hotel. I drive out and check on him every so often."

"So you figured out who he was?"

I shrugged. "I hung around the hotel's front desk a bit. He registered under the name of Daniel Findley, but there's no one with that name in the South Glengarry phone book. I looked up the plates some more, but I haven't had a chance to go any further than that."

"Good work," he said, smiling a little. "You've been busy." He handed me a thick manila envelope.

I opened it. "Darryl Robert MacEachern." That seemed to fit better than Daniel.

I read the report. Darryl was a single white male, 39 years old. Six feet tall, 190 lbs. That sounded right, from what I'd seen of him, and when I came across a photo, I nodded in recognition. Now we had a picture of his face, including the pale blue eyes that reminded me of a husky dog's. Except I'd prefer the dog.

I flipped through his social history. He did lots of farming-related odd jobs. He was a recreational hunter who got a license every year.

I paused at the firearms license, non-restricted type. Since I hunt with my teeth and jaws, I don't pay much attention to the gun registry. I tapped the paper. "What does this mean?"

Jefferson said, "It means he's allowed a rifle or shotgun, but no handgun. Legally."

Jack and I exchanged a look. Not that comforting, since the target might not bother registering his gun with the Canadian government.

206

I flipped through the pages. I wanted to know how the target had gotten his mitts on a million dollars. As far as I knew, no one became a millionaire milking cows or throwing around hay bales. And then I found the notice of his father's death.

"It's all private assets, but we assume this is where his money came from," said Jefferson. "He inherited it two months ago."

"Is it possible the assets are still frozen?" asked Jack.

Jefferson nodded. "Yes. I understand that's why he had trouble buying the land. But the paperwork will go through soon enough."

I said, "By that time, we should have closed the deal on the land. With any luck." I told Jack with my eyes not to mention selling Elena's van.

Jack lifted his shoulders slightly: *why would I bother telling this guy?* He said aloud, "I have some more news I was going to tell you both."

I raised my eyebrows. Why hadn't he mentioned it before?

Jack ignored the look, crossed the room, and pulled some paper out of his jacket pocket. "We got more in-depth readings on what was inside Elena's blood stream." He sat on the back on the futon and unfolded the paper so I could read it over his shoulder. Jefferson loomed over both of us, silently reading.

The first page was a toxicology report. "That's what I told you already. None of the usual drugs except pot." Jack flipped on to the next page. "Not even any of the rarer street drugs." He pointed to a column full of NEG results and flipped to the third page. "But they did fancier stuff like serum and urine protein electrophoresis and tests I can't even pronounce. See?"

I frowned at the graph. It reminded me of math class, with one big peak and a bunch of other, little peaks. I glanced at Jefferson, who maintained his poker face, and waited for Jack to explain.

Jack said, "They've included a normal graph, so you can see the difference. Her serum albumin is low, and she had an abnormal amount of globulins in the urine."

Jefferson cocked an eyebrow at me. I nearly smiled. He didn't get this mumbo-jumbo either.

Jack threw up his hands. "The bottom line is, they only did these tests because I was pressing them to do everything. But this was a weird result. I mean, they didn't expect Elena to have any blood or kidney disease like multiple myeloma. So I paid them to do some work on their own time, and they're isolating a strange protein they found in her urine that might be the cause of this."

I said slowly, "You mean you might have found the wolf bait."

He grinned at me. "Bingo."

I slammed my fist on the futon cushion. "I knew it! That fucking chicken!" Someone poisoned that chicken. Someone poisoned Elena.

Jefferson cleared his throat.

I glanced at him. "Um. Sorry."

"No offense taken," he said. "I wanted to let you know that we were concurrently performing tests on the chicken remains found at the site."

"And?" My heart drummed in my throat. Everything was coming together at once. My mouth dried out.

He glanced at Jack. "Our results are not final. However, we also believe the chicken had been tampered with, and we should isolate the contaminant shortly."

I stood up. Less than two feet of space remained between us, close enough to intimidate most humans. "How soon?"

He held up his hands. "It's not up to me. I don't control the laboratory."

"Gisèle flies back from Prague at 5:30. I'm closing the deal for the land next week. We need those results yesterday." I turned to Jack. "Would it help if your labs collaborated? Yours got a sample of the chicken and his lab got some of the blood or urine?"

"We have both," said Jefferson. "Dr. Flores supplied us with a sample."

Jack's nostrils flared and he stared at Jefferson with bald dislike before he shook his head. "My lab workers are used to working with human bodily fluids. If I sent them a chicken, they'd think I was whacked. We'll have to wait."

"Okay," I said. I turned toward Jefferson again. I leaned my upper body toward him, not in a sexual way, but in a domineering way. "You're not telling us all you know."

"I prefer to gather the information first." He didn't lean away from me. He stood his ground.

I shook my head. "Our lives are at risk here." I glanced at Jack and decided to put all my cards on the table. "Jack already brought up the question of someone hunting us. Tonight it occurred to me that he might be even smarter than that. We're doing all the leg work, but we're the ones who buried Elena and covered up her death. If he turns us all in to the cops and frames us for murder—"

Jefferson digested that. "We have no evidence he'll do that."

"Fuck the evidence," said Jack. He stood up too, facing Jefferson. He was shorter by a few inches, but I would have bet on him in a fight, based on the energy coiled in his body. "We're the ones whose lives are at stake. Tell us what you know."

Jefferson shook his head. "I came to give you information about Darryl McEachern, not to speculate about the contaminant." He nodded at each of us and turned his feet toward the front door.

"Wait," I said, reaching for his arm. I let my hand drop before I made contact. Jefferson was not a guy we could browbeat into giving us information. We had to change tactics. "I'm sorry. We're on the same team."

He didn't answer, but his breathing slowed a little. He kept his eye on Jack.

Jack nodded. Eventually, he said, "Thanks for telling us that your lab is on the same track." He paused. "What I'd really like to know is how we could detect this bait so that if this bastard tries it on any of us again, we'll catch him. Like if we could smell it—"

Jefferson shook his head. "Obviously, the chicken sample is no longer in its original state. But the first sample smelled like ordinary chicken to the human technicians and to the few wers present."

I filed that away. It still begged the question of how that baited chicken had lured Elena from the campsite. But I agreed that when Jack and I had checked out the "investigation site" even the next day, neither of us had seen or smelled anything out of the ordinary.

"Ideally, of course, we'd like to get another sample," said Jefferson. He glanced at me. I held up my hands. As far as I knew, I hadn't stored any wolf bait in my pockets from the campsite.

I mused aloud, "Maybe our noses aren't good enough."

Both men stared at me. I said, "I once read a book about the sense of smell. They said that dogs can smell so well, it's the equivalent of being able to find a chocolate bar in a city the size of Philadelphia. It's that acute. I don't know if we're that sharp in wolf form. And we're not sharp at all in human form."

"You want to get some dogs involved in this?" asked Jack.

I nodded slowly. "If we can get another sample."

He and I exchanged a look.

Tonight we'd learned a few things. First of all, we'd learned the identity of our public enemy number one. But we'd also found out that werewolf bait existed, and that we had no means of detecting it.

CHAPTER 54

After Jefferson left, I sat in his spot on the futon, and Jack dropped beside me. He draped his arm around me. "There's one more thing I wanted to mention."

"What's that?" I asked, slightly distracted by the scent of Jefferson lingering in the cushions, a slightly sweet, spicy smell that reminded me of pipe tobacco.

"I talked with the pathologist I know. He said that if the drug is a protein, it might load up our kidneys. And the liver and kidneys do most of drug metabolism anyway. He said it might be useful to do a kidney biopsy. So I talked to Dr. Flores, and she's going to do some more analysis on the samples she collected on the scene, but she warned me that since Elena, ah, passed away right after eating the chicken, she might not have had a chance to metabolize anything. So I volunteered."

I gaped at him.

He shrugged. "If the guy got Elena at the campground, all of us were probably exposed. It might be out of my system by now, but it might not." He paused. "I gave some samples a few weeks ago, and my serum and urine protein electrophoresis looked weird too." He glanced at me. "Maybe that's because we're werewolves. But in case it was the wolf bait, I got a kidney biopsy today."

"What?" Someone punched a hole in my man? I gritted my teeth. "That sounds painful."

He grimaced. "It only took a few minutes. She had an ultrasound to guide her, and she took a few samples, punching through the skin. Anyway, it's done."

"You got one of the doctors to do it?" I didn't like the sound of any of it. We'd always tried to keep our DNA out of the medical system if we could help it. Now Elena's samples had probably made the rounds of the McGill University Health Centre, and Jack's were about to join them.

He shook his head. "I got my vet friend to do it. Don't worry, she's one of us."

I relaxed slightly, hearing that she was a wer, but I had to ask, "A vet?"

"Don't look like that. Honestly, some of their equipment is better than the stuff they use on humans. It's all private system, you know. They can afford the best."

"You paid her for the biopsy?" Of course it was a her.

He blushed slightly. "She wouldn't take any money. I paid for drinks."

I stared at him. The flush rose higher in his cheeks, and he didn't quite meet my eye.

"One of your ex-girlfriends?" I asked, tapping my foot.

He shrugged. "We're still friends."

"I just bet you are." I didn't know what exactly a kidney biopsy entailed, but I imagined him peeling off his shirt and lying very still while a gorgeous woman leaned over him with a needle and cooed, "This won't hurt a bit."

"It's not like that, Leila. She's married now. We're running buddies."

I hoisted an eyebrow. He and I hooked up as running buddies oh so long ago.

"And anyway, I told you. That's old news. You and I are the current event. No room for anyone else."

I exhaled. Jack would always be surrounded by other women. Friends, ex-lovers, would-be lovers. I'd have to get used to it if we had an ant's chance of survival. I smiled slightly at him. "All right."

"More than all right." He kissed me thoroughly. By the time he finished, I'd lost my breath and my train of thought. I ran my hand over his back and encountered a bandage. "Does this hurt too much?"

He shook his head. His teeth gleamed in the dim light. "I'll go on top. Or we could try sitting with you on my lap." He peeled off my capri pants and underwear and guided me into position, sitting in his lap while he sat cross-legged.

"You're still dressed," I pointed out, even though I ground down obediently on him.

He squeezed my ass cheeks. "Just checking you out. And I have to say, Grade A."

I threw my head back and laughed before I unfastened his jeans. He lowered me down on the couch and licked and nuzzled me to near-orgasm before he sank his cock deep into my cunt, bringing up feelings so intense that tears sprang to my eyes.

While he rode me, I stroked his back. My hand ran into the bandage again. How far would Jack go to find this murderer?

And what would we do to him once we found him?

These thoughts should have sobered me. Instead, they aroused me more.

Jack met my eyes. His were black, almost blind with lust. That drove me over the edge, and I climaxed, a short, hard spasm before I rode him a few more times, grinding my way to two more peaks while he roared his own approval.

We lay in bed together, our legs tangled, sweaty, our chests pressed against each other, feeling our breathing. Jack said, "You're mine."

I didn't answer. I wasn't ready to admit it yet. I stroked his hair and kissed his forehead. If I'd opened my mouth, I might have told him I loved him. And right at this moment, I'd rather close my eyes and fall asleep like this, pretending we lived in a fairy tale.

Chapter 55

The Accidental Murderer

Darryl flipped through the motel's TV channels until one line caught his ear. "They say you can take the boy out of the country, but you can't take the country out of the boy."

Usually, Darryl would've snorted at the actors in cowboy hats, but tonight it made him think of his father, who ran so hard to get away from the country.

Dad took off to a fancy university with an even fancier research lab, but he ended up zeroing on one passion: wolf bait.

People had tried all sort of wolf bait over the centuries. Dad used to love telling war stories. In Russia, hunters sometimes took a live dog into the woods, sliced its flesh with a knife, and rubbed poison into its bloody wounds. The dog was left to die while spilling enough blood on to the ground to attract hungry wolves.

Darryl had nightmares about the poor, trusting dogs, stabbed and poisoned and potentially eaten alive, even before Dad described how a poisoned wolf might writhe and even run for several kilometres before dying in agony.

People tried other methods, too: scattering poison, which might get eaten by ravens, arctic foxes, raccoons, wolverines, or even a snowy owl or white-tailed eagle. They might go with leg traps instead or hunt wolves with dogs. Or nowadays, a lot of wolves just ended up as roadkill.

"It's simply not humane," said Dad. "What I want to do is build a better mousetrap. Or in my case, wolf trap. Lure the wolves and send 'em somewhere else."

Grandad hated wolves, too. He'd shot one years ago and hung its head above the wood stove. "They said there weren't any wolves in Glengarry, but they were wrong. There's the proof," he used to say, jabbing his index finger at the moth-eaten wolf's head.

Darryl sipped his lukewarm beer, remembering the way that wolf's beady black eyes caught the light.

Wolves seemed to be the only part of the country that stuck with Dad, but they stuck hard. He devoted his whole career to wolf bait, which was kind of nuts because no one wanted to fund it. Dad spent more time writing grant applications than he did mixing chemicals.

But one day he came home glowing. He thumped a case of beer on the kitchen table and called a bunch of his lab friends over. "They thought sodium fluoroacetate was the solution, but Osama bin Ladin could wipe us out if he got a hold of that one," Dad announced. "I like my poisons to be specific, and by George, I think I've done it. Even coyotes won't touch these crystals. Only wolves. I'm going to be rich!"

As usual, Dad didn't make much sense even before he got drunk and started singing "Bloody Mary Morning." Darryl snuck away and looked up sodium fluoroacetate. Took him a few times for Google to figure out the right spelling, but it turned out to be a tasteless, colourless, odorless poison. Yup, that could be dangerous in the wrong hands. Some psycho even killed 73 animals at a Brazillian zoo, including an elephant and a pygmy anteater, by poisoning their food with this substance.

So Dad had made a new poison for wolves. Darryl downed a few Molsons and didn't think too much about it until dear old Dad kicked off and Darryl found a locked box inside the safety deposit box.

Darryl unlocked the box with another key on his Dad's keychain and found an amber flask labeled DEW6374N.

Inside the flask? White crystals, rough and irregular, kind of like the sea salt one of Darryl's girlfriends used to sprinkle around the apartment to "improve the energy."

Darryl sniffed the flask. Couldn't smell anything.

He stopped up the flask, pressing the cork back in tightly, and re-locked it in the box. He shelved the box in his closet and almost forgot about it, until one night he got to thinking about the land. Grandad's land. Where the wolves used to roam.

Darryl didn't hate wolves like his Dad and Grandad did. Darryl saved his hate for the real problem: useless people.

Useless people about to steal his land, unless Darryl managed to scare them away.

Now, most people couldn't even stand coyotes howling at night, and coyotes are only about the size of a Collie dog. A third the size of a wolf.

If dear old Dad had actually made anything useful, this bait might attract some real wolves in the area and drive out the city slickers who wanted Darryl's birthright. The same thumb-suckers who were going to visit the land this weekend, as the Armenian guy let slip.

So Darryl bought a chicken. Based on Dad's stories, he should have bought a real one and cut its head off, which Darryl knew how to do, but he didn't want to pluck it or have feathers strewn on the ground. If Dad's bait worked, Darryl didn't need blood to lure the wolves, anyway.

Darryl wanted to turn the crystals into a liquid, but he didn't know if he should add water or what. What if the darn thing exploded? In the end, he shoved some pinches of crystal between the skin and the chicken flesh while wearing gloves.

On Friday, Darryl drove his pickup truck to the campsite, ignoring the PRIVATE PROPERTY. NO TRESPASSING signs.

He avoided the main building. The wolves might not come up to the bright light. Darryl just wanted the wolves close enough to scare away the city bastards.

He used wire to hook the chicken to a medium tree branch overhanging the river. He was pretty sure the average dog couldn't leap that high, and he didn't want any bear or fox to get the meat before the wolves could.

That afternoon, Darryl munched on a stale piece of bread while staked out at the abandoned farm across the river from the baited tree. He'd rigged up his camera to take infrared pictures and video. He'd found the instructions to make an infrared camera on YouTube—basically, fixing a piece of old-fashioned film over the camera lens—and figured it couldn't hurt. After the city bitches got scared off, Darryl might bring the film to the old Armenian guy and negotiate the price down some more. "I'm sorry, sir, but I'll have to decrease the price if you've got wolves running across your campground."

Darryl heard a van pull up around five o'clock, earlier than he'd expected. Soon afterward, he spotted movement on the campground side of the river.

What the—?

216

Darryl grabbed his binoculars. A tall, blond woman sprinted toward him, running faster than any woman he'd ever seen.

Darryl steadied his binoculars with his left hand and placed his hand on his shotgun. He'd never shoot a woman, but if she ran like that at him…

The woman dashed at the tree with the baited chicken.

Darryl's jaw dropped open, but he watched her crouch her legs. She sprang into the air, hands clawed in readiness for that chicken.

She missed.

She snarled.

Goosebumps rose on Darryl's forearms. She sounded like an animal. A dog, maybe.

No. Not a dog.

The woman grasped the lowest tree branch. Her shoes dug for purchase in the bark before she grabbed a toehold and started skimming up the tree.

This early in the year, no tree had properly unfurled its leaves, so Darryl got a clear view of her heaving herself on to the branch where he'd tied the chicken.

The branch swayed and bent with her weight as she started crawling along its length. Toward the chicken.

Holy—

Darryl he knew he should take off, that it was dangerous watching her, but his heart was thundering and he was riveted.

He watched her try to swing the chicken up toward her. Her hands slipped on the greasy skin. She sniffed and moaned in a way that made the hair stand up on the back of her neck. She sounded feral and frightening and sexual all mixed up together.

She licked her hands and made a high-pitched cry before she lunged at the chicken again. Somehow, this time, she managed to hold it and unloop the wire at the same time.

And then she started tearing into the raw chicken with her teeth.

Darryl could hear chicken bones snapping. He could hear her smack and chew.

It was like a horror movie, only Darryl was living it.

This woman was devouring his raw, baited chicken.

She sat on the branch, both legs dangling on either side, while she used both hands and bent her head over the carcass. With the binoculars, he could even see the blood staining her mouth and hands.

Darryl could almost smell the raw flesh. His stomach turned, but he didn't puke.

Instead, he finally grabbed his camera. Even with the strongest zoom, it didn't look like much, just a whitish blob in a tree.

Until she fell out of the tree.

It happened so fast.

She banged on the riverbank and made a wet thunk, like a melon smashing open.

Her front half, including her head, sprawled into the river.

Darryl didn't know what to do.

He couldn't just let her die.

On the other hand, he wasn't that good a swimmer himself, which meant he'd have trouble getting across the river. The chicken had bounced into the river too and was already out of sight.

And even though Darryl'd never admit it aloud, the way the woman ran and howled, the way she scarfed down the bloody, baited chicken— well, it didn't make Darryl want to approach her. Even with his .45 to protect him.

He dug in his back pocket. He could always call 911.

Her body shifted slowly but unmistakably. And then the river gave one last tug and her body swept downstream.

Darryl flipped open his phone. He had to prepare his story. Why was he camped out across the river, spying on an abandoned campsite? He could get arrested for trespassing at least.

Maybe he could just say he heard a scream. And then he could hang up.

But they'd trace the cell phone number and know it was him.

So he'd hung a chicken on a tree. They couldn't arrest him for that.

But he still had the flask of wolf bait on him. What if they took it away?

A man's voice called. Darryl closed his phone and raised his camera. Shadowy white shapes raced in the distance.

They'd noticed she was gone.

They'd take care of her.

He should drive away now, before they spotted him.

Instead, he stayed frozen in place. Would they find her in time? The river hooked around the bend, so it couldn't carry her too far, and in the spring, the water level rose high but didn't flow as fast. This year wasn't as wet as usual, so the water level was lower.

And the current was stronger.

Darryl tightened the laces on his boots. He didn't want to take 'em off, even though they'd weigh him down. He started to make his way to the river's edge, real slow. The light was fading fast and the moon hadn't risen yet.

One guy came running crouched over, bent close to the ground.

Darryl retreated, whispering a prayer.

The way the guy bent over, he almost looked like he was running on all fours. Like a dog. Or something Darryl might shoot when he went hunting.

The thing beat it back to the camp, shouting, "Mac! Mac!"

Darryl touched his gun again. How many of them were there?

Voices yelled in the distance. Four shapes burst out of the trees. They fanned across the river.

Splash. One guy waded through the water. And then he howled.

The worst sound yet. A sound that froze Darryl's blood and nearly loosed his bladder. A high-pitched cry of alarm and mourning.

Like a wolf.

Darryl reached for his camera. His hands shook, but he turned it on.

CHAPTER 56

Leila

When Jack rose off the futon, he paused, mid-bend, for fraction of a second. I knew the biopsy site hurt more than he let on.

"Hey," I said softly. Morning light spilled through the off-white blinds.

"Hey," he said. "I've got to get going. And I'm doing a night shift tonight. But I'll call you." He glanced at the manila envelope on the coffee table. "We're closing in on the wolf bait man."

I shook my head. "I hate that."

Jack quirked an eyebrow.

"Wolf bait sounds like we're animals. I thought of another name last night, while you were sleeping. As far as we know, it disappears almost without a trace. So far, we can't smell it and it's almost invisible." I hesitated. "Kind of like ice."

He nodded. "I don't know if you know this, but that's one of the street names for crystal meth. Have you ever seen it?"

I shook my head. "You're looking at one of the last goody-goodies in the world. But I've heard of it." Crystal meth. Crack for the new millennium.

"Right." He scowled into the distance. "Well. I guess this is like ice for us."

"In more ways than one," I said. "Get it? Icing someone used to mean killing them. So this is something addictive for us. Something that can kill us. Werewolf ice."

"Werewolf ice." He paused. "Wolf ice."

Wolf ice. I closed my eyes, thinking of how this might play out. We'd always talked about the government or paramilitary wackos getting a hold of wers and trying to control us. But if wolf ice got out, it wouldn't matter who employed it. They could out all the wers. And, judging from Elena's reaction, every one of us could be enslaved.

I stood up. Jack reached for my hand, but I shook it off. This was too big. "Armageddon," I said. Apocalypse right now.

"Not necessarily," said Jack. He kept his voice even. "So far, we've got one guy who knows how to use it. We need to figure out who's got the recipe and who's got the supply."

"And take him or her out," I said. I bit my lip and didn't realize it until I tasted blood.

I don't advocate murder, but for my species, I would do anything.

Jack nodded and checked his watch. "Let me tell the district heads. Yours, mine, and Bernard."

While he called and e-mailed and got the whole security chain on alert, I paced my apartment. This was bigger than all of us now. This could be the end of us. Worldwide.

Was it all linked to the land? It seemed farfetched, but someone had planted the wolf ice chicken on the campground. Either he'd figured out we were werewolves and had followed us to the site nearly a month ago, or the same guy who wanted to buy the land had tried to sabotage us.

I started with the millionaire. Darryl MacEachern. At least I knew the guy's ID, license plate, and practically his underwear size. He couldn't run or hide forever. I needed to track him down. I needed to pry the recipe and any leaks out of him.

I read through Jefferson's envelope more carefully. More photos. Even a few grade school photos, for whatever good that might do me. A copy of his rental agreement, which at least verified his address. That firearms card. No marriage license—apparently the guy was single.

I frowned. A lone wolf. Dangerous.

But, more importantly, where did he get that million dollars? If he inherited it, where did the money come from? No millionaire's kid I knew got his jollies shoveling manure.

I set the envelope beside my computer and started Googling. I hit pay dirt with the local Glengarry newspaper section. In addition to the obituary from Jefferson, I found a small article on Darryl II. (Our target was Darryl III. They couldn't even think of new names for their progeny. That gave me comfort.)

Where did the father used to work?

Wexler Pharmaceutical in Pointe Claire.

Even that might not be too lucrative, working for a drug company. Big pharma didn't get big by paying its employees all its profits. So I wasn't surprised to discover that Daddy's main research interest was wolf bait. In 1999, he scored a personal patent for a drug he developed on his own time. A Russian company paid him money for the rights and a few years later, so did a U.S. hunting group.

Still didn't sound like seven figures to me. I kept searching.

The original Darryl, the grandfather, owned a farm. Darryl Jr. sold it off. Although I couldn't track down the details, I bet my eyeteeth that the farmland had included our campsite.

Hmm. The land money plus wolf ice payouts, carefully invested, could easily reach a million dollars or more over the years.

Jack glanced over my shoulder. "Anything interesting?"

"You betcha. His dad passed on the wolf ice recipe and the million dollars to buy our campsite."

Jack whistled. "Time for another round." He started texting the group while I plotted my next move.

I couldn't put Elena's van officially up for sale without "her" signature. So I might as well put the finances on hold until she flew back from Prague.

In the meantime, I had to track down the wolf ice. I wanted to destroy any cache plus eradicate the recipe.

I glanced at Jack, who was talking on the phone and running this fingers through his already-tousled black hair. I remembered that bandage on his back. What if we'd all be exposed and we were about to die anyway from kidney poisoning?

I'd go down swinging. I'd go down protecting my pack, including Jack, until the bitter end.

He saw me watching me and smiled at me. I smiled back, showing my teeth more than necessary.

"Let's start with Wexler Pharmaceutical," I muttered to myself. I mapped it out. It sat on that same Highway 40. Darryl MacEachern must have driven right by it on his way to the truck stop. Was that why he'd turned around? To try and get a fresh supply?

I couldn't waltz in there and ask for a wolf ice recipe. But I might be able to sniff out a few details. Like who was working on that project.

Tracking through Google Scholar and patent applications, I figured out that Darryl Jr. had worked mostly on blood pressure medication in his final years. The wolf ice seemed to be a mostly solo project he'd explored up to year 2000 or so, on his own time, which explained why he'd kept the patent. In the 1990's, though, he shared some credit with a certain Dr. William Nash.

Dr. Nash, also of Wexler Pharmaceutical.

Dr. Nash, who had retired last year.

When I narrowed my search Dr. Nash, I couldn't understand a lot of his papers, but he seemed to do basic science stuff using animal models. Not wolves, except for the one time he helped out his colleague.

If anyone knew anything, it was Dr. Nash.

And then I downloaded a newsletter PDF and zoomed in on a picture of Dr. Nash grinning at a conference in Ireland. Although they'd cropped the photo, I noted pitchers of beer on the table in front of him.

I fine-tuned the map of Wexler Pharmaceuticals, plotting the bars and restaurants in its immediate vicinity.

Then I dialed Wexler and asked for Dr. Nash.

"I'm sorry, he's no longer with the company," said the receptionist.

My heart thumped. She didn't sound like a teenager, and she didn't say he wasn't listed in the directory. So maybe she actually knew who he was and where he'd gone.

"That's a shame. I wanted to talk to him about one of his papers on pupillary dilatation in mice."

The secretary hesitated. I could practically feel her reluctance. Ninety percent of staff would tell me to shove off right now. "We don't usually forward information to former employees, but if you want to leave your name and number…"

"Oh, that's okay. Does he still hang out at the Rusty Nail?" I named a local pub almost directly across the street from Wexler Pharma.

She laughed. "I'm not supposed to say."

Bingo.

CHAPTER 57

Jack popped over my shoulder after I hung up. "I've got to head. What're you up to?"

I shook my head and smiled. "I'm on the trail."

He paused, fingering his keys. "I don't like the sound of that."

I shrugged. "Someone's got to do it."

"Leila." He faced me and held both my shoulders in his hands. "I'm not leaving until you tell me."

I considered lying to him. I don't know why, except part of me wanted to run out to Pointe Claire, gunblade blazing, like something out of Final Fantasy.

"Don't bullshit me," he said, not unkindly.

"You can't come with me," I said. "You've got to rest before your night shift."

"What are you doing that you don't want me along?"

I sighed. He knew me too well. "I'm off to see one of the wolf ice wizards. Or that's what I figure." I showed him my Internet trail leading to Dr. Nash. "Darryl Jr. is dead and he's the main player. This is the only secondary one I could find."

He frowned at the picture of the grey-haired, balding main smiling over his pints of Guinness. "You don't think we should hit Darryl III first?"

"I will. But my gut tells me he's not the one making wolf ice. I could be wrong, but I think his dad had the recipe, and Dr. Nash might be the only one still brewing it."

Jack wrinkled his forehead. "I'll come with you."

"You said—"

"I don't have to sleep."

I looked into his slightly bloodshot eyes. I thought about how many nights we'd spent rocking our casbah instead of sleeping through the night. He'd spend his twelve-hour shift driving, hauling patients up and down stairs, and possibly saving their lives. "I know you don't have to. But I'd worry about you rolling your ambulance."

"It's no big deal. I probably won't sleep anyway."

I sighed and told him the truth. "I'm going to a bar in the middle of the day to try and meet a senior citizen. Nothing is going to happen. Please."

He shook his head. "I don't like it."

"I know, baby. But I think you need rest more than you need to worry about me."

He lifted his head as if something in my tone of voice caught his attention. Finally, he blew his breath out of both cheeks and repeated, "I don't like it."

I didn't answer. I squeezed his hand.

As I locked the door behind us, my cell phone rang. Mr. Tabassian said, "Hello, Leila. How are you?" Without pausing to hear an answer, he said, "Can we do the final papers on Friday? How does 10 a.m. sound?"

"You mean tomorrow?" I checked my calendar, but I already knew what the problem was, even without the bright white circle marking Sunday night. The night of the full moon. "Why don't we stick with our meeting on Tuesday?" That might give me time to talk to Gisèle and put up the ads for the van. Minimal chance of selling it in a few days, but if we had everything except ten grand, he might accept a later installment. Also, we'd have snapped back to fully human by then.

Jack watched me, eyes dark with concern.

Mr. Tabassian clicked his tongue in a way that made my stomach drop into my pelvis. "That's a shame, Leila. I hate to say this, but I need to close the deal with you this week. The papers and the money."

I'd never heard Mr. T talk like this. Normally he was much more jolly, like a nice old uncle. Today he sounded more like he'd taken lessons from Donald Trump. Or Machiavelli.

On the other hand, maybe I was getting too paranoid. A Friday morning meeting would still keep us more than 48 hours from the full moon. Elena used to work until a few hours before. Of course, she didn't start warping into wolf mode the day of, like Laurent.

I exhaled between my teeth. "I am absolutely unavailable on the Sunday. Even Saturday would be difficult."

He chuckled. "That's no problem with me, Leila. Like I said, I want everything wrapped up like a Christmas present on Friday. The weekend's all yours."

It sounded legit. And yet real estate is like renovations: always plan to spend twice as long and three times as much as you budgeted.

But the sooner we had the land, the better. And if Laurent literally got too hairy, I could find another lawyer for the meeting.

"Are you still there, Leila?"

"I'm here, Mr. Tabassian. I'll have to check Mr. Laforest's schedule. Could I get back to you?"

He sighed. "I didn't want to tell you this, Leila, but the other buyer, you remember him?"

My hand tightened on my cell phone. Jack moved closer to me as if he could protect me. I said, "Of course."

"He's been hanging around a lot. Trying to get me to change my mind. Now he's got the money and it's certified."

"I see," I said automatically, while my brain whirled. The land. Gone.

"I'm an old man, Leila. I'm close to my retirement. I don't need this kind of aggravation. You know what I mean?"

"Yes."

"I want this settled one way or another. This land, it's turning into a great big headache. The other guy pressured me into a meeting first thing Monday morning. I said okay, but I figured I'd get it settled with you guys first. Then I can cancel my meeting with him and not have to worry anymore."

My heart beat in my throat. "I understand." Jack raised his eyebrows questioningly, but I turned away from him. "I'm sorry to hear about these…high pressure tactics. We would never do that at Green Belt Montreal."

"I know, I know, Leila. Why do you think I'm giving you a break?"

"Thank you, Mr. Tabassian. We'll work out the details on Friday."

"You bring the money and the lawyers, I'll bring the papers. See you at ten in my office." He hung up.

"Mr. T?" asked Jack as I closed my phone.

"Wants the deal done on Friday."

Jack frowned. "You won't have the money yet."

"I'll have most of it. I'm more worried about climate change." That was one of our code words for the full moon. On our way out the door, I phoned Laurent and explained our latest pickle.

Laurent didn't speak for a long moment. "You and I should meet on Friday at 9 a.m. before we meet with him."

I tightened my grip on the receiver. So much depended on this. "Laurent, you don't have to come to this meeting. Maybe one of the more junior partners could represent the firm."

His voice dropped ten degrees into freezing territory. "Leila, I have worked on this deal since its inception, and I will carry it through. It is the least I can do." His voice dropped a little. He was thinking of Elena.

"I appreciate that, Laurent. I don't doubt your legal capacity or your integrity." Only your ability to stay 100 percent human lawyer. "I only thought the timing and the climate might not work out well for you."

His breath hissed out between his teeth. "I don't foresee any problems. I'll see you at 9 a.m., Leila." He hung up.

If anyone knew how well Laurent could handle moonrise, it would be Laurent. And we weren't even talking moonrise. Over two days before moonrise. He should be Just Fine.

Still, when I snapped the phone closed, uneasiness danced up and down my spine. And I shivered even though Jack reached for my hand.

#

The Rusty Nail sat between a chain bookstore and a sushi house in a sprawling mall. I stared at the black sign with gold lettering, complete with a red-speckled nail below the title.

Sheer cheese. I bet their beer cost over six bucks.

I pushed open the door. My eyes took a second to adjust to the dim interior and focus on the scuffed black floor and leather-ish booths. A few people dotted the bar, but at 4:30 p.m., it was a little early for the after-work rush.

I smoothed my hands on my dark wash jeans. I was aiming for fresh and pretty, not slutty, so I'd pulled my hair into a ponytail and picked a pink ruffled cap sleeve blouse that simultaneously said "I'm cute" and "look at my biceps." Low red heels added edge to my outfit, and when I clicked my way from the doorway, more than a few male heads looked up.

I walked up to the extra-tanned, too-cute bartender and asked for directions to a nearby Indian restaurant. When I feigned confusion, he drew me a map using the condensation on the bartop.

"Thanks," I said. "Hey, could I get a beer, since I've been so much trouble? What have you got on tap?"

I'm not a huge beer person, so I picked whatever sounded the least offensive, which turned out to be a blond beer. "A tiny one. I'm driving," I said.

Then I clicked my way over to a table and surveyed the room while I pretended to sip my drink. A few young guys clumped together around the sports screen. Nope. A serious, red-nosed businessman drained a pint without making eye contact. No, too young.

A white-haired man on a barstool glanced at the television, but his gaze kept tugging toward me, the interloper in the bar. I checked him out using my peripheral vision. He looked a little older and jowlier than his conference picture a few years ago, but his low-set eyes and even the light beard were still the same.

He probably wouldn't hit on me, since he was three times my age. It would have to be my move.

I picked up my glass and started walking toward the bathroom. About five feet away from the man of interest, I sloshed beer on my arm. "Shoot!" I held my drink at arm's length and dripped on to the floor.

Dr. Nash offered me a paper napkin. "Would this help?" My ears perked up at his British accent.

"If you had about ten more," I said, sinking into the chair beside him. I placed the beer on the counter and started mopping up my arm. He handed me another napkin, and I used that too. I made a face. "Now I'm going to smell like beer, and if the cops stop me for a breathalyzer, they won't believe a negative reading." I tossed the beer napkin balls on the counter. The bartender took them and handed me a few more. I smiled at him.

Dr. Nash smiled at me. "It's not as bad as all that. You can wash up."

I glanced at the bathrooms, where I'd been heading. "That's true. Would you mind watching my drink?"

His brows knitted together.

I explained, "To make sure no one puts anything in it. Like the date rape drug. I was trying to bring it with me, but I don't want to spill it on my head this time."

Dr. Nash shook his head. "I don't think you have to worry about that here, my dear. But of course I'd be happy to guard your drink if it would make you feel better."

"It would. Thank you so much." I sashayed to the restroom. When I came back, freshly scrubbed with watery pink soap, I slid back on to the barstool beside Dr. Nash, "Thanks. Am I interrupting you?"

"Oh, no." He folded up his newspaper and pushed it off to the side.

I pointed at it. "Did anything interesting happen today?"

"I'm afraid nothing but the usual misery."

True story. "So why do you read it, then?"

He shrugged. "An inveterate habit. I like to keep up with the world, no matter how foolish and haphazard it may seem to our human eye."

"You have a sophisticated vocabulary," I said.

"Thank you, my dear. A product of boarding schools, I'm afraid."

"You probably went to a lot of other schools, too," I said. "What university? I'm a McGill grad!"

He laughed and shook his head. "I attended an assortment of universities. I started my undergraduate studies in England, probably before you were born..."

I nodded, wide-eyed, while he gave me a more detailed c.v. After he wound down, I said, "Wow! So what did you do with all your degrees?"

"I became a biochemist."

"That's great!"

"I wish it had been," he said, taking a good taste of his beer.

"Did you discover anything famous?"

"No, my work focused on the basic sciences, which is the foundation for all the applied sciences you read about in the newspapers. I started at Oxford University..."

I waited him out, nodding and smiling, until I could work a word in. "You know what I studied? Biology! I love animals! Did you ever work with animals?"

"I did use some rat models in the '90s. You may have heard..."

I wouldn't have if I hadn't Googled him. I tried to steer him a little closer. Otherwise, I'd spend all afternoon talking about his glory days with rodents. "Rats creep me out!" I giggled with a little fake shiver. "But I know it's hard to work with any animals at all. All those ethics committees, right?"

He paused. "Well. I did work with other mammals at one time."

I lowered my voice and leaned closer. "Really?"

His eyes flicked down to the V in my blouse, even though I don't have a lot to show there. He said, "Er. Yes. With wolves, actually."

"Wolves!" I shuddered and leaned even closer.

"Yes. It was primarily the work of one of my colleagues, but I assisted him with a seminal paper on, ah, wolf attraction."

I frowned. "You mean helping them mate?"

He chuckled. "No, no." He coughed into his hand. "Luring wolves. Wolf bait. You understand."

"Ohhh. But what would you do with them if you caught them?" I tried to erase any condemnation from my tone and project innocent puzzlement.

"Well. As I said, it wasn't really my project. I'm afraid most people want to, er, trap them to prevent them from killing their livestock. But I worked on the distillation of the bait, if you will."

I bit my lower lip. "You helped mix up the recipe?"

"Oh, no! My colleague was far too...private for that. He was the only one who knew the precise concoction. I was strictly his assistant for the experimental arm."

I held up a finger. "Oh, I think I know what you're talking about. He couldn't tell you because only he and the company held that secret formula. Like, I saw these commercials on YouTube about the Cadbury secret?"

Dr. Nash nearly choked on his pint. I made a note to back off on the bimbo routine and offered him a napkin. He waved it off and cleared his throat a few times.

I said, "Sorry. I know you guys were working on something more important than chocolate bars. But I did hear that the company always hangs on to the recipes."

He smiled briefly. "Well. Ordinarily that is how it works, but my colleague did have his ways. He'd been recruited from another company and somehow managed to personally maintain the patent."

Ah. Perhaps that was how Darryl Jr. managed to become a millionaire. "He must've been rich!"

"You might think so. However…" Dr. Nash shook his head. "Suffice to say, I don't believe that was the case. Most patents don't amount to a hill of beans."

So if he was telling me the truth, Darryl Jr. held the monopoly on wolf ice. And Darryl Jr. was six feet under. Better and better. I switched tracks. "Well, anyway, it's pretty amazing that you guys figured out this wolf bait. I mean, if you were in a forest and a bear was attacking you, does that mean you could spray wolf bait on the bear? Then the wolves would attack the bear, and it would totally save your life in a cool way!"

He threw back his head and laughed out loud. "I love the way young people think like a television cartoon."

Oh, yes. Young people. So terrifically empty-headed. I grinned and shrugged and dimpled at him.

He dabbed his lips with the handkerchief. "Actually, it wouldn't work quite that way. The effect of the wolf bait was too distracting."

I widened my eyes. "What do you mean?"

"They wouldn't attack the bear." He took a few more gulps of beer. "They wouldn't be thinking of the bear. They wouldn't be thinking at all." He drained his pint and set it on the counter.

"What would they be doing?" I clasped my hands together like he was telling me a bedtime story. I would have bought him another drink, but I didn't want to interrupt the flow of the story.

The bartender slid another pint toward him anyway. I reached for my wallet, but Dr. Nash shook his head at me and took another long pull. I knew he was mulling over how much to tell me. I stayed quiet.

Eventually he straightened his shoulders and lowered his voice. "The problem was that the bait did work as a lure, but its effect on the wolves themselves varied considerably. We had to run many sample studies before we understood the variance within the population."

In plain English, I thought that meant that wolf ice didn't affect all the wolves the same way. I frowned and nodded, not acting this time. I turned my ear toward him to pick up every murmured word.

"To continue your theoretical example, if we gave twenty wolves some of the wolf bait, twelve wolves might attack the bear—or each other. The majority of wolves became aggressive and angry. Even if we placed other distracting elements in the area, such as fresh meat or females in estrus, about sixty percent of the wolves would attack the most convenient target."

My shoulders tensed, but I tried to stay airy and cheery. "Sixty percent, huh? That would be scary!"

"Yes. Even under controlled conditions." He swirled his beer in his clear mug, clearly remembering.

I kept silent.

He cleared his throat. "Not that we had access to so many wolves or would have been so foolish as to treat more than one animal at a time."

I nodded solemnly, although part of me wished a wolf had bit Darryl Jr. good.

"Approximately a quarter of them...channeled their energy in another manner. They would mate." His entire face turned red, not only his cheeks. Since he was balding, he looked like a red egg.

My hand jerked. I disguised it by taking a sip of the beer. My heart hammered in my chest.

Dr. Nash raised his voice and spoke more rapidly. "The remaining percentage seemed to get ravenously hungry. If we didn't have meat, they would try eating earthworms or grasshoppers or whatever was around them. One of them even sank its teeth into another wolf's leg."

I closed my eyes and stuck my head in my pint. Elena. Elena the eater turned super-eater. That was the missing link. She'd smelled the chicken and taken off to her doom.

What were the chances that, out of five werewolves, the murderer would manage to attract the one super-eater with a baited chicken?

Did he know the effect it would have?

If he'd wanted to kill us straight out, he should've poisoned the chicken. That would have been faster than luring us. Also less risky, since there was a good chance most of us would have turned aggressive and attacked him or someone else in the vicinity.

A smart guy would have baited and poisoned the chicken. Since as far as I knew, they hadn't found any trace of poison in Elena's body, maybe Darryl III wasn't the sharpest chisel in the tool box.

Or maybe he was smarter than all of us and we hadn't figured him out yet.

But I was getting closer, damn it. I had deciphered a few more pieces of the puzzle.

"Are you all right?" asked Dr. Nash.

"Feeling a little woozy," I admitted, leaning over my beer.

"I shouldn't have told you such bloodthirsty stories," he said, smiling sadly. "A nice girl like you."

If only he knew. But I liked the old guy despite myself. He'd helped Darryl Jr. with research that helped enslave me, but I still thought Dr. Nash was a good egg. How crazy was that?

But more importantly, he was a key source of information. I chose my next questions carefully. "I'm glad you told me. It's weird to think about. though I mean, is there any way to tell how someone—some wolf—might react? You know, like grey wolves get mad but black wolves get hungry?"

"No, no. That's a fallacy. There's more variance within a population than between a population. It would be like predicting red hair would make you angry." He smiled. "Stereotypes notwithstanding. Suffice to say, we were never able to find sufficient predictors using physical or breeding characteristics. Our sample sizes were small, of course, but in the end, that was what limited the utility of my colleague's work. Hunters and farmers don't want aggressive wolves or wolves that become even hungrier, in one manner or another."

They wanted wolves that they could trap and kill easily.

"So you never made a million off of it?" I asked, trying to look wide-eyed instead of sickened.

He waved his hand at the bar. "My dear. If I made my million, I would be cruising in the Caribbean instead of whiling away my days at the Rusty Nail, present company excepted. No, it never went into commercial production, and its inventor was extremely secretive. I'm afraid it will be one of the inventions lost in the sands of time."

I instinctively believed him. But once I left here, I'd alert my group and the district heads about Dr. Nash. They'd arrange to search his apartment and whatever else, looking for wolf ice.

I'd have to warn them about the multiple effects, too. It would be safer if a trusted human came along for the ride.

Or not, in case the angry or hungry wers turned on him.

Would the wolf ice have such an effect on us in human form? And how human did we have to be? The full moon rose in two days. Some wers theorized that instead of transforming bang, one hundred percent when the full moon rose, we waxed and waned over the course of the month, like the moon. In which case we'd be more and less susceptible to wolf ice in a somewhat unpredictable way.

"Are there any other crazy inventions you came up with? Or do you hang out here all the time?" I asked. I made sure I chatted with Dr. Nash for a few more minutes before I sailed out the door with his eyes following my ass.

I let him look. I had more important things on my mind. We'd search Dr. Nash's place, but more crucially, we could now focus on the murderer.

He'd managed to lay his hands on a supply of wolf ice and had no qualms about using it. It might be a diminishing supply of wolf ice, but one we needed to control and destroy.

CHAPTER 58

Right after I sent the e-mail alert, the calls started fountaining in. I pulled over at the next strip mall that pockmarked the West Island and answered the next ring.

"Leila," said Jack into my ear.

My bones felt like they melted, hearing his voice. I straightened my spine and tried to sound stern. "You're supposed to be sleeping."

"I did. Enough. But I had to answer your message. The district heads are going to try and figure out what they can from the patent application and from all the tissue samples."

"Good." I realized my cheeks hurt from smiling. Oh, no. Gotta turn down this love thing.

"Yeah. And like you said, they're tuning in on Dr. Nash. Good work." His voice cut out a little.

"Thanks. Hey, where are you? You sound funny."

He paused. "I'm at the airport."

I exhaled. Rage boiled in my stomach.

"Her mother wasn't going to make it in time. Her flight got messed up."

I bet Gisèle's flights always came in early or at exactly the right time. "So they decided to call you, right before your 7 p.m. shift? Instead of a taxi?"

"I told them I could pick her up and still make it to my shift."

"Really? You're going to get caught in rush hour traffic." I knew all about that after my Master Tracker chase.

"We're taking the shuttle. We'll be okay."

She could take the shuttle by herself. But what this meant was, Gisèle was returning to Montreal. With Jack.

I tried to sound calm. "I thought we agreed it made more sense for her to stay out of the city, since she's supposed to be overseas and all."

"Just for tonight," he said.

"What's the point in that?"

"It's for a debriefing."

"With whom?" I asked. A mom and kids passing by glanced in my rental car, and I realized I'd raised my voice loud enough to be heard through the closed windows. "You're going to be working all night. Right?"

"She and I will talk while I take her back—"

"On the shuttle bus. Sounds nice and private." Real great place to talk about werewolf Armageddon.

"—and then she'll spend the night at Mac's place, catching up the rest of the Montreal crew."

"Really? Why wasn't I invited?"

He sighed. "Leila. Check your messages. I'm sure you got them. You were busy talking to this doctor, which was totally worthwhile. But don't freak out on me, okay?"

"I'm not freaking out."

"Good. Because I've got to go."

I hung up on him before he could cut me off.

I bent over the steering wheel, breathing fast and hard.

Scum-sucking motherfuckers never change.

You can fall in love with them. Twice.

You can fuck them over and over.

But they don't change.

I'd wasted enough time on Jack Meng.

Now, thanks to Dr. Nash, I knew why we'd hooked up so many times at the campsite. Jack and I were obviously part of the wolf ice Viagra club.

Once we got rid of the murderer and the wolf ice, Jack and I would have no reason to chase after each other any more.

No reason at all.

CHAPTER 59

If the murderer had shown up in front of me right then, I would have tried to strangle him with my bare hands. I was that furious.

Closer to the full moon, I would tear his throat out.

I imagined that. The murderer reared back in surprise, but my fangs ripped the skin out of his throat. The blood splattered in a wide arc. He took a step back, his eyes still wide and disbelieving before he collapsed to the ground and I ripped his guts out.

My breathing slowed. I unclenched my fists, leaving deep fingernail crescents in my palms.

I could think again.

First of all, I checked my messages. Sure enough, they'd flown fast and furious while I cozied up to Dr. Nash. I quickly scanned the ones about "Elena" and noted that Mac and Laurent had declined to pick her up before Jack offered. I gave him a quarter point for that one. But only a quarter point. The woman was fully grown. She could take the shuttle bus or a taxi on her own.

I turned to the ones from the district heads. Most of them were like memos, statements issued rather than any true discussion. Hierarchy has its privileges. Reading between the lines, though, I noted one thing kept cropping up:

Bernard had a plan.

No details forthcoming, but a lot of reassurance that it was under control and he would take care of things.

Much as I would love to sit back and pretend Daddy knew best, I couldn't buy that one.

What was his plan?

And did it involve his daughter, which would explain why she was flying back today?

I considered confronting Gisèle myself, showing up at the airport to pick her up and sending Jack on his merry way to work. But I might bust my boiler if I saw Gisèle rubbing herself against him right now.

So I made a lateral move and called Mac. "Hey. Got a minute?"

"About two. What is it?"

"This plan of Bernard's. Do you know anything about it?"

He paused. "Not too much."

Since he was at work, where it was practically a religion to eavesdrop, I decided to supply most of the information so he could yay or nay. "Does it have something to do with 'E'? And the upcoming 'climate change'?"

He stayed silent.

"I'm going to go out on a limb here. I'm guessing Jefferson has supplied him—and the entire local community—with the information about our target. I bet Bernard knows who it is, has maybe even met the guy a few times or seen him around. This is the country, after all."

Mac said, "Is this a question?"

"You're answering it by not answering, buddy. So let's say Papa has triangulated in on the target. Only problem is, right now the target is in Montreal, trying to buy up the land. Off of Papa's territory and far from where he can bring him to justice. So Papa decides he needs the guy to get closer. How can he do that?"

Mac said, "Would you care to speculate?"

"Thanks, I would. I think that since the target is aware of our secret, Papa will try and lure him back on to the land. On Sunday night. Using his daughter as the lure."

Mac paused. "I have not been privy to all the information. However, your conclusions are consistent with the data I have received thus far."

"Thanks, man. I appreciate it."

"Wait." For the first time, he lost his office robot voice. "What are you planning to do about it?"

"I'll let you know," I said. "Later, dude."

I hung up.

So Bernard was willing to set his own daughter up as bait for the killer. And she was willing to fly from Prague to do it.

In a way, I had to admire their huevos. Like me, they were willing to do whatever it took to take that man down.

Only problem was, their plan hinged on too many ifs. They had to get the target back on to the land, for one. I could see why Bernard

238

preferred taking the man out on his own territory, but that was a werewolf blind spot, banking too much on territory.

We had to take the murderer out right now. Before the full moon on Sunday.

I drove until I found a gas station with an outside phone booth. No need for anyone to listen in. And then, thanks to Jefferson's meticulous detective work, I dialed the murderer's cell phone.

He answered on the second ring.

"Good afternoon, Mr. MacEachern," I chirped, assuming a slight Southern drawl. "This is Réal Realty calling. How are you feeling today?"

He paused. "Good," he said. His voice was deeper than I'd expected.

"I'm so glad to hear it. Now, I don't want to take up too much of your time on a beautiful Thursday afternoon, but I understand you're looking for a piece of land."

A longer silence this time. "What did you say your name was again?"

I tittered. "Oh, I'm sorry. I'm new with the business. My name is Mrs. Lofton, and I'm with Réal Realty. Now, I know you're looking for some acreage near the Ontario-Quebec border. At least 25 acres, would you say?"

Silence. "Where did you get my name?"

"Oh, well, a little birdie told me you were in the market, and with the economy the way it is, we've all got to chase down every lead. Now, the nice thing about the area you've selected is that there's lots of farmland for sale in the area, and some of it is up to a hundred acres. If you think you can handle that, I'm free tomorrow afternoon to do some viewings."

His voice sharpened, but what he said was, "Really?"

"Oh my, yes. We always make time for our customers at Réal Realty." I could smell my own sweat. I turned in place in the phone booth and banged into the plastic doors. The phone booth wasn't big enough for a cat to turn in, and it smelled faintly of urine.

"I'm sure glad to hear that. You sound like a real nice lady too."

"Thank you. You made my day."

"You made mine too. In fact, you made my whole life easier."

I tensed.

"I never did call any real estate agents. So where would you have gotten my number?" He paused. "I've never heard of Réal Realty. Your agency's not even listed."

"We're a new agency," I said, but I'd lost the Southern accent and most of my conviction.

"I know who you are," he said.

I clutched the receiver. I wished I'd altered my voice better. Suddenly, I felt naked. But I squared my shoulders. "That's nice to hear. Réal Realty is new, but I've made a few sales—"

He wheezed. After a minute, I recognized it as a laugh. He said. "Leila."

My breath froze in my lungs. I almost hung up on him. I whirled in the phone book, wondering if he could see me. Shoppers hustled past me, carrying plastic bags and barking on cell phones. I wished I'd called from a more private location. He could be anywhere. The battery had run out on the Master Tracker.

"Leila Fan. Did I pronounce it right?"

He hadn't, of course. He'd butchered the Chinese intonation.

I said, "Lofton. Mrs. Of Réal Realty. Now, as I was saying—"

"Leila Fan. Green Belt Montreal. You want the land."

I decided to drop the show. "I also happen to represent Green Belt Montreal."

He chuckled softly. "We meet at last."

I didn't answer. Tomorrow we'd close the deal with Mr. Tabassian. Let Darryl III think he had the upper hand. He'd hang himself with his own arrogance.

"That land is mine," he said.

"Mr. MacEachern, I'm sure that land means a great deal to you. Green Belt Montreal has many connections with our sister organizations. If you require a similar piece of land, we could help you negotiate for several. We have a file of comparable properties."

"No," he snapped.

"We would be prepared—"

"No other land!"

I held my breath. This was the guy who'd killed Elena. I wouldn't underestimate him.

"Unless…" he added.

240

I shivered at his tone of voice. Soft, knowing, almost caressing me like a lover's. But I'd never come within six feet of this guy. I'd never spoken to him before today. Why the hell would he talk to me like that? I waited for him to finish, but I knew I was breathing too hard, and he could probably hear it.

"Unless you were willing to play real estate agent." His smile transmitted through his voice.

I knew it was a trap. The guy saw through my ruse. He called me by name. He knew Green Belt Montreal. And he'd killed Elena.

But he was finally falling in line with my own trap. I said, "I told you, Mr. MacEachern, real estate is my business. I would be delighted to show you the properties at any time. However, I am not available on the weekend."

He snorted. "The wrong time of the month?"

I tensed. This man could blow our cover any time. I had to play him exactly right. "A scheduling conflict. You understand."

"Tomorrow night. Nine p.m."

Less than 48 hours before moonrise. That should be safe enough for me. Of course the safest was to wait until after moonrise plus a day, but I trusted myself more than Bernard's cockeyed plan of luring him out to the land using Gisèle. I'd take care of the problem first. I said, "I've got a piece of land in the West Island, on the South shore..."

"West Island."

"Off the 40?"

"Fine."

I gave him directions to a piece of land near Hudson. It wasn't really for sale, of course, but it was quiet and discreet. Acres of maple bush and farm land. Privacy was what we needed now.

He mouth-breathed some more. He said, "Fine. There's a motel not far from there, just off the highway, called Chez Brossard. I'll reserve a room and leave a key for you at the front desk. We'll meet there and go to the land together."

He was still trying to run the show. "It would be more expedient for us to meet at the piece of land. If you give me your e-mail address, I could provide you with some detailed directions." Straight to hell.

"No, this motel is nice. You'll like it. We can have a coffee before we go."

"That sounds nice. Why don't I bring a carafe of coffee to the land?" That way I could be sure it wasn't doctored.

He sighed. "Leila, Leila, Leila. You don't get it, do you?"

I kept silent. I did not make him call me Mrs. Lofton.

"Either you meet me at the motel, or you don't meet me at all. It's your call."

I rubbed the hairs standing on the back of my neck. My breath hissed in and out between my teeth. Mistake, mistake, mistake.

"Nice talking to you, Leila."

"Wait," I forced myself to say. "I'll meet you at a restaurant. I think there's a truck stop in the same area."

"Motel. Or nothing."

Jack would kill me.

Jack had nothing to do with this anymore. I was a big girl.

He said, "It's a public place. People all around. I just want to talk to you before we go out on the land."

There was no good reason for me to meet him at the hotel except that he insisted on it.

I'd have my crew scout out the motel before we met there. They wouldn't have the exact room number, but they could make sure it was a legitimate place of business and monitor me.

I said, "Okay."

CHAPTER 60

I called Mac from the car. "I'm going to do something risky tomorrow. Can you back me up?" While I told him, I shivered involuntarily. My body knew how dangerous this, more than I admitted.

"I'm going to tell the district heads," he said.

"No. They've got their own plan, using Gisèle as bait."

"We can't do this on our own."

I silently counted to five. I missed Jack. But Jack was picking up Miss Sweetie Pie from the airport. "We're not. I want you to rally all the wers. You've got to help me scout out that motel."

He sighed. "Leila. I'm in Boston. Remember?"

I didn't answer.

"I know you're tough. I know you're mad about Elena. But Leila, you can't do this on your own. Like you said yourself, you need backup. What did Jack say?"

"I got his voice mail," I lied.

"Okay. And Laurent?"

"I'll call him after you."

"You need to send a message out to everyone. We need all hands on deck for this, and I won't be back until tomorrow night, if my flight lands on time. By the time I drive out to the motel or the land—"

"Yeah, yeah, yeah." I rubbed my forehead. A headache started to build behind my eyes. "I'll call Laurent."

"And the district heads."

I didn't answer.

"Leila, if you don't message them and cc me, I'll call them myself."

"I'll cc you," I said finally.

"Great. Within the hour."

"Within the hour," I parroted. I knew a few ways to get around this puppy.

And I did. I wrote up a nice message about meeting the murderer, and I sent it to Mac and Laurent, pretending to alert the whole wer network, but secretly altering key addresses so the e-mail would bounce. Then I really did call Laurent, who cursed me out because he wanted to concentrate on tomorrow's morning meeting with Mr. Tabassian, but he agreed to come to the motel with me that night.

Perfect.

CHAPTER 61

Friday morning, I paced outside Mr. Tabassian's building as best I could in a jacket, skirt, and flats, while holding a briefcase. If I'd smoked in real life, I would have burned through a few cancer sticks. The closer I got to the full moon, the less I could control my nervous energy, even if I didn't physically 'shift until moonrise in two days.

"Cool it, Leila," said Laurent.

I glanced at him out of the corner of my eye. Freshly shaved, his facial hair barely qualified as stubble, but the way he surveyed the area set me on edge. He stood absolutely motionless, ears and eyes on alert, like he was stalking deer.

Once again, my instincts warned me to leave him at home, or at least in the car. "Laurent—"

He cast me a fierce look that quelled my objections. "Remember what we talked about."

We'd reviewed the legalities over and over. I said, "Yes."

His eyes flicked to his watch. "Let's go."

I glanced at my own watch. Five minutes to the hour. I half-ran to catch up to him. Laurent moved far too fast and fluidly for a human, despite his wool suit and carefully knotted tie.

By mutual, silent agreement, we took the stairs two at a time rather than waiting for the elevator. If we arrived breathless and slightly sweaty, well, at least we'd worked a bit of the edge off.

Someone stood outside Mr. Tabassian's door. He detached himself from the wall and walked toward us.

My first, fear-based instinct was to bare my teeth at the enemy.

But it wasn't. It was Jack.

Jack, eyes bloodshot, hair flattened on one side and sticking up on the other, walking toward us. He, too, flowed more swiftly and gracefully than an all-human would. "Hey," he said, nodding at both of us but keeping his eyes trained on me.

"What the—what are you doing here?" I whispered.

"Meeting with Mr. Tabassian."

"That's for me and Laurent!"

"Thought you could use some backup," he said.

"What—some backup snoring? Didn't you just get off your night shift?"

"We don't have time to argue about this," said Laurent. He looked at Jack. "Do you feel competent to attend the meeting? You must not speak or interrupt."

"I feel fine," said Jack. "You won't even know I'm here."

Then why bother showing up? I thought, but I bit it back and smiled rather toothily at Mr. Tabassian, who swung open the door.

He glanced at Jack, who'd dressed in a suit and tie, but when Mr. Tabassian glanced him up and down, I became conscious that Jack's navy suit was pulled a hair too tight across the shoulders and was made of some slightly shiny material, not wool. Mr. Tabassian's certainly looked a cut above Jack, topped with his neatly knotted brown silk tie. Mr. T glanced at me. "And who is this? You brought along another lawyer?"

"Another representative from Green Belt Montreal," I said. "A trainee. His name is Jack Meng. Don't worry, Mr. Tabassian, he promises he'll be seen and not heard."

Mr. T nodded. He'd been holding on to his belt, but now his hands relaxed. "Well, everyone needs to learn, hey?" He clapped Jack on the shoulder.

Jack moved a fraction of an inch away before he managed to grin and nod.

"Thank you for coming anyway, Leila. I know you and Mr. Laforest are busy people, but like I said, I want all this cleared up as soon as I can. My son's not well, and I'm tired of all this back and forth."

I nodded. The more he talked, the more sympathetic he'd be when I told him we were still ten grand short.

Laurent held open the door for the sixteen-foot wide windowless conference room, barely enough space for the rectangular table and a chair on each side. I entered first, followed by Jack. Mr. T and Laurent kept gesturing each other in before Laurent finally gave in and offered a little bow.

246

I thought Laurent was overplaying his manners a little, but I was glad he remembered them instead of licking his canines.

Jack glanced at me like he knew what I was thinking. I ignored him and settled into a seat at the head of the table while Jack took the chair on my right and Laurent on my left, closest to the door. I said, "Mr. Tabassian, we've signed all the papers you faxed to me."

Mr. T shut the door behind us and swung his briefcase on to the ten-foot long table, taking the roller chair on the opposite table head next to the door. Instantly, Laurent's nostrils quivered, and his features sharpened. I glared daggers at him, but he'd fixated dangerously on Mr. T, who was blathering about some new papers he'd drafted. "Some last-minute changes. No big deal. Your lawyer here can check it out and then we'll all be as free as a bird."

Then I felt it. Something in the air.

My gaze dragged over to Jack, seated on my right. His pupils had dilated, but more importantly, my gaze dropped to his mouth. Those knowing lips. That sinfully curious tongue. That chest, heaving behind his buttoned-down shirt. Those strong brown hands, capable of so much unspeakable goodness.

I raised my eyes. His nostrils flared. He was feeling it, too.

I bit my lip. Hard. That cleared my head long enough to think, *What the hell is going on?*

Of course I wanted Jack early and often. But at a business meeting? In front of Mr. Tabassian and Laurent?

Mr. Tabassian threw open his briefcase.

It was like he'd exploded a sex bomb in front of me. My vision blurred for an instant. All I could think of was grabbing Jack by the belt and fucking him over and under the conference table.

Laurent growled low in his throat. It was a warning sound too feral for a human voice box.

That sound tore me out of my sex haze for an instant.

I jerked my head to look. On my left, Laurent pressed both fists into the table so hard his knuckles whitened, but he eyed Mr. Tabassian like he was a juicy young deer with a lame hindfoot.

I dove for Laurent's arm. "Mr. Tabassian!" I screamed in warning.

Laurent sprang over the table, directly at Mr. T's throat.

CHAPTER 62

My hand closed on air. "No!" I called, and lunged again. I managed to encircle Laurent's ankle, but he kicked free.

I snarled.

Jack leaped on to the table and tackled Laurent across the waist.

Laurent landed hard, whacking his knees and his elbows, but he kept scratching the table, claws outstretched, snapping his jaws in anticipation of a kill.

I bashed Laurent on the head with my briefcase. He barely flinched. I smashed him again and yelled, "Move-move-MOVE!" to Mr. Tabassian.

Mr. T stood rigid at the foot of the table. He gaped at Laurent with the horrified fascination of prey.

"Get out of here!" I shrieked while Jack struggled to pin Laurent's arms and subdue him with his body.

Mr. T finally stirred, but stumbled and caught his foot under his roller chair. He fell hard on the floor.

I yanked Mr. Tabassian's wrist. "Get up!" With my other arm, I opened the door. We needed fresh air in here.

Not enough. This close to Mr. T's briefcase, longing surged directly into my groin. I moaned aloud, an ululation of desire and panic.

I dropped Mr. T's hand and slammed the briefcase shut. Too little, too late. By turning around, I spotted Jack out of the corner of my eye. My body was already surging toward him.

"Leila!" he gasped. He was straddling Laurent, trying to keep him still, but as he met my eyes, his hips started to work of their own accord.

We needed to fuck. Right now.

I started to climb up on the table. I wanted to rip open my shirt and press my breasts against his chest. I wanted to sit on his face and take his—

I bit my tongue. Nearly sliced the tip off it.

The pain and gush of blood jolted me back into my head for another second.

I wheeled toward Mr. T, curled up the ground on his back like a helpless beetle. He held his left knee, rocking back and forth. He stared at me in almost as much horror as Laurent.

I jumped on to the ground and seized Mr. T by both arms. "Come—"

Jack screamed a warning as Laurent leaped over the table, teeth bared.

I dropped on all fours over Mr. T, shielding him, while Jack lunged over the table too, shoulder-checking Laurent in mid-air.

Jack landed half on top of me and Mr. T. I ended up head-butting Mr. T. I felt something crunch. He cried out, but I was distracted by Jack grinding his hips against my side, dry-humping me. I turned and pushed myself against him before he dragged himself away.

Too late.

Movement caught the corner of my left eye. Mr. Tabassian bucked underneath me. Blood streamed out of both nostrils, but his hands scrabbled at his neck while he screamed and gurgled.

Laurent had pulled a 180 and reached under both me and Jack to seize Mr. T's silk tie in both hands.

With an evil, toothy grin, Laurent jerked his hands toward his body, strangling Mr. Tabassian.

I dived forward. If Laurent jerked too hard, he'd crush Mr. T's voice box and kill him.

I couldn't get a single finger under the tie noose. Laurent had pulled it too tight.

Mr. T's face reddened. He could no longer speak.

I clawed Laurent's hands. "Let GO of him!" I managed to bend one finger back, but he laughed. Bloodlust reigned in his eyes.

WHACK!

Jack smashed Laurent's head with a chair seat, barely missing my head.

I hit the deck, or in this case, Mr. T. His body convulsed under the impact.

Laurent shook. His body wavered, but his hands held tight.

WHACK!

Jack brought the chair down on his head again.

Laurent's hands finally relaxed.

I yanked the tie out of his grasp and worked it off of Mr. T's throat until I threw it against the wall.

Laurent's body crumpled on to us.

I shoved him away, toward the tie. He barely moved six inches, but he was still breathing, unconscious next to his instrument of attempted murder. Thank God.

Mr. T was purple-faced, bug-eyed, and still.

My heart nearly stopped, but Jack pushed me off Mr. T's body. I rolled off to the left, curling to avoid bumping into Laurent.

Jack tilted his head to listen to Mr. T's breathing while placing a hand on the man's chest. "He's breathing. No stridor. Heart rate regular. I think he fainted." The tendons in Jack's neck bulged as he stared at me with sudden intensity.

I felt it too.

Wolf ice.

"Let's get out of here," I blurted out. Whatever was in the briefcase kept permeating the air. Darryl III had outsmarted us.

"I think," Jack said, struggling to control his words, "it's on the tie, too."

I ripped my jacket off and covered my hands while I picked up the tie with one hand and Mr. T's briefcase in the other. I dropped both of those near the main office door and ran back, light-headed with lust.

After a minute, my breathing slowed. I still wanted to fuck, but it wasn't all-consuming.

I met Jack's eyes. He was slowly coming back to himself, too.

"You're right," I said.

"I know," he said, but he still had that look in his eyes. "Now you've got it on your hands."

I smelled my hands and, although we had two unconscious men at our feet, I had to rip Jack's shirt out of his pants and shove my hands down on his rigid cock.

He groaned. "We can't."

"I know." I gave him an extra squeeze, and his hips bucked. "We have to think."

"Leila. We have to call an ambulance."

That broke me out of my trance, although I held on to him. I managed to say, "But they'll arrest Laurent."

"I know."

"And Sunday's the full moon."

"I know."

It was the end of werewolf secrecy and our life as we knew it.

Part of me wanted to up and run. Grab Jack's hand—well, I already held on to a significant portion of his anatomy—and abandon Laurent and Mr. T to the rescue squad.

Even though I could never abandon my pack member. Even though we'd all probably been caught on hallway security cameras. For a second, I wanted to take off with Jack, and to hell with the rest.

Laurent stirred and groaned.

I threw myself in between him and Mr. T and called to Jack, "You call 911. You know what to say. I'd better tie him up before he comes to."

We heard a knock on the outside office door. A man's deep voice intoned, "Police. Open up."

CHAPTER 63

Jack shot me a look that said he'd handle it. "It's unlocked, officer."

I shook my head and called, "Coming, sir!" The door might have self-locked behind us. And we'd better play nice with the police, for whatever good it would do.

Jack frowned at Mr. Tabassian, whose breathing had evened out, but his face was still red, and a bright red line curved around his neck. At least his face wasn't purple anymore. And Jack could take care of him better than I could.

The door opened before I turned the knob.

Two white police officers entered the room. The balding, heavier one cast us a suspicious look. He looked kind of like Tony Soprano: a middle-aged guy you don't want to mess with. "What's going on here?"

"We're in the conference room," I said weakly, pointing them toward the second door on the right.

"I'm glad you came," said Jack, rising to his feet and holding out his hand. "We were just about to call you. I'm a paramedic, and we have two unconscious men here. They're both breathing, but they need to be checked out, especially this one." He indicated Mr. Tabassian.

The shorter one checked Mr. Tabassian while Tony Soprano kept a careful eye on us.

Jack continued, "He's breathing, but his heart's only going at 65, and it's a bit irregular. He needs a hospital."

Shorty said, "Yeah. His pulse does seem kind of slow." He looked at Tony Soprano for confirmation.

"Call an ambulance," said Soprano. From his badge, his real name was Shapiro. I smiled involuntarily at the near coincidence before he scowled at me. "But we need to talk to you. What are your names, and what were you doing here?"

Jack quirked an eyebrow at me. I said, "Leila Fan. I'm, um, an environmental—" Too late, I realized activist wasn't a profession that would immediately made the police grin. "Lobbyist," I said. "For Green Belt Montreal?" My voice rose involuntarily.

"Why were you here?" asked Shorty.

"We had a meeting with Mr. Tabassian. He was going to sell us his land." I pointed at Mr. T. "He gave us some papers to sign, and we were going to hand over a check and close the deal this morning. I can show you the e-mails if you like."

"We'll probably ask for that later," said Shapiro. He jerked his chin at Jack. "How about you?"

"I'm Jack Meng. I'm a paramedic and a friend of Leila's." He pointed at Laurent, who rolled on his side. Jack had bound up his hands with his belt while I'd gone to the door. "This is Laurent Laforest, the lawyer for Green Belt Montreal. He was negotiating the deal." Laurent's eyelashes fluttered. In a minute he'd wake up.

Shapiro eyeballed each of us in turn, including the two men on the floor, before he surveyed the mess of chairs, briefcases, and the tie strewn in the hallway. "What happened?"

"I don't really know," said Jack. "Our lawyer got very upset at Mr. Tabassian and, er, attacked him with his own tie."

I gave Jack a sharp look. He'd let Laurent take the hit for all of us?

Jack didn't acknowledge me. He was making earnest eye contact with Shapiro, trying to get him on our side. "He wouldn't stop, so I banged him in the head with the chair."

"Why didn't you call 911?" asked Shapiro.

"We didn't have time," said Jack. I nodded agreement. Between the two of us, we'd barely managed to keep Mr. Tabassian alive.

"Good thing one of the neighbors did," said Shorty. I nodded at him.

We heard sirens in the distance. Shapiro muttered into his radio. "That's the ambulance," he said to Jack. "Your buddies are going to take this one to the hospital." He indicated Mr. T with his foot. "The other one probably needs it too, but we'll wait for another ambulance and put him under police escort." He jerked his head at Shorty and nodded at Laurent. "Cuff him." Shapiro turned back to Jack and me. "We'll need you both at the station to make formal statements."

The police part passed in a blur. They interviewed me and Jack separately. I tried to stick to the story that we didn't know why Laurent had attacked Mr. Tabassian. I emphasized that we'd met many times before and always gotten along. No, I didn't know what provoked him. Laurent and I had met at 9 a.m. and he'd seemed normal. "He's an excellent lawyer. I'm sure he has many references. And he's my friend," I said. My voice climbed. I wondered if I should tell them that Laurent had been drugged. But what if they then took a bunch of blood and urine samples and somehow managed to reconstitute wolf ice?

My head whirled. I didn't know where Laurent was. He'd regained consciousness before his ambulance arrived, but the police led him away in handcuffs.

Mr. Tabassian still hadn't opened his eyes when the paramedics strapped him to his gurney and rolled him away.

At long last, they released me. I felt sweaty and dirty in more ways than one.

If Laurent 'shifted in custody, he was dead.

We were all dead.

I waited until Jack finally walked into the main lobby, wearing a crooked grin. I wanted to throw my arms around him, but I just touched his arm. "You okay?"

"Surviving. Let's get out of here."

We took a taxi back to my apartment. After the door was safely locked behind us, Jack said, "I need a drink. You mind?"

"I think I've got a beer at the back of the fridge."

He found it and gulped it down. "Okay. Now we've got to make up a Plan B."

I pointed to my briefcase lying at the front door. "That's the first part."

He raised his eyebrows quizzically at me.

"They confiscated the tie and Mr. Tabassian's briefcase as evidence, but I kept my briefcase and my suit jacket. Remember how I wrapped the tie in my jacket? Now we should have a trace of wolf ice. You can take it to your lab and analyze the hell out of it."

Jack kissed me. His stubble rubbed against my face, abrading it, but I didn't push him away. He said, "You're brilliant."

I shook my head. "I hope it's not too late. We've got to spring Laurent before he 'shifts."

254

Jack nodded. "We need a get out of jail free card for him. I texted everyone while we were in the taxi. We'll get the best lawyers on this. I think we can get him out on bail. He has no prior record, obviously."

"Before the full moon?" I asked.

Jack made a face. "That's the problem. It's Friday. Not much time before the weekend. They might try to sit on him."

"And then we're fucked."

He blinked in acknowledgement, but he said, "We'll do our best, Leila."

"There's one other thing," I said, taking a deep breath. "Laurent was supposed to help me out tonight."

"With what?" Jack gave me a funny look. He knew I wouldn't bring it up if it weren't absolutely vital.

I hated to tell him. The guy needed to crash. But right now, I had no other backup. I said softly, "I'm going to meet with the murderer."

CHAPTER 64

"No fuckin' way," said Jack, almost before I finished explaining my motel date.

I took a deep breath. I looked into Jack's eyes, which were so red now, they looked like he'd pulled an all-nighter at a rave with too many drugs. Stubble marked his face. I hated to lay this on him, too. "I'm doing it," I said. "But you don't have to come with me. I've taken self-defense courses. I've even gone on a shooting range or two."

He shook his head. "You're not doing anything without me."

I spoke over him. "He killed Elena. Laurent might as well be dead. Gisèle's willing to play bait, and she could end up six feet under. At this rate, even without the wolf ice recipe, we're all going down. It's genocide."

Jack grabbed the beer bottle like he wanted to smash it on the wall. Instead, he set it down very carefully and said, "You're not going anywhere. I would kill that guy with my bare hands before I let him touch you."

I didn't speak for a second. That was exactly how I felt about him.

I said, "You're working."

"I'll get out of it."

"You have to sleep. You're going to start hallucinating in about four seconds."

He shook his head. "I'd have worse nightmares about what would happen to you."

I took a deep breath. "Okay. Listen. If you can rearrange your shift, and if you crash right now, we'll figure something out."

Jack kissed me. "I knew you'd come around."

It took us a while to break off the kiss, leaving us both panting, and my newly-bitten tongue aching, but I didn't regret it. His hand had migrated under my bra. I pulled away.

256

He let me, but he said, "I'd sleep better with you next to me."

I laughed over my shoulders. "Baby, if we save the world, you'll be sleeping with me forever."

He smiled so wide, I didn't have the heart to take it back. And anyway, I still had to come up with a better plan.

When Jack finally crashed into sleep, he lay on his back, mouth open and snoring, but holding on to my hand. He'd managed to courier the wolf ice jacket to his lab lady, trade shifts with another paramedic, and even answer questions from Bernard before the Sandman sandbagged him.

I stroked his hair and tried to anticipate our next move. Together.

Clearly, the murderer had plotted well. He'd somehow gotten wolf ice on to Mr. Tabassian's papers and even his tie.

Which meant he knew Mr. T was meeting with us. The murderer was even thorough enough to ensure two different toxic sources.

Darryl III had pressured Mr. T into this early meeting, just before the full moon, when we'd most likely spin out of control, knowing full well that nothing would put our bid out of commission faster than attempted murder of the vendor.

A risky game, however. Laurent could have killed Mr. T. The land would have passed on to Mr. T's son, throwing the land into limbo.

But maybe the murderer didn't mind waiting a little longer, as long as he checkmated us.

Just to make sure, he'd arranged to meet with me as well. At a motel. Alone.

Jack rolled on his side, flinging his arm around me and burying his head into the pillow. I smiled. I wouldn't be alone this time.

He tossed his leg around my midsection. I lowered it down to my hips so he was no longer crushing my waist. And I decided what I would do.

I would alert the werewolf crew. It was foolhardy for Jack and me to go it alone, knowing how dangerous this man was. I would download some GPS apps for both our phones so that they'd be able to track us to the metre. But I wouldn't alert them until we were already on our way. Foolish, but I wanted us to have a head start in taking the murderer down. For Elena.

"This is for you, blondie," I said, raising an imaginary cooler to the sky.

Jack drooled his agreement into the pillow. I kissed his cheek. I loved him as a He-man, but maybe I loved him even better now, with his eyes closed and his face soft like a little boy's.

And then I tiptoed out of the bedroom. I had to prepare to meet the murderer face to face.

CHAPTER 65

Before I hopped into my rental car, a silver Nissan Versa, Jack said, "You sure about this, Leila?"

"Very."

"Okay." He glanced at his watch. "How 'bout one for the road?" From his crooked grin, he didn't mean a drink.

I walked up to him and poked him in his non-existent gut. "After I take this guy down and destroy his wolf ice—"

"After *we* take this guy down."

I rolled my eyes and continued. "—life'll roll back to how we know it." I choked up a little.

Jack's eyes narrowed. "I'm not quite getting you. Clue me in here."

I turned away so I wouldn't have to look at his face. "Nothing. Just that we won't have any more fake Viagra or a psycho throwing us together. Which is a good thing."

"Hey." His callused fingers touched my chin, gently forcing me back to his gaze. "You think that's why I'm here? Because of my hormones?"

I almost laughed. "Well, yeah."

He smiled. "Well. I guess that part is obvious. But if you think I'm only sticking around because of a psycho's machinations, think again. You're my mate, Leila. Simple as that. I'll prove it to you once we kick murderer ass. *Capice?*"

I nodded, not trusting my voice. Then I hopped into my rental car and peeled on to Chevalier.

This afternoon, I'd called my parents to say goodbye. Not that I expected to die, but you never knew. And that was one advantage I had over Elena: I knew this day could be my last.

I hopped on to Côte-Ste-Catherine with Jack's black Toyota in my rear-view mirror. To stay on my tail, he busted through a yellow light. I slowed down while I cut over to Décarie and eventually Highway 40.

Déja vu. All I needed was "Werewolves of London," but I refused to touch the radio. I wanted to concentrate on our plan.

Half an hour later, we wove through the 'burbs of the West Island. I wondered if Dr. Nash was nursing a beer at the Rusty Nail, and mentally saluted him before I sailed over the Île aux Tourtes bridge, squinting at the waves in the water. A few brave sailboats bobbed in the distance.

Jack stayed right behind me. No matter how I weaved in and out of the left lane, he remained glued to my bumper. It made me smile.

Whatever happened to me, I prayed Jack would stay safe.

Not safe enough to hook up with Gisèle, mind you. But alive and free to tackle the bad guys another day.

I waved at him in my rear view mirror. He lifted two fingers off the steering wheel in greeting.

Mr. Tough Guy. I had to smile. But his tight driving and fast reflexes reassured me that he'd caught up on his rest. We needed to stay on high alert tonight.

I signaled well in advance to exit on Highway 342, and we basically paralleled the highway until I turned into Hudson, a sleepy residential community. One of my friends had moved there and liked to bore me with tales about her idyllic country life, where she could canoe on the Ottawa River with her rugrats and speak English without getting any dirty looks. To me, it was too much like the suburbs, i.e. bored MILFs and barbecuing dads paying way too much attention to each others' business. But its big advantage was that, this far outside of Montreal, people still held on to large tracts of land. And my friend Kelly had told me all about this one acreage where kids used to drink and screw around until a boy got shot in the shoulder a few years ago. He recovered, but after that, the parents clamped down on the kids. The owner installed barbed wire and NO TRESPASSING signs. Which made it the perfect place to meet a murderer.

My phone buzzed. I'd stopped checking my messages after I alerted the pack. I knew they all wanted to kick my ass right after they mowed down Darryl III. But right now, I had to focus.

I pressed on the brakes and signaled to turn in to Chez Brossard, the murderer's motel of choice. The fading white sign and the red neon VACANCY sign didn't exactly inspire confidence.

The parking lot was almost empty, so Jack kept going. That was our plan, for him to join me if he could, but otherwise try and park nearby, somewhere inconspicuous.

I glanced at the dashboard clock. I was fifteen minutes early.

The moon already sat mid-range in the sky. I could see its dark spots, its basalt rock "seas." To the untrained eye, it already appeared full, but Jack and I still had another 20 hours or so before full moon rise.

"Wish me luck," I whispered to the Sea of Tranquility. I assembled the goodies in my purse and in my pockets. I checked my messages, ignoring the outrage and the "Don't do anything until I get there" warnings and focusing in on Jack's latest text:

Ready?

Ready, I texted back.

I climbed out of the car, wondering if the murderer was already watching me enter the motel office.

Probably.

I wondered where he'd stashed his truck, since only a white compact and a moving van squatted in the parking lot.

I opened the motel door. The jingle from the tinny bell affixed to the inside of the door was immediately drowned out by the TV.

I waved at the counter girl, who reluctantly turned down the volume on an episode of Taxi 0-22, but her froggy blue eyes kept drifting back to it even before I finished saying, "Hi. I think you have a key for me. My name is Leila Fan—"

I wanted her to remember me in case the police ever had to come a-knocking. Instead, she passed me the key for room number 18 and muttered, "Round the other side."

I paused for a moment before I took the key and its oversized white plastic room number card. I willed her to fix on me, my face, or at least my brown yoga outfit and my very best running shoes. "Thanks," I said.

She turned away from the counter, already laughing along with the TV.

No, this girl wasn't going to save me. I was.

I steeled my shoulders and turned toward the door and room number 18. I texted Jack the room number.

Got it, he wrote back. *I'll stay close.*

D-day.

CHAPTER 66

The sand on the pavement crunched under my soles as I crossed the parking lot slowly on foot. Maybe I should have driven across the lot and kept my car close, but as an environmentalist, I usually walked if I could.

I also wanted to give Jack more time to move into place.

Motels are creepy in general. The building lies low, flat to the ground, like a tigress skulking toward her kill.

I shook the image away. No tigresses dwelled immediately outside of Montreal. Jack lurked nearby, ready to back me up. I couldn't see him, but I could smell him, so he couldn't be more than fifteen feet away. I wished he'd thought to hide downwind, but it shouldn't matter. The murderer didn't have our sense of smell.

Between our heightened powers, our preparation, and all the wer packs on high alert, I'd take Darryl III down, with or without help.

I kept one hand closed around one of my goodies, hiding it from the murderer's view as I strolled across the lot.

Like many motels, this one was U-shaped, with all units huddling around the parking lot. Number 18 was the end lot opposite the office and my car. The white door paint had faded and the aluminum siding was slightly warped, but otherwise, it looked like a decent place to spend the night.

Or to avenge your friend's death.

I knocked on the door three times.

The knocks echoed through the room as if were empty. I knocked again, glancing out of the corners of my eyes in case he jumped me from behind.

I slid my key into the lock.

The knob turned slowly under my hand.

I held the door closed for a beat before I flung it open hard enough to bash anyone standing behind it.

I did not step into the room. I deliberately hung back, on the doorstep.

Still, an invisible cloud surrounded me, fogging my mind.

My knees buckled. I sprawled forward, on to a dusty beige carpet.

Wolf ice.

The entire room, from carpet to bedspread to free-floating air, was saturated in wolf ice.

My vulva throbbed. I yipped high in my throat and, with the last vestiges of my brain, clamped my nostrils shut with the pair of nose plugs I'd hidden in my hand.

When the haze lifted out of my mind enough for a few more neurons to fire, I fought my way to my hands and knees.

My legs wobbled. Jack. Even through the nose plugs, I could still smell Jack. And wolf ice.

Jack.

Wolf ice.

No.

I grasped the doorknob and levered myself up to standing before I slammed the motel door closed, breathing through my mouth.

Even though I was now outside the room, and I'd never gotten further than doorway carpet, my cotton yoga shirt, pants, hair, and face were now contaminated with wolf ice.

I ripped off my shirt. I was wearing a tank top underneath. I lobbed the toxic shirt at the front door step, away from me.

I turned toward my car across the parking lot. I was so weak, the murderer could have knocked me over with a nose hair.

I felt someone behind me even before I heard the footsteps.

I whirled, mouth already opened in a scream, my purse raised as a weapon.

Jack grabbed me under the arms. "Leila—"

I shoved him in the breastbone. "I can't be around you right now." Any other time or place, my nasal, nose-plugged voice would have made us laugh.

He didn't answer. His nostrils twitched. He stared at me and licked his lips, grabbing me closer.

"No, Jack! This is what he wants! Stay back! Put in your plugs!"

With effort, he backed away from me and patted his front pocket. After what felt like an eternity, but probably took only three seconds, he clipped the plugs over his nose and started breathing through his mouth. He was still staring at me.

A black Honda CRV screeched into the lot. Bernard and Jefferson leaped out of it.

"Leila, where is he?" Jefferson demanded.

I pointed at my key, still hanging in the knob of room 18, but I called to Bernard, "Wolf ice."

He understood. He let Jefferson stalk toward the motel door while he plugged his nose. Then he followed Jefferson, but not before I spotted the bulge on his hip. Bernard was carrying a gun on his belt.

Jack paused, torn between shadowing them and watching out for me.

"I'll get the car," I said. "You stay close. But not too close."

He nodded his understanding and trailed me from about ten feet away. Even with my nose plugged, even moving away from wolf ice central, my body ached for Jack. If we both got in the car together, I'd probably start riding him even if the murderer shot out the windshield. Jack had to stay away from me.

I reached the driver's door, but I paused, watching Jefferson from across the parking lot. He rapped on the door of room number 18.

I should have called Jefferson instead of Jack. As a human, Jefferson had immunity against wolf ice, while both Jack and I melted into sex fiends.

I cursed under my breath.

"Get in the car, Leila," called Jack. He jerked his head toward the office. Through the glass, I spotted the office girl on the phone. She must have called the cops, or at least her boss.

Jefferson shouldered the door in to room number 18 and immediately dropped into a crouch, surveying the scene. Bernard burst in behind him, gun held steady in both hands, like a pair of cops.

"Get him," I said under my breath.

Jefferson flipped on the light and advanced into the room, leaving the room door open. Bernard followed behind, still covering both of them with his gun. I lost my view of them when they skirted the bed.

"Leila," said Jack, but I held up my hand to shush him.

From the across the parking lot, I heard a snarl from room 18. A sound that ripped the night air.

From inside the office, the motel clerk screamed.

"Go help!" I yelled at Jack. "The wolf ice must've gotten Bernard! He'll kill Jefferson!"

Jack hesitated, glancing at me.

"No!" My voice cracked. "I'll drive up in the car. You can drag Bernard into the back seat." Or Jefferson, if Bernard had already ripped him apart, but I refused to think about that. "Go, go, go!"

Jack sprinted across the lot. Already, I could hear more snarls and the sound of furniture breaking. Maybe they were tearing apart the murderer and not each other, but I couldn't risk it.

I ripped open the door to the Nissan and jumped into the driver's seat, inserting my keys in the ignition. I gunned the engine. And paused.

Hadn't I locked the car doors?

Why was the steering wheel sticky?

I started panting through my mouth. I reached for the car door.

A dry voice behind me said, "Drive," just as cold metal pressed against the back of my head.

My gaze flicked to my rear view mirror. Darryl III looked back at me, holding a gun to my skull like he knew how to use it.

"Drive," he repeated.

CHAPTER 67

I didn't move.

Somehow, while I was getting the motel key and investigating room 18, this man had broken into my rental car and drenched it, too, in wolf ice.

In the close confines of the car, and maybe because less than 48 hours separated me from the rising moon, I could detect the wolf ice. A slightly musky odor.

The same smell I'd detected once in my apartment.

"The flyers," I said aloud. "You put flyers in my apartment with this shit on it."

He didn't smile, but something flickered in his dark eyes. "Right back at you."

A pressure built in my temples. Sweat pricked my armpits. The nose plugs wouldn't save me forever.

Not in this steel prison box filled with wolf ice.

I released the steering wheel, but I already knew I'd absorbed the toxin through my palms. He'd soaked the car seat upholstery. I didn't have to touch the gear shift to know that was contaminated too.

I didn't know what little game the murderer was playing, except that he played it very well. He'd managed to separate me from Jack, Jefferson, and Bernard, and potentially set them all up against each other.

I figured the nose plugs might buy me a few minutes, maybe even half an hour. I didn't know how long it took for stuff to absorb through the skin, but every druggie goes for the veins or the nose or the lungs, instead of bathing in their hit of choice, so skin couldn't be that effective.

With my eyes in the rear view mirror, I tried to gauge how to take the guy down, even though I was in the front seat and he held a gun to my head.

Couldn't do it.

I reached for the door instead.

All of a sudden, I felt something sharp prick the skin on the left side of my neck.

He said, "I'd rather not shoot you in the parking lot where everyone will hear. But I can do this." He traced a blade around to the front of my throat.

I gulped, locking into place, even as he scraped the delicate skin over my voice box.

In his right hand, he held a gun. With his left, a knife.

"Drive," he said. "Not to your boyfriend. Out of the lot. Listen to my directions."

"I need to put on my seat belt," I said.

He chuckled. It sounded like a door creaking. "You're not going to live through this anyway, Leila Fan."

He still butchered my name. I ached to correct him, but not as much as my neck already ached from holding rigid, trying to stay away from the blade and not breathe too deeply.

"Habit," I said. Somewhere, I'd read that you should try to talk to your captor and engage them. Couldn't hurt.

"Okay, little girl. Put on your seat belt."

He couldn't keep up the gun while I was driving. I glanced into the rear view mirror. He didn't have his belt on. Maybe I could use that to my advantage.

If I had to go down, I'd take him to hell with me.

"Both hands in the air. Reach your left hand out for the seat belt."

"I can't see it." I turned my head a fraction of an inch.

He jabbed me with the knife. I felt it cut the skin. It stung immediately, like a paper cut.

He said, "Reach back another inch. Higher. There you go."

I drew the belt across my body and dropped my right hand to hold the buckle.

"Stop right there, Leila Fan."

"I need the buckle."

"I know what you were doing. You were reaching for your pocket. Don't try this with me, Leila. You can do this the easy way or the hard way."

I'd do it the hardest way. As long as I made him suffer. But I released a tiny sigh. With him guarding me like this, I couldn't reach the gloves in my pocket. I said, "Okay, boss."

"That's right. Buckle it up with one hand, bitch."

I didn't flinch at his endearment. I checked the rear view mirror again, this time out the rear windshield. I saw shadows and heard some shouting from room 18, but I couldn't make out what was going on. While the murderer played with me, everyone could die in there.

"That's right, Leila Fan. They're ripping each other to shreds before the police can get here. Gotta love my father's invention, hey? Now buckle up and start driving, or I'm going to start cutting."

CHAPTER 68

I obeyed the letter of the law. I reversed half the length of the lot and swerved a wide left so that I could pass by room 18.

Jack roared from the doorway. He was wrestling with—Jefferson? I twisted my neck to be sure. Yes, Bernard clamped down on Jefferson's long, lean legs while Jack wound Jefferson's arms behind his back and hollered, "Stop, Leila!"

But I couldn't. Not with a gun to my head and a knife to my throat.

The murderer chuckled behind me. The knife hand jiggled slightly.

I sucked my breath in between my teeth.

"That's right, Leila Fan. Keep driving."

I cranked my neck forward and pressed gently on the accelerator, hoping that even in the dim light, Jack could spot Darryl in the back. Even if Jack couldn't make him out, he'd soon figure out something was wrong.

I hoped they'd manage to wrangle Jefferson into the CRV before the police came. If Jack had to explain for the second time in twelve hours why a friend of his had gone ballistic…

And why on earth would Jefferson be the one who freaked out on wolf ice?

"Turn right," said the murderer.

I did. But I said, "I know a faster way to the piece of land we're going to see."

"Shut up, Leila Fan. We're not going to play real estate agent. I've got something much more interesting in mind. Stay on Harwood."

I did. I expected we'd hook back on Highway 40, and then I'd put my plan into action. I should've been shaking in my shoes, but chances were pretty good I was going to die. I just had to save the pack while I was at it.

He still wasn't wearing his seat belt. Guess it's hard to hold someone hostage, especially with a knife, and still obey all the safety laws.

If I could get some good speed, I could roll the car into the ditch. Plenty of places like that on Highway 40. With any luck, he'd go flying before he had a chance to pull the trigger.

I didn't want to kill other innocent people. I'd have to wait for an empty stretch.

But on Harwood, a secondary highway, I ended up stuck behind a truck that couldn't do more than 80 kilometres an hour. I braked—slowly, I did everything slowly with that blade on my neck—and said, "I assume we're on our way to the campground."

He didn't answer.

I said, "We'd make better time on the highway."

He grunted. "Too many people."

So we made our slow, painful way through the back roads. My only comfort was that I wasn't feeling sexual at all. I'd risk a bullet to the cerebellum before I mounting this POS.

Was I developing an immunity to wolf ice? Drunks had to drink more to get the same buzz. Was it possible that after too many exposures, your wolf ice receptors got jammed too?

I frowned. *I wish.* Jack and I had gone gonzo as usual around each other. Only the nose plugs had saved us.

The murderer interrupted my thoughts. "I've got to thank the old man for one thing."

I couldn't bring myself to answer. I swallowed the bit of saliva I had left and grunted.

"This wolf bait sure works great on you." He cackled.

Fury made me clench the steering wheel, but my hands slipped on the wolf ice grease while he sniggered in the backseat. It was like he'd read my mind. I tried to slow my breathing and think instead. So his daddy had given him the wolf bait, like I'd imagined. I cleared my throat. "Did your...old man make a lot of it?"

He snorted. "Too much."

My heart stopped for a second.

"That's what I thought when I found the shit. But now I wish the stupid fuck had passed on the recipe instead of encrypting it."

I started to breathe again. Darryl III might have access to the motherlode of wolf ice, but no clue how to make it. Thank God for small mercies.

I realized I'd fallen behind the truck. I pressed on the gas.

The murderer leaned forward. "The road splits here. Stay left, on the 340."

I'd taken this back road once. Although a few towns pockmarked this local highway, there were a few stretches of long, straight pavement, and we were coming up to one now. I hit the gas harder.

"What are you doing?" asked the murderer.

"I'm going to pass the truck."

"No, you're not." He laughed. The knife blade trembled with his amusement. I tried to lean away from it without drawing his attention.

"You're going to stay under the speed limit, sweetheart. We don't need any cops on our tail. This truck is going to do us just fine."

Multiple yellow lights caught my eye ahead. Streetlights and store lights. Great. A small town. Even if I couldn't crash the car, maybe I could smash into an empty car. Even if the murderer shot me, he might a) die on impact, or b) get picked up for murdering me.

"If you try anything," he said, "I will kill you. Then I will shoot anyone who comes to help. It'll be a bloodbath."

I licked my lips. My heart thrummed in my throat. More mind-reading.

"If you try to pull over at the nice little cathedral, or if you try to wave over a family out for a night-time walk, I'll kill all of you." He chuckled. "Or maybe I'll shoot them and leave them. You'll have to keep on driving."

"You'll never get away with this," I said. My lips had cracked. I tasted blood. "What's the point? You want the land? You got the land. Why kidnap me? Why kill the bystanders?"

He laughed. It rasped in his throat. "I don't have the land yet, sweetheart. 'Green Belt Montreal' still has first dibs on that one, although with your buddy in jail, I don't know how much longer that'll last."

"You still didn't answer my question. You got Laurent thrown in jail. Mr. Tabassian's in the hospital. Why add kidnapping and massacre to your list?"

He didn't answer for a long minute. Then he whispered, "I guess you'll find out."

Crap. In movies and in books, the killer always spilled the beans before he tried to kill the brave protagonist. Just my luck to end up with the mute one.

After a few minutes, though, he started to speak again. "I didn't mean to hurt any of you."

My shoulders tensed. I knew he was talking about Elena. I pressed on the gas, keeping pace with the truck, while he flapped his lips.

He said. "How was I supposed to know you were a bunch of werewolves? I mean, that's fairy tale stuff, right?"

Yeah. Little Red Riding Hood, anyway.

I felt the blood start to tingle in my hands and feet again. Not lust. I hadn't felt aroused since we left Jack back at the hotel.

Something else built in its stead. Something burned in my stomach and made me clench my teeth so hard, my jaw ached.

"I wanted to scare you away from the land. That's all. It was my grandfather's land and his grandfather's before him."

Boo fucking hoo. It was the Indians' land before that and the trees' and the wild things' land before that. No one owns anything.

I pressed on the accelerator, moving the gauge up to 110 clicks an hour. I pulled out to pass the truck.

"Hey. Wait a minute. I said not to pass!"

I ignored him, sliding ahead of the truck.

"Leila Fan, don't you ever disobey me again, or I'll cut your face off."

I tried not to picture that. My eyes flicked over the landscape. We were still about five minutes from town.

Time for quick right into the ditch, or into a telephone post.

If I could aim it right—

"Slow down!" he said.

I heard a click. He'd cocked his gun. He jammed it against the base of my neck so hard, it snapped my head back.

"We're going to end this. I know you want the land. I also know you're not the kind of girl who'll give up without a fight. So sorry it has to end this way, but if it's me or you…"

Suddenly, I recognized the feeling coursing through my body. My hands gripped the contaminated steering wheel. My thighs clamped together. I stood very straight in my seat. Even though it was barely May, sweat sprinkled my forehead.

Rage.

He wanted to kill me. The way they put down dogs when they don't want them anymore. The way they "cull" elephants who compete for farmland. The way they hunt wolves on their skidoos, riding and riding them for hours, until the wolves die of exhaustion.

"Take it nice and easy through the town, Leila Fan, unless you want me to kill you and all the little kids eating ice cream too."

Instead, I slammed on the brakes.

The truck behind me honked its horn. Its yellow headlights bore down on us.

I gritted my teeth and ducked right, away from the knife.

The murderer fell forward from the sudden decel. He grunted and slashed at me with the knife.

I tried to knock him away and crouch behind the seat as a shield. The car veered right, but I wasn't driving anymore.

The knife blade gashed open my left arm, right below my shoulder. Warm blood seeped out of the wound. Its smell filled the car. It hurt like an SOB, but I'd choose that over a blasted-off head any day.

"You filthy cunt!"

HOOOOOONK, HOOOOOOONK, HOOOOOONK....

I braced myself for impact. The truck should smash us like a tin can. Rear passengers first.

HOOOOOOOOOOOOOOOONK.

The truck's lights pulled up short in my rear-view mirror, honking like an angry 60-foot duck, while the murderer burst out of the back seat and grabbed the wheel.

It shocked me so much, by the time I decided to fight him for it, he'd already managed to sit on me/push me offside while he mashed the brakes and stopped us off on the shoulder.

The truck passed us, still blaring.

The murderer slid into the passenger seat, training his gun on me. "One more stunt like that, and I'm taking you out," he said.

My hands shook. My left arm throbbed, still dripping blood. My throat ached like I'd been screaming.

But I signaled left and merged back onto Highway 340, biding my time.

Chapter 69

Soon I noticed the signs for Highway 401 and for North Lancaster, Ontario. Back to Glengarry county, as I thought, without a single car in sight.

"Take a left here," he said.

As if I didn't know the turnoff to my own piece of land. The land marked by Elena's blood.

I took the left.

As I turned into the lane and started bumping over the gravel potholes, I felt better. I know most women would panic away from civilization and bright lights, but the shadowy trees soothed me.

I'm not most women.

The target had three advantages: wolf ice, which I'd partially blocked with the nose plugs; his size; and his weapons. Four, if you counted my injured left arm.

I'd take my chances.

"Now, I know you're wondering why we didn't meet here in the first place. But to tell you the truth, I wanted you good and distracted first. Like my dad might say, there's no reason not to play before you pay."

My frozen brain took a full minute before it managed to compute what he meant. He'd infected me with wolf ice on purpose. He wanted to fuck me before he killed me. He figured the wolf ice would make me a nice, easy target.

"Stop at the building," he said. "In there." He gestured at the overhang where they'd done the autopsy on Elena's body. "And take off those nose plugs. I let you keep them for the driving, but no more."

"Let me park first," I managed to say. I was not going to drive in there like a lamb. I was a wolf, God damn it.

"Go in the overhang."

"I'm going to have to back up. I overshot it." I threw the car into reverse while I surreptitiously unclicked my seat belt.

"What kind of driver are you?" A whine lifted his voice.

A driver with a gun to her head.

A driver who's going to kill you.

I hit the gas one last time.

At the same time, I launched myself toward my door. I threw it open and sprang into the darkness.

He fired.

The windshield exploded.

Since I was already out of the car, he was the one fighting the broken glass to scramble out of the car while I ducked behind the vehicle slowly rolling to a stop.

When he clawed his way out, waving the gun, I kicked him in the back of the knees.

His legs buckled. He fell forward. Before he could complete the fall, I karate-chopped him in the back of the neck and managed to partially knee him in the throat on the way down.

He gasped. His chest heaved. He couldn't even make a sound. It felt fucking good after he'd held me hostage for the past hour.

He crashed on the ground. His gun splayed on the dirt, gleaming in the light of the nearly full moon.

I leapt for the gun. It felt heavier than the one I'd practiced with at shooting ranges. Good. I made sure the safety was off. "Now talk. Where'd you hide the wolf ice?"

He grabbed his throat. He shook his head and wheezed at my feet.

"Where is it, you fucker?" Not the best plan, I admit, cutting off his airway before I asked him questions, but I figured he'd talk in time. I kept an eye out for the knife, too.

He shook his head. Then he scrabbled to his knees and lunged for the gun.

I danced backward, so he sprawled on the dirt before I kicked him in the eye.

He cried out and grabbed his head.

Even in the darkness, I saw and smelled blood welling behind his hand. I felt a twinge of conscience, even though he was a murderer and would-be rapist.

The gun weighed heavy in my hand. I'd learned how to shoot a few years ago, because lots of hunters frequent the same areas wers do, and I wanted to familiarize myself with firearms.

But it felt wrong.

Foreign.

Human.

I smash-kicked him in the nuts.

He howled.

I savored the sound. That was the sound Elena would have made, if she could have. That ululating, that desperation.

Then I shot him in the head.

Explosion.

The smell and spray of blood and bone. The thump of his body hitting the ground.

I felt, more than heard, my own panting breath. The gun had temporarily deafened me.

I stared at the body of Darryl III with the moon as my only witness.

It was over so fast, it felt unreal. I would have shot him a few more times to be sure, only I was pretty sure he couldn't survive the hole in the back of his head.

I'd have to bury him here or risk blood in the rental car. He'd share the same burial ground as Elena.

Despite all my preparation, I'd forgotten to bring a shovel.

Headlights bumped up the gravel road.

Shit! Someone was coming. I'd better hide the body.

I hooked under the target's arms and started dragging his body toward the trunk. I was still ten feet away when I decided to drop the body and bolt for the trees.

And then I froze in mid-leap. I recognized the black Toyota.

Jack hit the brakes, spraying dirt and gravel. He barely waited for the car to stop before he sprang out and sprinted toward me.

"It's over," I said.

He looked at the body. He'd killed the car's headlights, but in the moonlight, the body's motionlessness was obvious. Not to mention the bizarre angle of his neck. Even so, Jack dropped to his knees and leaned over the body, checking for breathing. He pressed a hand against the neck.

I watched him. It reminded me of our CPR on Elena. I felt numb.

Jack whistled soundlessly. Then he looked up at me and said, "I love you."

I fell into his arms. My body shook, but I couldn't cry. I pressed my nose against his neck and breathed in the smell of his sweat and testosterone. Instead of answering his declaration, I said, "I think two things saved me. I don't think the murderer"—I refused to give him a name—"realized that wolf ice affects everyone differently. He thought I was going to be his sex slave. But after he pulled me away from you, Jack, I didn't want sex. I wanted to kill that guy's ass."

"Plus you'd figured out the wolf ice and brought nose plugs and gloves," Jack pointed out.

My hands started to shake. I'd shot "the murderer." What did that make me?

Jack's fingers dug into my arms. "Look at me. Don't think like that. The man was evil. He killed Elena. He got Laurent put in jail. He would've killed us all, just so he could get a piece of land that his father had sold off fair and square."

Evil.

But I'd looked into the murderer's eyes. I'd heard his voice. I'd felt his testicles squish when I kicked him. I'd shot him through the brain.

"Forget it. You saved the day. Our pack, our land. Bernard's going to give you a medal."

"I don't want a fucking medal." I looked into Jack's eyes, which looked nearly obsidian in the shroud of night. "Tell me one thing. If you'd been the one alone with him, would you have held him for the police or the district heads?"

Jack shook his head slowly. "No. Because if he'd escaped, he would have come after you again. And if there's one thing I couldn't stand, it's someone hurting you."

"Jack," I said. My voice trembled, even though my eyes stayed desert dry.

"I love you," he said again.

I couldn't speak. I didn't want to. But he folded my rigid body against his warm chest until, molecule by molecule, I started to relax against him. I muttered into his shirt, "I love you, too."

Epilogue

Mr. Tabassian dropped the charges. Laurent's lawyer convinced him that someone had spiked Laurent's Red Bull that morning. So even though I had to get a new lawyer, the land deal went through.

Elena's bones were safe.

We were safe. For now.

And so Green Belt Montreal hosted a "housewarming" party on our land on the long weekend in July. While I picked up a few things at the local grocery store, I ran into Jefferson. He was pushing a cart dominated by a good-sized roast, fingerling potatoes, gourmet mustard, and ready-to-eat organic spinach. My stomach growled, looking at his choices.

"Hey," I said.

He nodded at me.

"Coming to the party?" I nodded at his cart.

Jefferson shook his head. "I'm on a case."

Of course he was. I glanced at his long, lean body. Even through the miasma of the store's prepackaged meat and cheeses, the detergent and dog food, I could still smell Mr. Jefferson.

Every bit as toothsome as the first time I'd met him, and now I recognized why.

He carried that werewolf tang in his sweat.

"Could I ask you a question?" I said. "Do you know what happened to you that night?" The night he'd gone into the motel without nose plugs and turned into a raging animal. It had taken two wers to subdue him and whisk him out of there before the cops arrived.

He smiled. "That's part of my next case, figuring that out."

And then he pushed his cart away. I watched him go. So he had no idea, either.

Jack had theorized that werewolf genes could run in a family, like mine did, or they could spring up out of nowhere, like his had. However

278

it worked, it seemed like Jefferson carried werewolf tendencies, even if he couldn't 'shift like us.

Jack walked up to me, holding a baby watermelon. "Hey, you want one of these? They're not in season yet, but—"

"Sure," I said. I smiled at him. He touched my hand with his free one, his skin warm against mine. I laced our fingers together. "After all we've been through, we can handle an unripe watermelon."

He grinned at me. "Are you making fun of me, woman?"

"Always," I said and kissed him in front of the yogurt display until his heat erased the chill.

Author's Note

Melissa Yi likes werewolves (warm, furry) better than vampires (cold, dead). She practices emergency medicine and dotes on her kids and her Rottweiler in South Glengarry, Canada.

You'll get a free gift if you join Melissa's mailing list. Plus, leaving a positive review makes the wolf pack stronger. Aroo!

Connect with Melissa online:
Twitter: http://twitter.com/dr_sassy
Facebook: https://www.facebook.com/MelissaYiYuanInnes/
Website: http://www.melissayuaninnes.com/